W...
Laura V. Hilton and *Firestorm*...

"*Firestorm* is Laura Hilton's best accomplishment to date! I became so deeply involved with Gabe's life that I found myself in tears several times. Penned with s........ ......nelted emotionally. My h........ ......ther. Amish fiction at its ve........

........*Marchinowski*
........ds, Michigan
perspectivesbynancee.blogspot.com

"*Firestorm* is a great story about faith and trust! It was interesting to read about the Amish in a little-known settlement area. As always, Laura Hilton does a wonderful job bringing her characters to life. I was easily swept away in Gabe and Bridget's story and couldn't put the book down! I strongly recommend *Firestorm* to anyone who loves Amish or inspirational fiction."

—*Cecilia Lynn*
Goodreads reviewer

"If you haven't read the Amish genre because you think you can't relate to them, I'm sorry to tell you that you are wrong. The Amish are just like us—human beings who go through life trials that include temptation, birth, loss, death, grief, marriage, teasing, financial struggle, and health issues, as well as natural disasters like floods, fires, and storms, and so much more. Laura V. Hilton writes an action-packed book that keeps you on the edge of your seat! The characters come alive in scenes that seem to place you right there in the moment. Emotions, thoughts and dialogue all pull the reader in with each turn of the page. I know I wanted more of Gabe and Bridget's story. I can't wait for book two in the Amish of Mackinac County series."

—*Tina Watson*
Founder, Amish Book Previews on Facebook

"I love how Laura Hilton shares about the research that goes into her books, because she makes the settings seem more authentic, which, in turn, helps bring the characters to life. This story took its sweet time drawing me in, like a good family friend. I found that I could relate to the characters when it seemed they just couldn't catch a break, which seemed to mirror my week. Sure they are just characters in a book, but they could be real people working toward a goal as they overcome roadblocks and detours along the way. Fathers providing and doing what they feel is best for their families, but then realizing something is missing. Young adults thinking they have it all figured out, but then discovering that they missed a step. I am jealous that they get to figure out these issues and resolve them, but then I also hope we get to visit them again to see how they incorporate these lessons into their next big roadblocks."

—*Christine Bonner*
Sheffield Lake, Ohio

a novel by
LAURA V. HILTON

FIRE STORM

Where There's Smoke, There Is Fire

The Amish of Mackinac County

WHITAKER
HOUSE

FIRESTORM

Laura V. Hilton
http://lighthouse-academy.blogspot.com

ISBN: 978-1-64123-031-5
eBook ISBN: 978-1-64123-033-9
Printed in the United States of America
© 2018 by Laura V. Hilton

Whitaker House
1030 Hunt Valley Circle
New Kensington, PA 15068
www.whitakerhouse.com

Library of Congress Cataloging-in-Publication Data
Names: Hilton, Laura V., 1963– author.
Title: Firestorm / by Laura V. Hilton.
Description: New Kensington, PA : Whitaker House, [2018] | Series: The Amish
   of Mackinac County ; 1 |
Identifiers: LCCN 2018016697 (print) | LCCN 2018019966 (ebook) | ISBN
   9781641230339 (ebook) | ISBN 9781641230315 (paperback)
Subjects: LCSH: Amish—Fiction. | BISAC: FICTION / Christian / Romance. |
   GSAFD: Christian fiction. | Love stories.
Classification: LCC PS3608.I4665 (ebook) | LCC PS3608.I4665 F57 2018 (print)
   | DDC 813/.6—dc23
LC record available at https://lccn.loc.gov/2018016697

1 2 3 4 5 6 7 8 9 10 11 **UJ** 25 24 23 22 21 20 19 18

ACKNOWLEDGMENTS

Thanks to Michael (USCG and Volunteer Firefighter) for information about the Upper Peninsula of Michigan Amish, for the snapshots of buggies taken with his cell phone, for actually driving out to the area where the Amish live, and for information on fighting wildfires.

Thanks to Jeanette for all the pasties she made for us when we lived in Michigan, and for giving us a copy of the recipe she uses.

Thanks to Cliff and to Carl for their unintentional help with Gabe's ankle injuries, and especially to Carl for actually living through the pain, surgery, and recovery.

Thanks to Jenna, Steve, Carol, Joy, Candee, Lynne, Linda, Heidi, Marie, Christy, Kathy, Julie, and Marilyn for your parts in critiquing, offering advice, and/or brainstorming. Also to my street team for promoting and brainstorming.

Thanks to Jenna for taking on the bulk of the cooking while I approached my deadline.

Dear Reader:

I read a series of books a year or so ago that were set in Michigan's Upper Peninsula. As a Michigan native, I was curious, and I researched but found nothing about Upper-Peninsula Amish, except for a notation that one community had tried and failed. So, I contacted the author. She told me that she'd never been there, and her research had all been based on hearsay. Figuring there was nothing to see, I didn't make plans to visit the Upper Peninsula for myself.

Then God intervened. My son who is in the United States Coast Guard was stationed in the Upper Peninsula during the summer of 2017. He reported seeing Amish driving around in buggies, and he confessed to feeling "like a stalker" as he followed one buggy and drove through the surrounding area. He even sent me some pictures. (Shhhh.)

Yes, there *are* Amish in Michigan's Upper Peninsula—at least, there were when this book was written.

As a Michigan native, I used some terms in this story that may not be familiar to non-Michiganders. A Yooper is someone who lives in the Upper Peninsula. A Troll is someone from the Lower Peninsula. Pasties are kind of like Hot Pockets, except that they're meat pies made with root vegetables such as carrots, potatoes, and rutabagas. They are so good. And "the straits" refers to the area of the Great Lakes connecting Lake Michigan and Lake Huron.

As for the wildfire, the earliest wildfire I could find any documentation on in the Upper Peninsula was in April. It is generally a snowy area—trust me. I lived near the Muskegon area and saw snowdrifts as late in the year as May. We occasionally saw over six feet of snow on the ground at one time. So, to get the wildfire when I wanted/needed the wildfire, I used artistic license. Yes, fires really happened in Michigan's history, just not in the month mentioned in the book.

Thanks for reading *Firestorm*!

Laura V. Hilton

GLOSSARY OF AMISH TERMS AND PHRASES

ach:	oh
aent/aenti:	aunt/auntie
"ain't so?":	a phrase commonly used at the end of a sentence to invite agreement
Ausbund:	Amish hymnal used in the worship services, containing lyrics only
boppli:	baby/babies
bu:	boy
buwe:	boys
daed:	dad
"Danki":	"Thank you"
der Herr:	the Lord
Gott:	God
grossmammi:	grandmother
daadi:	grandfather
dawdi-haus:	a home constructed for the grandparents to live in once they retire
dochter:	daughter
dummchen:	a silly person
ehemann:	husband
Englisch:	non-Amish
Englischer:	a non-Amish person
frau:	wife

grossdaedi:	grandfather
gut:	good
haus:	house
"Ich liebe dich":	"I love you"
jah:	yes
kapp:	prayer covering or cap
kinner:	children
koffee:	coffee
kum:	come
liebling	darling
maidal:	young woman
mamm:	mom
mammi:	grandmother
morgen:	morning
nacht:	night
nein:	no
"off in den kopf"	"off in the head"; crazy
onkel:	uncle
ordnung	guidelines for daily living
ser gut:	very good
sohn:	son
verboden:	forbidden
welkum:	welcome
wunderbaar:	wonderful
youngies:	young unmarried individuals in the Amish community

1

Mackinac County, Michigan

It was a nacht-mare.

Lightning flashed across the black sky. Thunder boomed so close that vibrations shook the ground. Rain, mixed with pebble-sized hail, pelted the van's windows with enough force, it seemed the glass might not withstand the impact.

Bridget Behr stared in dismay at the haus Daed had bought. Illuminated periodically by the bright flashes of lightning, along with the beams of the headlamps of the vehicle that had brought them here, the building appeared gray. Run-down. Forsaken. Abandoned.

Maybe it wouldn't be so bad during the day.

Or maybe it'd be worse.

"It's a nacht-mare. A nacht-mare, I tell you!" She hadn't meant to blurt out those words aloud. Her parents, her older brother, and the driver all stared at her. Still, her family had kum here seeking a safe haven, and they'd found *this*. Unbelievable.

Daed grunted. His frown spoke volumes. *Don't converse in our language around Englishers,* he was saying. Also, *We're doing this for you, Bridget.*

Maybe she should be grateful instead of assuming the worst. She had probably been reading too many mystery novels by flashlight while curled up cozily under her covers. But this seriously had "creepy," "scary," and "unnerving" written all over it.

A complete disaster.

Granted, there probably wasn't a dead body hidden halfway under a bed. There weren't any beds, because the moving truck bearing all their worldly possessions wouldn't arrive until tomorrow. Provided the bridge across the Straits of Mackinac was open. It'd been closed down for hours today due to gale-force winds.

The driver cleared his throat. "I can take you to the house next door, if you wish. Things might appear more attractive in the morning light."

There didn't appear to be a haus next door. Just a thick expanse of ever so many trees. Maybe home to bears. Wolves. Cougars.

Bridget shivered. The book she'd read most recently had featured the hero battling grizzlies in a high-stakes adventure.

"Jah...yes. The neighbors' would be fine." Daed surveyed the spot-lighted wreckage once more as he tugged at his beard. "Let this be a lesson to you, kinner. Never buy a property sight unseen."

Hadn't Bridget argued that very point when Daed had announced his plans?

Daed had ignored her. Other than to say, "We can't stay here, Bridget. It's not safe. Not for you, not for your sisters, not even for your mamm."

Indeed.

At least Daed had semi-admitted his mistake, albeit in a roundabout way.

Bridget sighed and leaned back against the van seat. Getting as far away as possible from the atrocity that was to be her new home.

"The next-door neighbors...are they Amish or Englisch?" Mamm clutched the cushion of her seat as if worried it might catapult her out toward the forsaken-looking haus.

The driver chuckled. Not a comforting sound. It almost sounded sinister. "Amish."

That was gut, ain't so?

Mamm relaxed.

Bridget glanced over her shoulder into the rear seat of the van, where her two younger sisters and her younger brother slept. Seated next to her, her older brother stared out the window and shook his head. He'd have plenty to say away from Daed's hearing, nein doubt.

"Off we go, then," the driver said. "Neighbors live about half a mile down the road." He adjusted the gearshift and drove off.

Long before Bridget could mentally prepare herself for meeting strangers, the driver pulled the van in front of another dark haus.

At least this one appeared to be in better shape. The window glass was still intact.

Wait. Nein windows? That meant the new haus was already home to any number of creatures. And now thoroughly drenched, thanks to the driving rain.

"Daed—"

The driver cleared his throat. "Should be unlocked. No one locks doors around here. The family is in Mio visiting relatives. Probably won't mind your staying overnight."

A sensation of unease slithered up Bridget's spine. A sharp contrast to their home in Ohio, where the Amish locked their residences because of all the tourists always about. And because of the stalker. Around here, were strangers welkum to just barge in and camp out over-nacht?

"Thank you." Daed handed the man some money. "Appreciate your picking us up at the bus station."

"No problem. Welcome to the area." The driver laughed as he pocketed the cash. "Of course, you might not like it as much once the snow starts flying, in a week or so. Might want to go back where you came from."

There was a thought. They may have removed themselves from one type of danger, but what if they'd jumped from the frying pan straight into the fire? Bridget waited for Daed's response.

Daed grunted.

After a few moments of silence, the driver coughed. "I'll wait to be sure the house is unlocked."

Bridget climbed out of the van, then reached back inside to help her youngest sister, Roseanna. The heavy rain soaked Bridget's dress and kapp, turning her into a cold, soggy mess. Too bad their hand luggage hadn't made it to the right bus going north. But they had received assurance it would be found and delivered as soon as possible. Maybe the family who lived in this haus wouldn't mind their borrowing something dry to sleep in.

Daed led the way up the porch steps and opened the door. He flicked on the small flashlight he always carried in his pocket.

"Where are we?" Roseanna rubbed her eyes. "Is this our new home? I don't recognize the furniture."

From upstairs came the sound of a door closing. A man appeared at the top of the steps, holding a flashlight lantern. He had crazy bed head and nein clothes, other than some psychedelic-looking lime-green pajama pants.

He stared down at them and blinked.

Bridget lowered her head, her cheeks heating. But then she darted a glance upward again, fascinated by the sight.

"Uh…there's a lantern on the table," the man in the lime-green pajamas said. "Go ahead and light it." He set down the flashlight at the top of the stairs and then disappeared inside a door.

Seconds later, he reappeared, tugging an undershirt over his head as he scrambled down the stairs.

~

Gabriel Lapp stumbled to a stop halfway down the stairs, turned a second time, and went back up to grab the flashlight he'd left behind. It wasn't every day he woke from a sound sleep to find a family of seven standing in his living room.

Technically speaking, it wasn't his living room. It belonged to the Zooks, who'd left town two days ago. But he'd already been with them a month. Surely, the family would've mentioned something to him if they were expecting company while they were gone.

He scooped up the flashlight, then turned and eyed the hunting rifle hanging above the front door. The rifle Samuel Zook kept loaded and ready. The older man and the oldest-looking bu—his sohn, probably—stood between Gabriel and the rifle. Not that Gabriel would use it, but—

"He said you were Amish." The older woman wrung her hands as she stared at Gabriel's pajama pants.

"I am Amish. Gabriel Lapp. Gabe, to those who know me. This is the Zooks' home, but they're in Mio, so I'm staying here." For now. Until he could escape this frigid land for the warmth and sunshine of Florida. And it wasn't even winter yet. But it was November, and the locals said they sometimes had snow as early as September. Gabe couldn't imagine. He lit the lantern on the table, since it seemed nobody else was going to.

The woman's wary expression hadn't changed. But why was she the one ill at ease? She wasn't having her temporary home invaded by a large family from who knows where.

"Hosea Behr," the oldest man said. "This is my frau, Elisabeth; our sohns, Noah and Jonah; and our dochters, Bridget, Shiloh, and Roseanna."

Gabe nodded as the names went in one ear and out the other. He didn't need to know these people. Not if he would be out of here before the first snowfall of the season, as he planned.

Granted, the likelihood of that happening seemed unlikely. Gabe had helped his Englisch boss, Patrick, fix his snowblower just the day before. According to Patrick, snow was in the seven-day forecast. Gabe shivered.

His gaze skimmed over the group, and locked on the green eyes of the golden-honey-brown-haired girl—woman—staring back at him. Pretty, that one.

He struggled to recall her name. And came up with…nothing.

He shook his head. "I'm sorry. The Zooks must've told me you'd be coming, and I forgot." But he was 99.9 percent positive they hadn't mentioned it before they'd left, two days ago. And they certainly hadn't made any preparations for company. Nein menu planned. Nein extra bedding set out. Nein instructions. Nothing. Except for the candy jar crammed with homemade goodies, all of which were already gone. Gabe had inhaled them. Nein point in even thinking about them. It only made his stomach rumble. "But seems to me the first step would be to find you places to sleep to-nacht, and we'll figure things out in the morgen."

The older man nodded. What was his name, again? An Old-Testament prophet, ain't so? Obadiah? "We'd be obliged. And, actually, the Zooks don't know us. We bought the place next door."

"Next door?" Gabe scratched his head. "You mean…." Nein. Surely, they didn't mean the haus in such disrepair.

"Afraid so," the oldest sohn muttered. "We bought it sight unseen."

Pure foolishness. Gabe shook his head. "Well, maybe the preachers will organize a frolic to get the haus whipped into shape." He shrugged. "Or maybe they'll take one look and suggest tearing it down and starting over from scratch. That would be my recommendation."

In which case, Green Eyes would be in close proximity for a while.

"They actually used it as a 'haunted haus' for Halloween, three and a half weeks ago, you know," Gabe added, "and for gut reason." He looked at Green Eyes and winked. "Do you believe in ghosts?"

Bridget stared at Gabe. At least his handsome looks made him very pleasant to gawk at, even if he sounded like a foolish Englisch bu when he spoke.

Daed frowned at Gabe. "We'll be staying in our new home tomorrow nacht."

Hopefully, Daed would take a trip to a local lumberyard or hardware shop beforehand, to cover those open windows. Bridget didn't want any bats flying in and roosting in her bedroom. Or owls swooping inside in pursuit of mice.

Gabe shrugged again. "Suit yourself. But you should know there's a big hole in the floor of one of the second-floor bedrooms. If you don't watch your step, you could fall right through." A slight grin appeared on his face, as if he thought the whole thing was a joke.

Daed's frown deepened. He grimaced, glanced at Mamm, then cast his eyes at the floor.

"Best thing to do now is get some sleep," Gabe added. "Things are bound to look better in the morgen. It'll be an adventure, for sure." He gestured overhead. "My room is the first door on the left, but the rest of the rooms are up for grabs, and the beds are made up with clean sheets. The Zooks' dochters occupy the second room on the right. Might be the most comfortable for the girls. Preacher Zook and his frau have the room across from mine. The other room is…uh, well, there's a hide-a-bed in there. Or a fold-up sleeper sofa. Whatever it's called. Might have to move the sewing table out of the way."

His eyes flickered around the room, then lit on Bridget. Lingered. "Gut nacht, all. See you in the morgen, Green Eyes." He added another wink.

Just like the stalker in Ohio used to do.

Gabe was ever so bold, but Bridget didn't get the same uneasy vibes from him as she had from the creepy man back home. Gabe seemed more like a….

A flirt.

Bridget shivered and looked away.

If she wasn't careful, he might stir up a lot of gossip.

2

The next morgen, Gabe went downstairs and was greeted with the welkum aromas of koffee, eggs, and bacon. The four females who'd arrived last nacht bustled about in the kitchen. The middle girl hunted for something in the cabinet, while the littlest girl wiped the table.

Gabe cringed. That was a job he should've done, but hadn't, since the Zooks would be gone another week and a half.

The girl stopped working and stared at him, as if he were a strange creature who'd stumbled in from the marshes.

Whatever.

His gaze went to the sink, where Green Eyes washed the dishes he'd dirtied in the days since the Zooks' departure. Oops. Another job he should've done already.

He'd been afraid he'd dreamed Green Eyes into existence. Her gut looks, at the very least. And maybe he had. The way she stood, he couldn't see her face. But her figure...those curves accentuated by that damp dress...he hadn't dreamt those.

Damp dress? He glanced around. Everyone wore the clothes she'd had on yesterday. In the rain. He should've thought to offer them towels—directed them to a hot shower—but he couldn't have done anything about their clothes. He couldn't—wouldn't—go through the Zooks' personal items. Would they object to loaning things to this family? But the patriarch of this family had expressed an intention to stay in the family's new home to-nacht. Maybe their belongings were expected to arrive today.

Gabe shook his head. There was nein way they'd be in that haus to-nacht. Unless they were made of sterner stuff than most. It'd be interesting to tag along and observe their reactions as they explored the haus by light of day. He was pretty sure that what the darkness had concealed, the sun would expose.

A twinge of pity worked through him when he realized they probably wouldn't get their money back from the sale of the haus. And if they left, he'd also miss the chance to gaze at Green Eyes. Not that he'd have much time to do so, anyway. Why would a family of seven move to an area where they know nobody?

"Morgen," he said to the four women, though only the youngest had acknowledged his presence so far. "Smells gut."

The mamm nodded stiffly from her place at the stove. Green Eyes froze, as if she hadn't realized he was there. Maybe the clatter of the dishes had masked the sound of his approach. The middle girl dropped something with a shatter—not the candy jar, thank goodness—spun around in the pile of glass shards, and gaped.

What? Was his appearance so unusual?

He glanced down at his white T-shirt and lime-green pajama pants. He'd pulled on a pair of socks and his work boots....

His face heated. Maybe he did look odd.

Best just to go with it.

With a wink and a jaunty grin at the two little girls, he shrugged on his old coat, clapped his hat on his head, and opened the door. "Time for the chores."

The yard was full of mud puddles and downed tree limbs, but there was freshness to the air, and a tiny hint of sun peeked through the clouds. The wind was still pretty strong, though. Gabe held his hat in place with one hand.

He found the three males of the nameless family in the barn. The chores were mostly finished: cow milked, eggs collected, animals fed, stalls mucked. It reminded him of the days before the Zooks left town, when he was one of several men doing chores, as opposed to his solo act of the past few days.

It meant he'd get back to the warmth of the haus and the heavenly-smelling food a lot sooner.

"Danki for the help. I'll take you to your new home this morgen after breakfast." Gabe took hold of the wheelbarrow full of manure, preparing to push it outside, as the daed hung the shovel back where it was kept on the wall. "Then, maybe we'll go to a hardware shop, or to the lumberyard to order your materials and have them delivered, if you need to." Or a bulldozer.

They'd need to. Unless they'd brought building supplies with them. And, judging by the daed's reaction last nacht, they hadn't.

Or maybe he would take them to the bus station if they decided to head back to where they came from after a second look at the "haunted haus."

"Do the men in this district usually do chores in their pajamas?" The oldest bu—who looked to be close in age to Gabe—followed him out to where he usually dumped the manure behind the barn.

Gabe's cheeks burned at the question, which brought to mind the gaping girls in the kitchen. "Nah, but the Zooks are gone, and I thought I'd dreamed you guys up last nacht. Since today's Saturday, and I'm off work, I figured I'd do what I need to, then stay home and read. Doesn't matter what I look like, right? Well, at least until the frolic to-nacht. And once I was downstairs and saw your sisters' facial expressions, I couldn't resist coming outside in these pants."

The young man grunted. "I'm Noah. Not sure you caught that in the introductions last nacht."

"Nein." Gabe stopped short of asking the name of Green Eyes. Didn't matter, anyway. He'd always struggled with names, and most of the girls around here answered to endearments with giggles and the batting of eyelashes. Those who didn't, answered to "Hey, you."

Gabe missed his friends in Florida, and had tried to keep an emotional distance from the people here in order to protect his heart. Those efforts weren't working very well, though; he'd made some close friends at work and among his fellow volunteer firefighters. Still, he was glad for the reintroduction. Because, for some reason he couldn't explain, he *needed* to know these people's names.

"Frolic?" Noah sounded interested.

"Birthday party for one of the maidals. Perhaps you and your sister would like to go. You'll get to know people. And tomorrow's Sunday, but not a church Sunday…uh, well, don't suppose you'll have visitors. But you might if anyone knows you're here."

"Don't know if Daed will let us go to the frolic. Depends on…." Noah frowned.

Gabe lowered his voice and said, "Sight unseen? Really?"

Noah slumped. "Jah. But he had gut reasons. And the person he bought it from painted this beautiful picture of white pines, sand dunes, the lake, unlimited game and fish, and privacy. A land virtually flowing with milk and honey."

Gabe laughed. "The description actually fits the land. Nein mention of the haus, though, huh?"

"Stupid of us not to notice, but nein. Not a word. Other than 'four bedrooms.'" Noah shook his head. "And Daed and I need to find work. We can't afford to spend months remodeling."

"I can help remodel your haus in my spare time." Since his dream of leaving town before the snow started wouldn't kum true. "Construction is one thing I'm gut at." That, and getting into trouble. But he wouldn't go there.

Gabe dumped the contents of the wheelbarrow in the compost pile next to Frau Zook's fall vegetable garden. He'd arrived in Michigan in time for winter squash and pumpkins galore. "I think breakfast is almost ready. We all should head inside."

"Daed and Jonah already did, while we were talking."

Gabe returned the wheelbarrow to the barn, then stopped at the outdoor pump to wash up. The water was frigid, but Frau Zook preferred that the men wash outside rather than in the kitchen. She kept a bar of lye soap in a covered container beside the pump. She usually kept a small hand towel out here, too, but Gabe must've forgotten to take care of it, because it was gone. Carried off by the strong winds yesterday, nein doubt. He felt a pang of guilt at his negligence. He should have been taking better care of things. After all, his hosts were letting him stay here for free.

He scrubbed his arms and face, shook the water off, and followed Noah inside. He should've mentioned Frau Zook's rule to them. Yet another failure.

Gabe took off his boots, coat, and hat, then put on his slippers that he kept by the door. He eyed the table, filled with serving dishes of food. His usual seat was already occupied by the eleven-year-old-looking bu. Jonah, presumably. So Gabe lowered himself into the empty chair next to Jonah, and as Noah sat on his other side, he bowed his head for the silent prayer. *Danki, Gott, for this food, and for the unexpected gifts—I mean, guests. Help me to be of service to them. And…. Would it be wrong of him to ask Gott to let Green Eyes notice him? Probably so. Amen.*

He raised his head. His glance caught Green Eyes' wide gaze. Her lips were parted slightly, as if she'd just pulled in a quick gasp.

He couldn't think of anything overly shocking he might have done. He shrugged and reached for the bowl of scrambled eggs.

The daed cast a stern look in his direction, reminding Gabe of the many times his preacher father had done the same. He was in trouble again. Couldn't seem to avoid it. What had he done this time?

"Let's pray." The daed bowed his head.

Ach.

⌒

Bridget took the bowl of eggs Shiloh passed to her, but she couldn't look away from Gabe. She knew she shouldn't be so fascinated by the man seated across the table. But she had never met anyone like him. His light brown hair had natural blond highlights from hours spent working in the sun, and his blue eyes twinkled as if he found joy in the ordinary. His not-too-thin, not-too-full lips had an upward curve as if a smile came naturally to him. When he did smile, a dimple flashed.

And he was comfortable enough in his own skin to wear psychedelic-lime-green pants with his black felt hat and work boots. In an Amish haus, nein less!

Bridget could only imagine having such a degree of self-confidence.

She glanced down at the damp, dirty gray dress she'd worn for three days straight. Their belongings couldn't arrive soon enough. A fresh dress would seem like a luxury.

At least she was appropriately attired, even if her clothes smelled of dampness from yesterday's rain. She glanced out the window. The sky was overcast, the color a darker gray than she'd ever seen before, and the wind whistled through the trees with such force that they swayed. Despite the heat from the woodstove, cold air crept in from somewhere. The windows, maybe.

"Long-range forecast predicts snow early next week," Gabe volunteered.

Bridget looked at him. His gaze was locked on her. A fluttery mass like a flock of Canada geese landed in her stomach. Weird.

Daed grunted.

Nobody else verbally acknowledged Gabe's comment. Her sisters and younger brother stared at him with wide eyes. They seemed paralyzed by utter shock.

Or maybe it was awe. Fascination. Because she—they—had never met anyone as carefree as he. This district must be a lot more lenient than their former one, in Ohio. Not that it had been particularly strict. Still, it seemed appealing to live in freedom instead of always hiding from strangers behind locked doors.

Gabe glanced at Daed. "You're going to want to get the haus—"

Daed violently shook his head, and Gabe clamped his mouth shut. He fumbled his fork, and the utensil fell with a clatter to his plate, launching a piece of scrambled egg into the air. It landed next to the plate.

"The haus isn't—can't be—as bad as it looked last nacht. It must've been the storm. The lightning. The heavy rain." Daed straightened his back, firmed his shoulders, and shot Gabe a firm look. "I appreciate your offer to take us there. We'll leave after breakfast."

Gabe nodded. "Wouldn't miss it." He retrieved his fork from the mound of eggs on his plate. The corners of his lips slid upward. His dimple flashed. "This is going to be fun. An adventure."

Daed growled deep in his throat. A sound he made when he was beyond frustrated. Maybe Gabe should tone it down a little.

Bridget didn't know how much fun it would be. She just hoped Daed was right. It couldn't be as bad as it had looked in the middle of a thunderstorm.

But an hour later, after the breakfast dishes were washed, dried, and put away, she sat in the cramped buggy, Roseanna on her lap, and gawked at the big, gray monstrosity, and realized she'd been wrong.

It was worse.

⌒

Gabe climbed out of the buggy and surveyed the abandoned haus with a fresh perspective. The covered front porch sagged and twisted. The front door hung open, and most, if not all, of the windows were broken out. A new roof was an immediate need, with many of the shingles missing. The crooked chimney appeared ready to crumble. The haus probably had gut beam support, keeping it standing, but it would require an extreme do-it-yourself makeover to become livable.

If it were up to Gabe, he'd level the structure and start over. But it wasn't his home or his decision. And the daed acted upset every time Gabe opened his mouth to voice his opinion. As if his opinion were worthless.

As if he was worthless.

A dart of pain pierced his heart. He shrugged it off.

Still, it'd been used as a "haunted haus" last month, so the local officials must've deemed it safe enough to handle a stream of visitors. Gabe had staffed it, despite Preacher Samuel Zook's objections. The proceeds helped to fund the fire department where he volunteered. And all he'd had to do was jump out at the thrill-seekers and scream while wielding a dull ax.

He'd gotten in plenty of trouble for doing it. The local bishop had written home to Florida, complaining about Gabe's awful behavior. Gabe, in turn, had received a letter from Daed berating him for his actions. But he didn't regret the decision, even if he had gone overboard and left his gut sense behind. It seemed that nein matter what he did, he found himself in a familiar heap of trouble, facing judgment. Too bad Daed still didn't think Gabe was man enough to act responsibly. Too bad the gratefulness of the fire department or the praises from his construction-crew boss weren't enough to qualify him as being responsible.

He shook his head to bring himself back to the present. The family stood in silence as they stared at the building.

"Do you want to go in?" Gabe shifted a tiny bit closer to Green Eyes, in case she needed help walking over the uneven ground.

"Is it safe?" she whispered, darting a cautious glance at her daed.

"If you watch where you walk, I suppose," Gabe put in. "Though they made all the haunted-haus visitors sign a disclaimer stating they wouldn't hold the village responsible for loss of life or limb, and acknowledging they were entering at their own risk."

This statement earned him another glare from her daed.

Nobody moved.

Gabe sighed. "I'll go in first, if you want."

3

There's nein barn." Bridget's teeth chattered as she studied the trees surrounding the "haunted haus." Which meant a barn raising would take precedence over remodeling—or rebuilding—the dilapidated structure in front of her.

And their animals were supposed to arrive on Monday. They'd have to tie them outside and hope the bears didn't eat them. If there were any bears nearby.

There was nein way Daed seriously expected her family to live here. And yet his desperation to protect his family had led him to jump on the chance to buy this haus, sight unseen. Too bad it was worse than any worst-case scenario they might have envisioned. Bridget admired how hard Daed tried to provide for the family and keep her safe, and how determined he seemed to stay positive about the situation, even though it was a far cry from what he had hoped and expected.

She should try to be positive, too. What had Gabe called it? An adventure?

Even though Daed's shoulders slumped and his face was drawn, he stoically turned away and trudged after Gabe toward the structure masquerading as a haus. Both of them ignored the "Do Not Enter" signs posted outside. The yellow tape strewn across the front door that read "Crime Scene. Do Not Cross."

Bridget shivered, not yet feeling brave enough to risk life or limb by entering the accident-waiting-to-happen. Yet nor did she want to remain outside, with the possibility of bears peeking through the pines. Were grizzlies native to these woods?

When her brothers glanced at each other, then hurried after Daed, Bridget took a faltering step forward. Mamm stood a few feet away, holding Shiloh and Roseanna by the hand. None of them moved.

Bridget took another faltering step forward, then stopped and turned around. Rumbling down the dirt road toward them was a yellow moving truck. The same kind of truck Daed had rented. Was it the one bearing their belongings?

Except, it was too soon. They weren't ready to move in. And even if the place were structurally sound, Mamm would insist on scrubbing down the entire haus before they unpacked. The boxes of cleaning supplies had been the last things to go on the truck so that they would be the first things out and put to use. But then, dirt and cobwebs might be the only things holding the place together.

Bridget stepped out of the road as the moving van drove down the lane. It slowed. Stopped. The driver—an Englisch man from Ohio Daed knew and trusted—lowered the window. "The GPS tells me I've reached my destination. But that can't be right. I'm going to see what's down this road." He waved as he drove past them, following an overgrown, two-track lane deeper into the woods.

⟋

The village council hadn't cleaned the building since the October holiday almost four weeks prior. Gabe pushed past a plastic skeleton hanging in a doorway and shouldered his way through a fake spider web with a creepy toy tarantula suspended from it.

He knew it was fake, since tarantulas didn't spin webs. Still, he kept his distance.

Noah followed him. "Guess they didn't expect this place to sell."

A noisy truck rumbled past. Gabe peered out a glassless window. Through the trees, he made out the insignia of a well-known move-it-yourself company.

Noah appeared at his shoulder. "They're going to the wrong haus!" He darted toward the front door.

"See where they stop, because maybe…. Where did your daed go?" Gabe turned and left the room. He pushed past a Frankenstein double, climbed the stairs, and found Jonah and his daed peering over a circle of yellow caution tape surrounding a gaping hole in the floor.

"This is so cool." The young bu grinned at Gabe. "We could install a fireman's pole, and slide downstairs in the morgen."

"Sounds like fun." Gabe actually liked the idea.

"I made a terrible mistake." The older man shoved his hands into his pockets. "It was a foreclosure, you know. Got it dirt cheap. Now I know why."

"Maybe not so terrible." Gabe stood beside him. "What address did you give the driver?"

The daed glared. "I don't see why it matters, but I told him this address. And I saw the number on one of the mailboxes out on the road."

"Jah, but the truck we just heard? It passed on the other side of the trees." Gabe pointed to the east. "And the driver would be using a GPS, which would tell him when he's reached his destination."

Hope lit the man's eyes. "You mean, we might be at the wrong haus?"

Gabe grinned. "I'd say there's a gut chance. I've been in town just over a month, or I might have caught the mistake."

An answering smile appeared. The daed clapped Gabe's shoulder. "Danki, bu. You've given me hope. Let's go see if you're right."

Gabe nodded. But if he was correct, he would miss seeing Green Eyes on a regular basis.

On the other hand, she might be able to attend frolics if she didn't have to worry about helping renovate a haunted haus.

Bridget froze as her eyes followed the path the truck had taken. Mamm moved beside her, and both her sisters crowded close. Hands— she didn't check to see whose—grasped hers. "Let's follow it," Bridget murmured.

Noah burst out the front door of the haunted haus, not bothering to duck under the crime tape. It came untethered and flapped in the breeze. He jumped over the half wall surrounding the porch, barely missed a bush on the other side, and dashed around the haus in the direction the truck had driven.

Bridget glanced at Mamm.

"Has the world gone mad?" Mamm muttered, then released Bridget's hand. "Go on. Follow."

Bridget took off at a run, following the tracks through the woods. Her sisters did, too. She was glad for their presence.

Ahead of them, Noah disappeared around a curve in the lane.

Bridget was panting by the time she skidded to a stop on the other side of the curve. She pressed a hand to her heart as if to slow its pounding.

There, in the clearing, stood a white two-story farmhaus with a covered porch. The roof was gabled on the three sides Bridget could see. A stone's throw from the haus stood a faded green barn. The family's buggy had already been unloaded off the truck and was parked in front. None of their animals had arrived yet. That'd happen Monday, maybe.

Noah came toward Bridget and her sisters. "Go tell Daed he's at the wrong haus. Girls, kum. Fill a pail and start scrubbing down the cabinets, as Mamm said." He turned and strode back toward the truck, Shiloh and Roseanna behind him.

It hadn't seemed so scary, running through the woods with her sisters. Walking back was a different thing. Bridget balled her fists, her breath still coming in pants, and studied the woods on either side, hoping nothing would jump out at her.

Mamm sauntered toward her. "Well?"

"There's a haus…and a barn…and they've unloaded our buggy. Noah told the girls to scrub the cabinets and sent me to tell Daed." She bent double, hands on her knees. "I'm out of shape."

Mamm laughed. "Why do you think I didn't run? I'd probably trip over a tree root and fall flat on my face. Go on and tell your daed. I'll help the girls with the cleaning."

Bridget walked toward the haus that, thankfully, wasn't theirs. Daed, Jonah, and Gabe came out the door. Jonah ran toward her. "Gabe says we can add a fireman's pole in the bedroom!"

"Actually, buddy, I said it'd be fun." Gabe lifted Jonah's hat, ruffled his hair, and then returned the hat. He winked at Bridget. "And we'll let Green Eyes go first."

"I want to go first." Jonah looked up at him. "Why do you keep calling her 'Green Eyes'?"

"What, isn't that her name?" Gabe grinned.

"Her name is Bridget," Jonah said.

"Bridget." Gabe repeated it once.

"Nobody is sliding down any pole." Daed cleared his throat. "Where did the truck go?"

Bridget pointed. "There's a haus, and a barn, and…and…and it's a real haus. Not a nacht-mare!" Her eyes burned with tears of joy.

"Can we add a fireman's pole to the other haus, Daed?" Jonah asked hopefully.

"How about if I take you to the fire station in the village?" Gabe said. "You can see the engines, too. And maybe your brother and sisters would like to kum." He glanced at Bridget and lifted an eyebrow.

Interest sparked for a moment.

But, nein. She couldn't. Bridget ignored him, turned away, and started the return trip through the woods.

Gabe fell into step beside her as they trailed Daed and Jonah. "There's a frolic to-nacht. A birthday party. Mentioned it to your brother. He'd like to go, if he can. Will you join us?"

Bridget shook her head. "Nein, danki." Something about the look in his eyes made her tremble. She stepped a little further away from him. Hopefully, he could take a hint.

"Aw, kum on. It'll be fun."

Gabe was cute, but his winks reminded her of the man who'd started her own personal nacht-mare. The last man who'd winked at her was the reason her entire world had been uprooted. If only she hadn't smiled back the first time, then maybe he wouldn't have started stalking her. Sneaking into her bedroom. She shuddered. And then, they wouldn't be stuck here as bear-bait in freezing Michigan.

Better off to never date at all.

Gabe might be handsome, but she wasn't interested.

She glared at him. "I. Don't. Date."

4

Gabe shivered, and not only because of the weather. The cold shoulder and extreme brush-off from green-eyed Bridget chilled his heart, shooting shards of ice through him. Maybe she'd thaw out once she realized this move wasn't the nacht-mare she'd imagined.

On the other hand, if he couldn't waltz in and save the day, she'd have nein reason to look up to him. And, for reasons he couldn't identify, it was important she did. That someone did, anyway. And not just because he was being held up as a bad example.

Bridget's two brothers trailed him on the rutted track, strolling, as if, now that the housing situation had been made right, there was nein reason to hurry.

Gabe glanced at the tall pines standing at attention on either side. Something gnawed at him, demanding his attention, but he couldn't figure what it might be. He sighed heavily. *Lord....* What should he pray for, when he didn't know what was wrong? *Help me...to help them. Help me to be a friend, and maybe they could be friends with me. Help me to do something right for a change, and win Bridget's—and her daed's—favor.*

The prayer didn't bring the peace he'd hoped for, maybe because it was selfish. *Help me. Me. Me. Me.* Daed would have plenty to say about that, if he knew.

Gabe came around the curve in the road and stopped. They'd started unloading the truck. Boxes sat in the yard. Bridget's daed carried a box out of the back of the truck. But there were telephone wires connected to the haus. Lacy curtains fluttered in the windows. And a satellite dish sat on the roof. This was clearly an Englisch residence, and it looked vaguely familiar. Gabe narrowed his gaze at the oversized built-in grill, the wrought-iron benches, the cement birdbath....

He'd been here before, the day after Halloween. For the fire chief's annual barbeque, hayride, and bonfire. It didn't matter that Gabe had attended only to celebrate the huge amount of money they'd made from the haunted haus—he'd still gotten in trouble.

He sighed. It seemed that ever since Daed had sent him here, he'd been under constant watch. A stream of visits for the smallest of infractions. He shook his head and forced his attention back to the haus, this time focusing on the motorcycle parked beside the barn.

This was not the haus Bridget's daed had purchased.

As if to verify his conclusion, one of the girls came outside and said, "There's furniture in there. And a television. And a ringing…I'd say phone, but it looked like a small computer screen. And a meal cooking in an electric pot of some kind. It smells really gut. Kind of spicy, but—"

"This haus belongs to the local fire chief." It hurt to admit. Especially when the patriarch of the family set down the box and turned to glare at Gabe. As if it was his fault.

Then again, he had encouraged the man to believe this haus was truly his. He should've checked it out before saying anything.

"Load it back up, men," one of the movers said. And then he looked at the daed. "What do you want it to do, Hosea?"

Hosea. That was his name. At least Gabe had been right about the prophet part.

"Should we go ahead and unpack it at, uh, the correct address?"

The politest way possible of referring to the disaster waiting at the other end of the lane.

"Uh…." Hosea hesitated, and again looked at Gabe. This time, he raised an eyebrow.

Did he expect Gabe to offer some suggestions, just so he could shoot them down? Trouble was, Gabe had an abundance of ideas. Which one should he toss out to be rejected first?

He decided to appeal to the man's logical side. "You'll need a barn first, nein matter what you decide to do with the haus. You could have your things stored inside the haus until the barn is built, and then move them over there while you work on the haus."

"Hmm." Hosea sounded dubious.

"Or you could store everything in the Zooks' barn for now, and move it when your new—or newly remodeled—haus is finished."

The older man rubbed his bearded chin.

Might as well say it. "Or you could go back where you came from, and call this what it was: a mistake." A bit harsh, but….

"We're staying here. At the haus." Hosea firmed his shoulders and turned to the truck driver. "Unload everything at the haus, please."

"Maybe you could sleep in tents. Might be more pleasant for the ladies." It was a joke. Sort of. But even the hardiest of men would hesitate to bed down in the disaster Hosea had bought. Then again, they would freeze in tents unless they had plenty of blankets.

Hosea's brow furrowed. "Do you know where we could get a couple of tents, bu?"

"If you want to go that route, I can round some up."

"Start rounding." Hosea shoved his glasses higher on his nose.

Gabe scratched his neck as he tried to think where to start. Then he nodded. "Okay. You'll have them by nacht-fall." That is, if Gott was still in the miracle-working business.

Hosea made a disbelieving snort, then picked up the box he'd set down and put it back on the truck.

Gabe hesitated another moment. Should he help repack what had been unloaded? Or start tracking down tents?

The tents won. Most of the outdoor enthusiasts Gabe knew had hunting cabins. Or campers. *Hmm.* He headed back along the weedy tire tracks, and didn't acknowledge Bridget when she passed, other than to give a jaunty wave. Hosea could have the honors of breaking the news about the haus mix-up.

Not his job.

⌒

Bridget's heart closed in on itself as the door of the moving van slammed shut. It seemed the nacht-mare had gotten worse. The haunted haus was theirs, in all its horrific glory.

A "land of milk and honey." She scoffed. And she hadn't even gotten a glimpse inside the prettier haus. Though maybe it was better this way.

Grasping her sisters' hands for support—and not for protection from imaginary bears this time—Bridget trudged back toward the worst-case scenario that was their future.

The Zooks' horse and buggy had vanished, presumably with Gabe, by the time she and her sisters returned to the haus. The men were making quick work of unloading the boxes. Mamm examined each box as it came off the truck, making sure the pantry items and kitchen supplies were kept separate. How Mamm planned to cook anything was a mystery, because the chimney likely posed a fire hazard. Although she hadn't been brave enough to venture inside to check it out.

Then she noticed Jonah arranging rocks in a circle. Ach. An open fire pit.

She wouldn't have made a very good pioneer.

Maybe Daed would let them bunk at the Zooks' haus again, with interesting, unconventional, handsome Gabe; a functional woodstove; and plenty of food.

Or not. Daed's frown, pursed lips, and ramrod-straight posture informed her there'd be nein warm haus to-nacht.

And the way Mamm blinked her bloodshot eyes and bit her lower lip to keep it from quivering showed that she disagreed with some, if not all, of Daed's decisions.

Would returning to Ohio really be so bad? A gut guard dog could've kept the intruder out of the haus. Or what about a service dog? One of Bridget's Englisch friends had a dog that had actually served in the military. Somehow. If this town had a public library, she'd look for a book about military dogs and find out what they were used for. And then maybe suggest the family adopt one when they returned home.

When. Not "if."

Although Daed might object to both the book and the dog.

A gust of wind set the trees to swaying and the haus to creaking. Loudly. The men paused in their work to stare at it, as if afraid it might topple. But nothing happened.

"Kum help with dinner, Bridget," Mamm called. "We need kindling gathered from the woods."

Bridget eyed the trees pitching back and forth in the breeze. "Do you really think we can get a fire going with such strong wind?"

Mamm looked at the jar of home-canned tomato soup in her hands. "I don't know what else to do. We don't have any bread left for sandwiches. Cold soup wouldn't be very appetizing. We could take a chance on the chimney being safe, and start a fire in the woodstove. But we'll still need wood."

Bridget summoned her courage and went to check out the kitchen. It was worse than she'd imagined, with rodent droppings everywhere, nests in every corner, and the chimney pipe hanging loosely from the wall. The stove was dirty and dilapidated. She shuddered as she went back outside.

"I guess the worst that can happen is, this place will go up in flames," she said to Mamm. "And I'm thinking it'd be a justifiable homicide."

~

Gabe loaded two tents into the back of the Zooks' buggy. Well, it was technically one piece—two rooms connected by a tunnel. He'd borrowed it from his boss, Patrick. According to him, it slept eight, so it ought to be plenty big for a family of seven. Not only that, but Patrick had also loaned him an RV that slept four. Five, if two people shared the overhead bunk and one slept on the sofa. The RV would be delivered tomorrow. But with nein electric hookup, the family wouldn't be able to cook, so Gabe also managed to procure a portable propane stove from a fellow volunteer firefighter, an Englisch man named Ed. Ed shown him how it worked, and Gabe was sure he would be able to demonstrate for Hosea's frau.

"Don't forget, now," Ed said. "The stove needs to be used in a well-ventilated area."

Gabe didn't think that would pose a problem, considering the haus had nein windows. But he would remind the mamm, just in case she didn't know not to cook inside a tent.

Gabe climbed into the buggy and took the reins. "Thanks, Ed. I know the family will appreciate this." At least, he hoped they would. He needed to do something to get on Hosea's gut side. The man seemed to have judged him and found him lacking without knowing anything about him.

Granted, his first impression on the family hadn't been made under ideal circumstances. He'd been awakened from a sound sleep and had gone downstairs in his pajama pants to investigate. Not a gut way to start a relationship. Especially when the judging party had been at the top of his game—except for the bad decision of buying a house, sight unseen, and moving without at least checking it out first.

Okay, so Gabe was guilty of judging, too. The man *might* have had a gut reason. And, as Daed always reminded him, "You need to show grace."

Jah. And that grace apparently applied to everybody but Gabe, because he was the one separated from his family, scolded by the church officials, and sent to live with strangers in the frozen tundra of Michigan. Even there, he had nein escape from the eagle-sharp eyes that watched for any perceived infraction.

"Manhood often grows in the soil of hardship," Gabe mused aloud, echoing the last words Daed had said to him when he dropped him off at the bus station in Pinecraft.

The horse snorted.

Gabe wasn't sure if Cherry Blossom agreed with the proverb.

He wasn't sure if he did, either.

But he knew his circumstances qualified as a hardship.

Though not as hard as having to live in a tent outside a haunted haus.

5

Bridget gathered a boxful of twigs and three or four armloads of broken branches. Some of the pieces were too long for the wood-stove, so Daed would have to find his ax or his saw before they could start supper. She pulled a fallen log out of the forest, inch by painstaking inch, as the moving truck roared to life and rumbled down the drive.

Leaving them here. Alone and unprotected.

And with nein way to get around. Even though they had their buggy, their horse hadn't been delivered yet.

Not to mention, they didn't know their way around the community. One wrong turn, and they'd be lost in the woods.

Bile rose in her throat. But talking to Daed would be of nein use. Mamm had already tried that. Tried begging. Pleading.

Daed wanted a small, secluded community.

Emphasis on *secluded*.

How would they ever find friends in this place? And would a garden even grow this far north? Would they need to invest in a sleigh to get around in the winter? So many questions. So few answers.

Back home, she'd had lots of girlfriends. And Isaac Hershberger had asked to court her. An offer he'd quickly withdrawn once he'd discovered they were moving to Michigan. How would she ever find an ehemann here?

An image of Gabe Lapp flashed into her mind—complete with his psychedelic-lime-green pants. And nein shirt. She closed her eyes, her breath quickening. So inappropriate. *But oh, my word. He is so hot.*

What would it be like to be courted by him?

He'd asked her to join him and Noah for a frolic that evening. And she'd refused. She winced, recalling the harshness of her response. But

35

it was probably a nonissue, anyway, because Daed wouldn't let Noah go. Not now. Not to-nacht. Too much to do.

Not to mention, too much uncertainty.

Besides, how would Gabe introduce them? "Behrs den in haunted haus"? "Behrs hibernate in haunted den"? "Behrs share den with ghosts"?

Bridget grimaced. She'd read too many newspaper headlines as they'd wrapped dishes for the move.

He'd be a bit wordier, surely, and say something like, "Meet Noah and Bridget Behr. Their daed is off in den kopf. He bought the haunted haus."

Irritated at her thoughts, she gave the log a hefty tug, and landed on her rump on the cold, damp ground. She stifled a sob of frustration. But she really wanted to climb to the ridge of the roof and scream, letting the world know just how she felt.

Maybe Isaac would kum to her rescue.

Isaac? Never mind him. Gabe would do quite nicely.

"Everything okay, Green Eyes?" As if summoned by her thoughts, Gabe crouched beside her. His gaze roamed over her face, then his hand reached out, fingering several strands of her hair. One long, heart-thumping, spine-tingling moment later, he tugged at something tangled in her kapp. A small pine twig. His eyes twinkled as his knuckles blazed a trail down her cheek.

Her heart pounded. "Just…just try-trying to gather wood to start a fire." She hated the way her voice trembled. But really. Wood? Who needed wood with this man around?

She swallowed a lump in her throat and stared at him.

His gaze shifted to the log lying across her lap. "I brought a propane camp stove. Showed your mamm how to set it up." His Adam's apple bobbed. "It'll be safer than attempting to use the woodstove. Figure the haus will likely be leveled. I'd recommend it, but…." He shrugged. "Your daed's got to decide. Of course, he could shore it up and keep renting it out to the fire department for the annual haunted haus. As a source of income."

Income. Jah, they'd need that, too. Had Daed put any forethought into this at all?

Gabe stood and tugged the log off her lap. "Need help?" He held out his hand.

Bridget looked at it for a moment, her thoughts whirling, as mud seeped into the only dress she had available to her right now. But how embarrassing would it be to stand and let this man see her filthy back end?

Of course, the alternative meant staying put, sitting in the mud. *Nein, danki.*

She closed her hand around his, and he effortlessly pulled her to her feet. He tugged her a little closer than was necessary—close enough for her to breathe the piney scent of the soap he must've used that morgen—and held her hand a little longer than was polite.

Her first impression was correct. He was a flirt. Not to be taken seriously. She sucked in a breath, her chest rising and falling with the deepness of it. Disappointment filled her.

Still, she didn't give her hand a tug to free herself from his grasp. Instead, she let him clutch it, his gaze holding hers, and imagined him raising her hand to his lips and brushing a kiss across her knuckles, as was done in several of the historical romances she'd read recently.

He didn't do that.

His fingers were just beginning to release her when Daed cleared his throat.

"She doesn't want anything from you, Gabriel Lapp. We heard about you and your reputation before we set foot here. Hope you'll soon be gone." He narrowed his eyes. "Unhand my dochter."

What had Daed heard? He hadn't shared anything with her.

Gabe stared, unblinking. Pain filled his eyes. His hand fell to his side.

Bridget wished for it back.

⌒

Gabe climbed into his borrowed buggy and sat there in the cab, watching Hosea fight against the wind as he set up the tent. He had his younger sohn sit on it while he tried to shove random poles together. Noah frowned at the poles in his hands.

And there hadn't been a single word of thanks for the tents or the camp stove. Not even a nod when Gabe had mentioned the camper due to arrive the next day. Just a hint of gratitude in the frau's eyes.

As much as he wanted to leave this ungrateful man to his mistakes, Gabe couldn't do it. Instead, he gritted his teeth and climbed out of the buggy. "The haus would serve as an excellent windbreak if you sent up the tents on that side." He pointed. "Be a bit warmer, too."

Hosea glared at him and opened his mouth, but Noah nodded and quickly said, "I agree."

"The least you can do is help us move it all." Hosea pursed his lips.

Gabe silently counted to ten. And then to twenty. Then he quietly helped them move the tent, and showed them how the poles hooked together.

A short time later, the tent was up, the pegs hammered securely into the ground. The youngest girl emerged from the haus through a side door and carried out an armful of blankets, which she set inside the tent. "Be right back with more. Shiloh is looking for the pillows."

Gabe glanced at the haus, looking for Bridget to follow. Maybe with an armful of stuff, so he'd have an excuse to go to her. To help her. To let his fingers brush against hers. He'd felt the zing of their earlier touch from the top of his head to the tips of his toes, and everywhere in between.

Bridget didn't appear.

Gabe fought back his disappointment and looked at the tent again.

Hosea rubbed his back and stretched. "Probably time for you to go on home, bu."

Noah glanced at his daed, frowned, and scuffed his feet.

"Jah, need to get ready for the frolic to-nacht." Gabe tried to keep the bitterness out of his tone. Evidently, he wouldn't even be invited to share a meal with them. So be it. He had better things to do than help an ungrateful family.

Noah didn't try to follow him to his borrowed buggy, though he looked as if he wanted to. Gabe released the brakes, backed up, and turned toward the road. Since tomorrow was the Lord's Day, nothing would get done, except what was absolutely necessary. But what counted as necessary?

A visit to the bishop was in order. Immediately. The man should know the Behr family had arrived and needed a barn, so that word would get out and plans would be made.

Gabe also wanted answers to his big question: What had he done that was so bad, complete strangers considering a move to the area needed to be warned about his presence? He'd simply been in the wrong place at the wrong time and made some unfortunate choices of "friends." Friends quick to abandon him when they were caught. And for that, Gabe had gotten the reputation, the exile, the punishment....

He blew out a breath of frustration.

Then again, what would kum of his asking the bishop to back off? Nothing gut, for sure. Instead, he'd get a lecture about disrespecting his elders. Another letter would be sent to Daed, resulting in yet another scolding. And Gabe would be subjected to even more scrutiny from the powers-that-be as he struggled to prove himself upright and sincere.

Struggled in vain, because someone spotted every slight infraction to complain about.

It was almost enough to make him want to pack his bags with his few belongings, disappear in the dark of nacht, and find a ministry that helped those desperate to escape the Amish adjust to the real world.

But running away would solve nothing. It'd only serve to further estrange him from his family, his faith, and maybe even Gott.

"I will never leave thee, nor forsake thee."

Gabe exhaled heavily as he directed Cherry Blossom to turn into the bishop's driveway.

It was gut to know Gott hadn't forsaken him. Because almost everyone else had.

The bishop exited the barn as Gabe climbed out of the buggy. He tugged on his long, graying beard. "Kum to confess something?"

Gabe frowned and shook his head. "The Behr family arrived in the middle of the storm last nacht. They need a barn."

The bishop snorted. "They need more than that. I'll talk to them. Staying with you at the Zooks' haus, I presume?"

"Nein, someone warned them to stay away from me. I rounded up some tents and a travel trailer of some sort. It will be delivered tomorrow."

The bishop's eyes widened. What, was he shocked Gabe had helped them? Wow. He hadn't realized his reputation was that bad.

"I'll check on them tomorrow," the bishop told him. "Danki for stopping by. And anytime you need to confess, I'll hear you."

What did he have to confess? "I...uh...I ate all the candy in the Zooks' candy jar."

The bishop's eyes bulged a moment before he snorted, then gave way to a spurt of laughter so intense that he bent double, gasping for breath. "I'm guilty of that sin, too. Go in peace."

Gabe nodded and climbed into the buggy. He'd go "home" and stay far away from the Behr family for this afternoon. For always. He knew where he wasn't wanted.

"Ach, Gabe." The bishop waved to him. "I'm putting you in charge of the Behrs until we get them settled. Check in on them daily and help out if they need it. You're the closest Amish neighbor."

Gabe blinked. Dread filled his chest. But so did something else. Excitement?

The bishop chortled. "Let me know if Goldilocks shows up."

She already had.

~⌒

Bridget shivered into her frozen-stiff dress the next morgen. Mamm had insisted on washing it when she noticed the caked-on mud the previous day, but with nein fire to speed the drying process, she had little choice but to put it back on while it was still wet, and cover it with her coat. After breakfast, she planned to burrow in blankets and read the book she'd had the foresight to drop into her purse instead of into a moving box.

Since it was Sunday, work was verboden, making it an ideal time to read. Too bad Gabe hadn't thought to bring any camp chairs. But she was grateful for the tent and the camp stove. They were out of the wind and had hot oatmeal for breakfast.

Now, they all huddled in the tent as Daed read a portion of Scripture from Genesis, emphasizing the verse in which der Herr tells Abram to leave his homeland and travel far from his father's haus into a land Gott would show him. He illuminated it with a verse from the book of Hebrews: *"By faith Abraham, when he was called to go out into a place which he should after receive for an inheritance, obeyed; and he went out, not knowing whither he went."*

Bridget's teeth chattered as she drew her blanket more tightly around herself. Daed was really going to use the Bible to justify this move to Michigan? It would be rude and disrespectful to point out that his name wasn't Abram or Abraham. Bridget glanced at Noah. He frowned so fiercely, his nose and forehead were wrinkled. She quickly looked away so she wouldn't get in trouble for giggling during morgen devotions.

Daed droned on for a few more minutes about how Gott would surely bless them for following Him, and then he bowed his head. "Let us pray."

A horse whinnied outside the tent, and Bridget's heart jumped. Was it Gabe?

"Knock, knock," came a man's voice outside the tent flap.

Daed quickly said, "Amen," then rose from the blanket he'd been sitting on. He unzipped the flap and lifted it. "Hallo. I'm Hosea Behr from Ohio."

A man with a graying bushy beard peeked his head inside and glanced around at all of them. "Nehemiah Brunstetter. Most people call me Miah. I'm the bishop in the district. Welkum. Young Gabe Lapp stopped by yesterday afternoon to let me know you'd arrived and to inform me of your need of a barn."

Daed scratched his neck and looked at the blanket-strewn canvas floor. "I'd offer you a seat, but...."

The bishop waved his hand. "Nein, I'm fine. The men and I will meet on the morrow to discuss when we can build you a barn. Have you made any decisions regarding the, uh, haus?" He cleared his throat.

Daed shifted. "As we read in the Scriptures this morgen, Gott has given us this land, and we're not going back."

"All well and gut, but...." The bishop surveyed the group once more. His gaze paused on Bridget before moving on. "Young Gabe Lapp is getting a reputation around here as someone who knows construction. Ask him what he thinks."

"We were warned to keep our distance from Gabe Lapp," Daed said tersely.

The bishop chuckled. "He's somewhat of a rebel without a clue. But he's got a gut head on his shoulders. And if he survives the proving, he'll make a gut man."

"The *proving*," Daed muttered.

"Every man must live with the man he makes of himself. We're making sure this bu has some rough waters to navigate so he'll know how. A smooth sea never makes a skillful mariner."

"I've been wrong." Daed bowed his head. "I treated him like the idiot I assumed he was."

The bishop shrugged. "His daed wants him to learn a lesson. Down south, he had too much time on his hands. Idle hands are the devil's playground, you know. He found trouble. Nothing serious, mind you, but enough so his daed decided to send him north. Nein time for idleness here. And he's finding even more ways to keep busy than I dreamed." He glanced at Bridget. "He'll make a fine ehemann, someday."

She felt her face flame red. She quickly dipped her head so nobody would see.

But, despite her interest, Gabe was a flirt.

And she didn't date.

6

Gabe's stomach hurt when he came home from the singing Sunday nacht. Some food might help, but he could still taste the awful dried venison the hosts had served. It was so leathery, he'd had to chew the one bite he'd taken for an eternity before it softened enough to wash down with a gallon of sour lemonade. He wasn't used to eating wild game, but if he had to, he much preferred the Englisch barbequed dish the fire chief had served.

He settled for a bowl of bland cereal with a heaping spoonful of sugar. That would tide him over until morgen. Maybe.

Stomach satisfied, for now, he went up to bed. If only he could wake up to the aromas of breakfast being cooked by a beautiful woman. With green eyes, like Bridget. Well, alright. Bridget herself would be nice.

But the next morgen, when Gabe wandered downstairs, nobody puttered around the kitchen. The dishes from his late-nacht snack still sat where he'd left them. He missed the Zooks. And, if it was possible, he missed the Behrs, even though they'd stayed with him just one nacht.

What he really missed was real food. His memory conjured the platter of fried seafood he'd dreamed about during the nacht. What he wouldn't give for a meal at his favorite restaurant back home in Florida.

He'd been assured the locals here ate seafood, especially smoked fish. But it'd been too cold to go fishing, in his opinion. A friend from the fire station had offered to take him out on his vessel in the spring. Someone else had suggested ice fishing, but said it wasn't cold enough for that yet.

Gabe glanced at the frost-covered windows. Hard to imagine it being any colder. The "Yoopers," running around in only sweatshirts and pants, often teased him about his "thin southern blood" as he shivered and wished for a parka.

Gabe added another log to the fire, then set a plate of leftover scrambled eggs and bacon from yesterday on the woodstove to warm. *Danki, Gott, for real food.* Even if the meal didn't get steaming hot, it would still be better than whatever else he might manage to scavenge after he'd finished the chores.

He put on his boots, slipped his coat over his pajamas, and went out to the barn, moving quickly to minimize exposure to the sleet slanting down from the sky. When he finished his work, he carried the bucket of milk to the haus, poured it into jars, and put what he wouldn't drink for breakfast in the antique "icebox" on the back porch.

He knew that nobody would kum by to visit if he bothered getting dressed, but if he stayed in his pajamas—he chuckled, remembering the Behrs' shocked expressions—it was almost a given someone would, causing embarrassment all around and probably getting him into more trouble with the preachers. Unless he hid upstairs in his bedroom.

But then, someone would likely go investigating and find him.

Of course, if it was Bridget....

Nein. He wouldn't go there. He shouldn't even entertain such thoughts.

Maybe little Jonah. Gabe chuckled as he recalled the bu's wide-eyed shock when he saw Gabe's green pajama pants. Wouldn't he love to see Gabe's firefighting gear?

Gabe held his numb fingers over the woodstove as he bent his head for a silent prayer. Then he carried the plate from the stove to the table and ate his slightly warm meal.

The silence was almost deafening.

And he had nowhere to go today. Nothing to do.

Except...oh, jah, Bishop Brunstetter had given him orders to check in on the Behrs daily. Gabe wouldn't mind having a chance to see Green Eyes, maybe to tease or flirt with her. Or a chance to visit Noah, who had the potential of being a friend. And/or their cute, fire-pole-fixated little brother.

Then he remembered Hosea, and his excitement waned.

He sighed.

Best to get it over with.

He washed up his few dishes—just in case someone stopped in while he was gone—and ran upstairs to get dressed and find an extra blanket for the buggy. Once appropriately attired, he went outside and harnessed Cherry Blossom.

Sleet bit at his skin as he traveled through the piney woods to the "haunted haus." Dread filled him. What would he find? Had Mrs. Behr remembered his warning to use the camp stove only in a well-ventilated area? Or would he arrive to find the tent he'd borrowed a charred, worthless mess?

Gabe shook off the worry and steeled himself for another unpleasant exchange with Hosea. Full of complaints, judgment, and demands, with not even an iota of thanks. And why was he so eager to see Bridget? She'd been more than clear in her rejection of him and his attention. And even though he was sure he'd seen a brief flare of interest in her beautiful green eyes yesterday, she wouldn't act on it, thanks to whoever had warned her family about Gabe.

Either that, or she had a beau back in…wherever it was she came from.

Gabe shrugged as the buggy turned by the rusted mailbox. The wheels slid sideways on an icy patch before they regained traction. Winter here would be bad. His teeth chattered as a gust of freezing rain came in through the open window and hit him in the face. He used his damp sleeve to mop it off as he traveled the overgrown road to the haunted haus. The tent still stood, evidently uncharred, but there was no sign of life. Nein conversation. Would he find a pack of frozen Behrs?

Strains of a conversation met his ears. And then came the noisy rumble of a running motor.

Had the RV arrived? A burst of excitement warmed him.

He parked the buggy, climbed out, and followed the sound around the back of the haus. The family had gathered around the large, class-A motor home.

"And that's how you turn on the generator." Patrick reached for a switch and turned it off.

Hosea had a deer-in-the-rifle's-sight look in his eyes. He stared at the RV as if he expected the devil himself to open the door and step out. Would he refuse the offer of the motor home on principle? "I know how to work a generator, but thanks for showing me this, uh, particular model." His voice was husky, raw, as if his throat might be sore.

"I'll show you how to operate the interior generator in a moment," Patrick told him. "But, like I said, it has about two thousand hours of use, so you'll need this one as a backup in case the interior one needs charging. I realize you Amish don't use electric, but even if you don't use the lights, you'll still need electricity for the water heater, the stove, and the oven. Not to mention heat."

Hosea grunted.

Gabe cleared his throat and stepped forward. "Actually, Amish in Florida use electric for refrigerators and air-conditioning. Too hot down there otherwise."

Patrick glanced up, his eyes lighting. "Hey, Gabe."

Everyone looked at him. Stared, really. Gabe resisted the urge to glance down at his clothes, to make sure he'd remembered to change out of his pajama pants. He focused on Patrick, but out of the corner of his eye, he noticed Bridget take a tiny step in his direction. Two steps. Then Hosea strode toward him.

"Like I told Gabe yesterday, I just had it serviced, but my family doesn't need it this winter, so you folks can use it until your house is…." Patrick's gaze darted to the gray monstrosity behind the RV. "Um, inhabitable."

Gut word, that.

Hosea's hand came out and landed on Gabe's back with a hard pat, then settled with a squeeze on his shoulder. "Appreciate your doing this for us. And everything else you've done. You've gone above and beyond."

Gabe shifted away from him, dislodging his grasp, and frowned, waiting for the "but…."

"I was wrong, and I say I was wrong. I'd appreciate it if you'd talk with me about my options with this haus, tomorrow, if you're free then."

He was wrong? What had happened during the over-nacht hours?

"But I'm still not prepared to give you my dochter's hand in marriage."

Bridget's face flamed. She pressed her hands to her burning cheeks. "Daed!"

Gabe turned away, coughing hard. He sounded like Grossmammi when she'd suffered from emphysema.

Noah laughed. So did the Englischer.

Bridget would have run away if she had anywhere to go. Instead, she turned to the bearded *Englisch* man. Patrick. "Can we see inside?" She hated the squeaky pitch of her voice. How could Daed say such a thing? If Gabe had been entertaining any interest in her, Daed had just killed it. Murdered, in cold blood.

Although that might've been his intent.

And she should be grateful. Really. It was only a silly instance of attraction thing she had going, and nothing would ever kum of it.

"Oh, sure, sure," Patrick replied. "I need to show you how to work the interior generator, anyway." He reached for a thin, shiny handle, and a set of metal steps came out of the side of the RV. He climbed them and opened the door. "Come on in. It sleeps six. Think I told Gabe it sleeps four, but I forgot about the sofa bed."

The interior was the fanciest place Bridget had ever set foot, with overstuffed chairs, a built-in table and bench seats, a tiny kitchen, a supersmall bathroom, and the biggest bed she'd ever seen. "It's a king," Patrick said proudly. Plus, there was a bunk over the front seats with a metal ladder right behind the driver's seat. Patrick demonstrated how to open the sofa bed.

Bridget figured this was the end of the tents, unless Noah and Jonah slept out there. If the RV slept six, they could squeeze in one more.

Mamm sank into the seat behind the steering wheel, tears flowing down her face. She wiped her cheeks with her sleeve. "This is so nice…the nicest place I've ever lived."

Jah, it was. As well as the tiniest.

Gabe stood silently in the doorway, not attempting to jostle past anyone in the narrow passageways. A small smile played on his lips as he glanced at Bridget. His dimple flashed. She quickly looked away. It wouldn't do for him to catch her staring.

"I'll leave you all to get settled." Gabe backed out of the doorway and descended the metal steps.

Patrick nodded. "If you have any questions, Gabe knows how to reach me. But you shouldn't have any problems. We were planning on taking the camper south this winter." He swallowed hard. "The good Lord had other plans. Guess He knew you'd have need of it."

The good Lord? Did Patrick mean that Gott had His hand on them, even here, with all that had gone wrong? And what, exactly, had kept

Patrick's family from using the RV as they'd planned? She couldn't think of a tactful way of asking. Maybe Gabe would know, if she ever got up the nerve to inquire.

And that reminded her.... She pushed past her little brother and rushed out the door after Patrick and Gabe.

The two men stood by the Zooks' buggy, talking. Bridget hesitated, not wanting to interrupt. But when Patrick climbed in, and Gabe after him, she had nein choice. She walked quickly toward the buggy.

Gabe shifted the brake, and the horse started backing up. Then Gabe noticed her approach, and pulled on the reins. "Hiya, Bridget. Is there something you need?" There was nein hint of flirtation in his voice. Not in his facial expression, either.

Why was she disappointed?

She shook her head. "I want to thank you both for all you've done. We really appreciate it."

Gabe blinked. A half smile appeared. "Danki for saying that."

"You're welcome," Patrick told her.

"I owe you. *We* owe you. If there's anything we can do to help you, just let us know."

Gabe's smile widened. "Anything?" The flirting had returned. Along with his adorable dimple.

His low chuckle sent a shiver down Bridget's spine. "I'll hold you to it, Bridget Behr."

Her face burned. "Except dating. I don't date."

"You've made that clear. But you also promised." He winked at her, then made a clicking noise at the horse.

The buggy headed toward the road.

What had she just agreed to?

And why was she looking forward to it?

Gabe pulled the buggy to a stop in front of Patrick's home. "You want me to bring back your tent? I've a feeling they'll all stay in the RV."

Patrick pursed his lips as he climbed out of the buggy. "Give them a few days and see what's happening. I think they'll find seven crowded in there is a bit too much. Even six might be, but it's doable." He shrugged.

"No rush. The tent belongs to my son, and he won't use it this winter. He does his camping during the summer, between Memorial Day and Labor Day, like most people."

Gabe chuckled. "I'm sure the Behrs were mighty cold last nacht. But they didn't want to stay with me at the Zooks' haus, and I'm pretty sure it'd take nerves of steel to stay in their own haus. If they decide to renovate, the work will be the least of their concerns. I didn't say anything, but there's a nest of raccoons in one of the closets. One of them hissed at me. And there's evidence of other animals living there—bats, squirrels, and other rodents, to name a few."

Patrick grunted. "Between the wildlife infestation and the structural deficiencies, I think they ought to level the place and start over. Can't believe it was approved to be used as a haunted house this year, considering the people going through it were either drunk, high, or too young to know better."

Gabe nodded. "Starting over was my recommendation to Hosea."

Patrick nodded. "I suppose, if Hosea Behr has the means, he could build a right fine place there. What does he do for a living?"

Gabe stilled and shook his head. "I don't know. Noah mentioned he and his daed would need to find employment, but he didn't say where or doing what. And I didn't ask." Hosea's finances might need a remodel rather than a rebuild. If that was the case, Gabe wasn't sure where to start.

Patrick sighed. "Too bad I don't have need of anyone right now. Sawmill might be hiring. Or one of the logging companies. But they might have to commute to Indiana and stay there during the week to work at the RV factories. Or they could join a fishing crew, but they'll be closing down for the season soon, if they haven't already." He shrugged. "Well, I'll see you tomorrow."

"I'll be there."

"You'll be laying laminate flooring after you tear up the orange shag carpet that reeks of cat urine. The former owner was an elderly woman who fit the 'crazy cat lady' cliché. Her kids are renovating the house for sale. There's a buyer already in the picture if the things he demands are fixed or replaced."

Gabe nodded. He was thankful for the work, and even ripping out stinky carpet beat trying to figure out how to fix the haunted haus.

Patrick's laughter startled Gabe. "So, what're you gonna ask that girl to do? Date you, even though she says she doesn't date?"

"No idea, really." A gust of wind drilled tiny ice shards into Gabe's face. That reminded him… "The fire chief mentioned something about a polar bear plunge happening the first of January. If I'm still here." Not that he'd ask Bridget to participate, but it'd be interesting to see who was crazy enough to risk losing limbs to severe frostbite. The weather in January would be ever so much colder than it was now.

"You'll still be here."

Patrick didn't need to sound so sure, as if he were privy to information unknown to Gabe. As if he assumed Gabe wouldn't be welkum back home, even if he earned the money he needed to. As if perhaps Gabe had been traded to the Mackinac County Amish for new blood.

Wasn't this community too recently formed to require new blood already? Or was it the case that everyone who moved here from wherever it was they came from was related, and therefore…

Daed would've told him, ain't so?

The sick knot in his stomach said otherwise.

7

The RV was such a luxury. The heater worked great, and for the first time in twenty-four hours, Bridget thought she might thaw out. In the morgen after their first nacht in the camper, she stretched lazily in the king-sized bed beside her sisters and listened for signs indicating Mamm and Daed were up. They'd chosen to sleep on the sofa bed, while her two brothers had taken the bunk.

She didn't hear any conversation, but the strong scent of koffee indicated at least Mamm was awake.

Bridget slipped out of bed, pulled on her dress, and padded barefoot out of the dark bedroom. The brightness of the electric lights caught her by surprise. She stopped and squeezed her eyes shut, her hand pressing against the wall. Then she opened her eyelids, blinking rapidly.

Daed sat in the kitchenette, an odd-shaped ceramic mug on the table before him. It looked as if someone had taken the soft clay and squeezed it before firing it. Though probably the mold had been shaped that way. Bridget's job back in Ohio had been painting ceramics for an Englisch lady who sold them to tourists. It'd been enjoyable, especially when she was allowed to sketch idyllic rural scenes on some of the items. Pictures of buggies, barns, flowers, animals, and the like. This particular mug wasn't pretty. It was a plain brick-red color with gold trim on the edge, and bore a logo, also in gold.

"Gut morgen, Bridget." Daed peered at her over the top of his glasses. "Do you recall what time Gabe said he would kum by to talk to me today? And why did the bishop call him 'Young Gabe'?"

What, did Daed expect her to have all the answers when it came to Gabe Lapp? Granted, she probably would've remembered if he'd mentioned a specific time—and would've been watching the windup clock, too, watching the seconds crawl by as she awaited his arrival.

Her face heated. "I…I don't think he said," she stammered. "I don't know."

Daed smirked as he pushed a notepad toward her. There were some words written on the paper, but she couldn't see them clearly for her sleep-blurred vision. She rubbed her eyes.

"What features would you like to see in a new haus if we decide to rebuild?" He raised his eyebrows.

"If"? Not "when"?

Bridget glanced out the nearest window at the monstrosity they were parked beside. Little specks of white floated by in the dim beginnings of the early-morgen sunrise. A flutter of excitement worked through her. "It's snowing!"

Mamm spun the whisk around in the mixing bowl. "I'm thinking we'll see enough snow here to make flurries nothing to get excited over."

Bridget turned to her mamm. "How can I help?"

"I don't think you can, just now. Maybe when I get further along. This stove is too small for two people to stand at, so I figured I'd do all the cooking today. Tomorrow, you can cook. Help your daed. He's trying to design a rough draft of what we want in our new home."

That sounded more positive. Bridget poured herself a mug of koffee from the pot. She opened the refrigerator in search of cream, but there was nothing inside. Ugh. She'd have to drink it black.

Daed pushed the sugar bowl toward her as she sat. Followed by a can of milk.

Ach, she'd forgotten that Mamm had purchased some shelf-stable milk to use until their cow arrived.

Powdered eggs, too, until the chickens came and started laying.

And ready-to-eat bacon.

"So. What would you like in your dream home?" Daed pushed the neglected notepad closer and slid a pen across the table.

It didn't really matter, because this place would belong to her parents. Not her. She would eventually marry, move in with her ehemann, and have a family of her own.

Not if you never date.

She cringed. But what could she do now? Gabe had asked her out. Twice. And she'd rejected him with absolute clarity. What were the chances he'd ask her out again?

She sighed and glanced at Daed. "I don't understand."

"Do you want your own bedroom, or are you content sharing with your sisters? Do you want a porch with a swing for sparking with your beau? Do you want a bathroom with a shower upstairs?"

"A bathroom upstairs would be wunderbaar." Their old haus had only one tiny bathroom for the seven of them. "I don't mind sharing a room. And who am I going to be sparking with?"

Maybe she shouldn't have asked that question. She could almost see Gabe's name forming in Daed's mind. Mamm's, too.

Before either one of them could say anything, Noah climbed down the ladder. "If I have any say, I'd like my own room." He lowered himself into the chair next to Bridget's.

Jonah scrambled down the ladder and plopped down on the bench beside Daed. "I'd be lonely all by myself." His lower lip trembled.

"What are we supposed to do with ourselves today, Daed?" Noah spread his hands out on the tabletop. "Seems pointless to unpack anymore, and we have nein chores."

Daed cleared his throat. "We'll be plenty busy. After breakfast, we're going outside to decide where we want the barn. The bishop will be by sometime today to discuss it. And I suppose we should ready a room of the haus to use as a temporary barn, since the animals will arrive later today."

"Gabe Lapp offered us the use of the Zooks' barn until we have one built." Noah said this respectfully, but with an underlying edge that clearly recommended they take him up on the offer.

"Jah, but then he'd have to do the chores." Daed took a sip of koffee. "I hate being beholden to him more than I already am—and will be. Not to mention, he probably should clear it with the Zooks before he goes offering use of their facilities."

Mamm placed a full mug of koffee in front of Noah, then gave Jonah a sideways hug. "Pancakes will be ready soon."

"Yum! I'm starving." Jonah looked at Daed. "Can I have koffee, too?"

"It'll stunt your growth." Daed edged his mug a little farther from Jonah.

"I'd love a workroom in the barn." Noah leaned forward. "Someplace to try my hand at woodworking."

Daed grunted.

"Bridget needs a hope chest. I could make her one."

Bridget gave Noah a gentle punch in the arm. "I don't need a hope chest."

Noah grabbed his mug, got to his feet, and moved to stand by the stove. "Jah, probably too late for that, with the way Gabe Lapp looks at you. Maybe a marriage chest, instead."

The words provoked an odd fluttering sensation in Bridget's heart. But she scoffed. "I'll never marry. I don't date. Remember?"

But she might be persuaded....

⌒

Dusk was falling when Gabe got off work and drove his borrowed buggy to the Behrs' campsite after stopping briefly at the fire station. He parked in front of the haus and noted some stakes in the ground about 150 yards to the right, evidently placed to mark out the location for something. Probably a barn. Someone had built a ramp, of sorts, leading into the haus. He heard a horse whinny.

He would give the family credit for imagination and spunk, but it hurt to realize they had decided to reject his offer to use the Zooks' barn. Didn't they trust him to take care of a few extra animals? Granted, he might not be an expert on livestock. His family in Pinecraft didn't own a single animal. Not even a dog or a cat. Horses and buggies were verboden there. The Amish either walked, biked, or traveled by bus. But he'd learned quickly how to care for animals when he arrived in Mackinac County.

He skirted the outside of the building to where the RV was parked. The generator rumbled, and some lights were on inside the vehicle. Someone had dissembled the tent, and Gabe wondered where it had gone. Maybe inside one of the camper's many storage compartments.

Gabe heard someone laugh as he rapped on the door, then opened it. "Hallo?"

"Gabe!" Jonah raced toward him, stopping just in time to avoid tumbling down the steps. "Our animals came today. And the preachers came and helped us lay out a barn. Then they took Daed to order supplies."

"Wow. Sounds like you've been busy."

"Did you kum to take me to the fire station?"

"Ah, nein. Not today. I just went by there, and it was closed up tight. But sometime, for sure. Is your daed here, or is he still with the preachers? He wanted to discuss the haus."

"He's here." Jonah sobered. "Kum in."

Hosea stood from the table as Gabe approached him. "Gut of you to kum by. Wasn't sure you would, considering the late hour. Have you had supper yet? I think there might be a plateful left."

"I just got off work. Sounds gut, if you're sure."

Hosea shrugged. "One of the preachers brought along a casserole his frau made. Mixture of tuna, rice, and broccoli. Not too bad. And definitely appreciated, with things being as they are right now." He raised his voice and called, "Bridget, warm a plate for Gabe."

A door at the end of the hallway slid open, and Bridget emerged. She wore the same gray dress she'd had on when she arrived. Their luggage must not have caught up with them yet.

She brushed her kapp strings off her shoulders and, without looking at Gabe, opened the refrigerator, removed a plate, and stuck the plate in the microwave. The back of her neck was pink, as was the portion of her face visible to him.

The microwave beeped, and as she took out the plate, his nostrils registered an aroma that smelled beyond delicious. His stomach rumbled in anticipation. She took a fork and a knife from a drawer and set them in front of Gabe in a manner even the most seasoned server would be proud of.

"Danki, Bridget."

Her face flamed brighter. "Sure."

Hosea fell silent, and only then did Gabe realize the man had been talking the entire time Gabe had been gawking at Bridget. His own face heated. He quickly dipped his head for the silent prayer, and then, as Bridget retreated—with frequent backward glances—to where she'd been hiding, he turned his attention to Hosea. Sort of. Half his attention was still on his dochter. "Sorry. My mind was on something else. You were saying?"

Bridget stopped in the doorway. Turned. And very slowly slid the door shut, her gaze on Gabe the entire time.

The latch clicked.

"Something? Or someone?" Hosea said wryly.

Gabe pressed his lips together and glanced around, strangely glad to find himself alone with Hosea. He didn't know where Jonah had gotten to. But it was a small space, and their voices would carry easily, even beyond closed doors.

Gabe spoke quietly. "Look, I know you don't consider me worthy of your dochter. To put your mind at ease, rest assured I'm not going to make a play for her. Besides, she's already made her status clear. And I'm aware of your opinion of me. When it comes to brains, you think I got the short end of the stick." Seemed that opinion applied to his family, too. He set his jaw. "But I'm *not* a dummchen, and I won't intrude where I'm not wanted. Including on the plans for your haus, and involvement with your family." Harsh, but it needed to be said. Now Hosea could agree, and Gabe would go on his way without eating a single bite of dinner.

Or maybe he'd be able to get down a bite or two before Hosea kicked him out into the cold.

Nein, he should resist the temptation to eat their food. He could make a sandwich or warm a jar of soup. And he could survive without this family.

The acute pain of loneliness stabbed him. His eyes burned. What he wouldn't give for a hug from Mamm. A pat on the shoulder from Daed, even if it was accompanied by a scolding. At least they loved him.

Hosea let his breath out in a hiss. "I apologized, bu, for misjudging you. I value your opinion. But I can understand why you think of me as a judgmental old man." He sighed. "I am one."

I am one. The three words echoed in Gabe's thoughts, reaching out and taking root. Jah, Gabe was, too. He'd judged Hosea harshly because of the situation he'd gotten himself and his family into. At least Hosea had had the grace to apologize. Gabe needed to do the same. *Forgive me, Lord.*

He reached across the table and rested his hand briefly on Hosea's arm. "And I'm sorry for judging you. I'm sure you had gut reasons."

Hosea nodded, his eyes filling with moisture. "There's an older man in our previous district. He's married, but he's also the bishop's brother, so the bishop won't kum down harshly on him. He's been stalking the dochters. One family moved to Missouri. We stuck it out until Bridget awoke to find him standing in her bedroom, even though we'd locked the doors. He must've crawled through an open window. She screamed, and he left the same way he'd kum in, but I worried what would become of us. My frau, my dochters...they weren't safe. If the bishop wouldn't protect us, then I had to do something. I couldn't stand by and watch my dochter be violated. I had nein choice."

Gabe blinked. He hadn't expected Hosea to share so many details. But that explained, at least in part, why Hosea had been so desperate as to jump at cheap land, and a "haus."

"Why not go to Missouri, like that other family?"

Hosea shook his head. "Lack of land. They are staying in a rented dawdi-haus with their large family until they can find something. It was easier and simpler—or, rather, it seemed so—to buy this property."

Gabe pushed his now-cold dinner away, even as his stomach grumbled in complaint. He rose, studied the microwave for a moment, and reheated the food. "Okay, what did you decide to do with the haus?"

"Level it, as you suggested. I've asked my family what they want in a new haus. My frau wants a big, roomy kitchen with lots of counter space and cabinets. Two full-size bathrooms are on the list. As well as a front porch with a swing for the purpose of courting."

"With a window within easy eavesdropping distance?" Gabe only half joked, but as he said the words, he realized the older man hadn't denied having deemed Gabe unworthy of Bridget.

Hosea chuckled. "But of course." He slid a piece of notebook paper across the table. "Let's see what you kum up with."

Gabe could do a rough sketch using the specifications Hosea provided, but the real one would need to be done on graph paper by a true professional. He nodded, took a bite of his dinner, and went to work.

Who would be the lucky man courting the lovely Bridget on the front porch swing?

Only thing he knew for sure: Even with Hosea's recent thawing, it wouldn't be Gabe.

⌣

Bridget hated that she and her sisters had been hidden away back in the bedroom with the king-sized bed while Gabe was there. Mamm, too, but she didn't seem to mind. Instead, she'd curled up on the bed with a romance novel she'd selected before the move and hadn't had time to read on the long trip.

Her sisters huddled on the other side of the bed, heads together, doing a word search.

Only Bridget paced, wanting to go out and listen in on the quiet conversation in the main part of the RV, to be privy to whatever it was that Daed and Gabe were discussing. She couldn't hear clearly from here, with the rumbling of the noisy generator right outside. She'd even sit next to Daed, but mainly she wanted to look her fill at the handsome man.

But that would do nein gut. Men weren't to be trusted, and they tromped on women's emotions, wants, needs, and desires, as if women were insects. Inconsequential.

If women mattered, the married man stalking single girls would stay home with his frau and love her the way Christ loved the church.

If women mattered, the bishop would put the safety of women ahead of his brother's lecherous thoughts and actions.

If women mattered, Daed would've talked to his family before deciding to uproot them and move to the edge of civilization.

If women mattered, Isaac Hershberger would have asked her to write, and made plans to visit, instead of promptly breaking up with her when he learned of the impending move.

If women mattered....

She slumped against the wall.

The point was, to most men, women didn't matter.

Therefore, she wouldn't date.

But, ach, she wanted to.

8

The following evening, when Gabe returned to the "haunted haus," several men were unloading lumber, shingles, and other building supplies from a delivery truck. A package of tarps waited to cover the building supplies, though Gabe wasn't sure how much gut those would do if the predicted hurricane-strength winds Patrick had mentioned kicked in.

Noah hurried over to greet Gabe. "They're building the barn tomorrow."

"That's great. Once the barn is done, and you can move the animals, the next step is to move the RV away from the haus and get a bulldozer in." Gabe eyed the monstrosity.

"Someone from the township came by today and reclaimed the Halloween decorations—spiders, bats, and other spooky stuff—saying it would be reused." Noah frowned at the haus as if he expected someone else to emerge carting miscellaneous Halloween items.

About time, too, considering Thanksgiving was this Thursday. Thanksgiving...Gabe's first without any family around. Nein friends, either, since the Zooks planned to spend the holiday in Mio, and nobody had invited Gabe to join them.

Of course, the Behrs would be alone, too. Probably. They might've gotten an invitation from the bishop or one of the other preachers to enjoy some freshly killed venison. Not the store-bought turkey Mamm would've stuffed and baked, along with innumerable pies....

Gabe's stomach rumbled, and he forced his attention to the roofing shingles lined up in a sheltered area. Nein point in dwelling on Thanksgiving. Or the feast he would miss. For him, it'd be a normal day, except without work to detract from the loneliness.

Hosea shoved his glasses further up the bridge of his nose, and adjusted his hat. Flurries fell from the sky, but Gabe's boss had informed him that a "real" snowfall was imminent. Flurries were real enough for Gabe. Blizzard warnings had already been forecasted. And if those forecasts proved true, he wouldn't take the horse and buggy out. Patrick would need to drive over in his four-wheel-drive truck—or his snowmobile—and pick him up for work.

That would be an adventure. Almost worth the troubling thoughts of snow. And the bitter cold.

Almost. He pulled his coat tighter around his body and glanced around. None of the female Behrs were anywhere near the construction site. It was possible they were holed up in the RV.

"They'll start with the haus after Thanksgiving. Next Monday, Bishop Brunstetter said, weather permitting...and if you agree to head up the construction crew." Hosea stopped next to him. Eagerness filled his eyes, and an expression close to a smile lit his face.

"Ah." Gabe's mind whirled. "I work for someone. Patrick, the Englisch man who loaned you the RV. I can't direct the construction crew."

"But a haus is necessary."

Gabe puffed out a breath. "Jah. And so is my continued employment. I can't quit a permanent, full-time job for a temporary one I'm not qualified for. That would be foolish, on both our parts. And you do have shelter, even though it may not be ideal."

Hosea's eyebrows shot up. "You would refuse the bishop?"

The men slammed the back of the delivery truck closed, and the engine rumbled to life. Moments later, the vehicle disappeared down the lane.

Gabe looked back at Hosea. "Nein, I wouldn't refuse the bishop. But I would point out you don't have real plans for a haus. And it's not the same as building a barn."

"You drew plans on the notebook paper." Frustration filled Hosea's voice.

Whatever it was Hosea had done in Ohio, it hadn't been construction. Gabe frowned. "I sketched a basic outline. The real floor plans will require much more detail. Square footage; locations of windows, doors; and plumbing. Among other things." He'd done it before, working at Daed's construction company. But it took days of planning. Weeks.

Of course, this project would give him something to do over Thanksgiving.

Hosea slumped. "So, we won't be in the haus next week?"

Gabe sighed. "Honestly? You won't even be in by Christmas. And the weather will only get worse from here."

A gush of wind grabbed Gabe's hat and made off with it. Noah and Hosea both managed to grab their hats.

Gabe turned to chase his hat. At the edge of the tree line, Bridget jumped and snagged it. She turned to face him. And very deliberately put the hat on her head. Held it there, to keep the wind from reclaiming it.

Gabe caught his breath as he remembered something his mammi used to say. *"A woman who puts on a man's hat is giving him a sign she wants to be kissed."*

Except, that couldn't be the case for Bridget.

Everything she'd said was to the contrary.

Then again, wasn't it true that actions spoke louder than words?

Her behavior said volumes.

Bridget pranced nearer to Gabe. He met her halfway and, with a swoop of his arm, reclaimed his hat. His eyes lit with humor. "I'll hold you to it someday, Green Eyes."

I'll hold you to...? Huh? "What?" She stopped her retreat and planted her fists on her hips. "I don't understand."

"Ach, you know. A woman who puts on a man's hat is giving him a sign she wants to be kissed."

Ach! She'd forgotten about that old proverb. Her face burned. She avoided looking at Daed, but she caught her brothers' smirks as she lowered her gaze to the ground. "Nein, I was just teasing. I didn't mean...." Actually, she had meant to flirt a little, just to see if she could find a spark of interest—or whether what she'd thought she'd seen before had merely been a figment of her imagination. She hadn't meant she wanted a kiss. Nein, not at all. But then, why did her lips tingle at the thought?

Now that the idea had been planted in her head, it was more than intriguing. She couldn't keep her gaze from rising to Gabe's well-formed lips.

Daed cleared his throat as he approached. He stopped beside Gabe, his stare boring into Bridget. Disapproval was written clearly in his raised eyebrows, in the lines etched in his forehead, in the frown dominating his jaw. She would get a lecture later, for sure, about how a man pursues a woman; how she shouldn't have dangled herself in front of him, begging for attention.

She cringed and stared at the ground, waiting, waiting for the proverbial hole to appear and swallow her. Or for a brilliant idea she could use to escape.

Had that been what attracted the married man in Ohio? Watching the youngies flirting with each other? Teasing, playing, doing the ageless courtship dance that even animals do to catch the attention of the opposite sex?

Despite her earlier thoughts about not wanting a man to control her and her life's decisions, the reality was, she had nein choice. If she didn't marry, she would live under Daed's rule, or her brothers'. Forever. Nein reprieve.

And always, always under the rule of the bishop and the preachers.

Really, there was nein escape, whether she dated or not. Whether she married or not.

She sighed. Backed away, the heat giving away to icy coldness.

"I'm sorry." She made her back ramrod stiff, her tone overly formal. "I didn't mean to mislead you, making you believe I was interested in a...a kiss."

And there went that blasted heat again, at her mention of the "k" word in mixed company.

"Interested...in you," she whispered. She looked up again, hoping he might somehow understand her mixed-up emotions and thoughts, and discern that she might truly be interested and just didn't know how to behave, how to proceed, and, to be honest, even what to think. She confused herself.

Some of the light faded from Gabe's eyes, but something about them still held her captive. Drew her in. Pulled her to him, until it was just the two of them.

She stood there, suspended in time, her heart reaching out for his.

Reaching, grasping, and coming up empty.

Daed cleared his throat, and she ran off to find a pile of sand in which to bury her head.

～

When Gabe returned to the Behrs' place as evening fell the day after Thanksgiving, the new barn had a fresh coat of dull red paint and a Pennsylvania Dutch hex sign painted near the top. The haus had been razed and now lay where it had fallen. Bringing in a dumpster would be the next step.

Gabe couldn't keep from doing some mental planning. The idea of running a construction crew was both flattering and enticing, as a chance to prove himself. His mind had drifted in that direction several times while he ate his lonely, yucky Thanksgiving meal.

He had deliberately stayed away until after the holiday. He knew the Amish community would reach out with its loving arms and embrace the Behr family, since they were rebuilding the barn and had nothing.

Nobody had reached out to him. It hurt, but his stomach was filled. With burned soup and scorched eggs because he'd gotten the fire too hot and had forgotten about the food when he'd gone to feed the animals and do other chores. But filled nonetheless. During his day off work, he'd read devotions and thanked Gott for His blessings. For food on the table and shoes on his feet. A roof over his head and a gut place to sleep.

He shook off the feelings of rejection and looked around. The barn doors stood wide open, and someone had backed the RV into the big building. The vehicle was too long for the space, so the front stuck out of the building by about five feet. The barn would provide additional protection from the elements, but it would be dangerous to run the generator with the scant ventilation afforded by the building.

Gabe walked around the side of the RV. Gut, someone knew what to do. The generator was inside the barn, but just barely; it was covered just enough to stay protected from the elements. The exhaust was aimed toward the outdoors. That was fine, as long as the wind didn't change direction and blow the fumes back inside.

With that worry as gut as eliminated, Gabe entered the new barn and looked around. Stalls on one side, with a milking room for the cow, stalls for the two horses, and a pen for the hog. On the other side, a small chicken coop with a few hens clucking.

"Nice, isn't it?" Noah came up behind him. "Much nicer than the barn we had in Ohio. We saw you walking around out here. Want to kum in? Someone brought by chicken and dumplings, and Daed suggested playing board games. Mamm plans to bake cookies and make hot chocolate."

"Sounds gut." Much better than the burnt eggs he'd eaten for breakfast. Or the scalded soup he'd eaten last nacht, with leftovers planned for lunch today. Supper was to be a nein-fuss, impossible-for-him-to-ruin sandwich.

"Kum in." Noah opened the door.

"If you're sure I won't be intruding." Gabe followed Noah into the RV.

One of the younger girls—Gabe couldn't remember her name—set out bowls on the counter, while the other removed the silverware tray from a drawer. Where was Bridget?

"Thanks for inviting me for supper," Gabe said.

"We appreciate all you've done." Bridget's mamm smiled at him. "Do you take butter on your dumplings?"

Gabe glanced at the kettle full of fluffy dumplings floating on a creamy sea of broth and vegetables. He nodded. "Jah, that'd be gut. Danki."

"Tell me when." Mrs. Behr ladled some out, then nodded toward the seats when his bowl was almost full. "Let the young ones sit at the table." She added a generous pat of butter to the top.

"Danki." Gabe nodded, took the bowl, and sat on one edge of the sofa.

Noah brought his bowl over and sat down next to him. "Never expected people to bring food in, but it's wunderbaar. We were invited to the bishop's home for Thanksgiving. Where did you go?"

Now would be a gut time to pray. Gabe dipped his head. *Lord, forgive me for my envy. Help me to remember to be grateful for what I have. Danki for providing dinner to-nacht.*

He raised his head from the prayer and took a bite, hoping Noah wouldn't bring up the subject again. It'd be hard to admit that nobody cared enough for him to invite him for a Thanksgiving feast.

Bridget appeared then, passing by with her own bowl of food. She swiveled the passenger seat around and sat down, facing him and Noah.

"Barn looks nice." Gabe grinned. "Surprised to see it painted already. Red, at that." A lot of Amish communities felt a red barn shouted "Look at me." Prideful. But the Behrs had gone for a more muted hue than some he'd seen. Not that he'd seen a lot. They didn't have very many barns in Pinecraft.

"The paint was thrown in, free." Hosea sat next to Noah. "And one of the youngies is an aspiring artist. He's the bishop's gross-sohn, so he gave him a nod of approval, since our place is secluded and not visible from the road. Not sure how well the paint's drying, though, since it's been spitting snow and sleeting for the past...." He shrugged. "However long."

What would life have been like if someone had encouraged artistic expression with Gabe? Even if all his work was destroyed by uncooperative weather?

This meal was turning into a private pity party. He sighed and spooned another bite of food into his mouth.

Hosea cleared his throat. "Let's pray."

Gabe grimaced and lowered the spoon. When would he learn? He quickly ducked his head again. *Lord, help.*

He'd have a talk with the bishop about whether Daed had traded him to this community. If he had, then Gabe would probably be expected to marry Preacher Zook's dochter, Agnes. And while her candies might be beyond gut, it'd been nice to get a break from the chunky, stuttering woman, from her staring eyes that followed him everywhere.

Gabe sighed again.

If he hadn't been traded....

He cast a glance at Bridget.

She blushed and looked away.

The game just got a lot more interesting.

9

Mamm sat in a chair near Bridget. "Where are you from, Gabe? I heard that this community is only a few years old, so everyone came from somewhere else. Is your family here with you? Or did you come alone?" Mamm scuffed her stockinged feet on the carpet.

Gabe's eyes darkened with an expression that seemed to indicate emotional pain. "I came alone. My family lives in Pinecraft, Florida."

"Wow. You're really far from home. This must be a huge adjustment," Mamm said.

Gabe nodded and shoveled a spoonful of chicken into his mouth.

"How many brothers do you have?" Jonah piped up.

Gabe almost smiled. "Two older ones. Both married. And three younger sisters."

"So, what made you decide to kum up here? Alone?" Bridget blurted out her question.

Gabe glanced over, his gaze skimming her. Warming her. A teasing light lit his eyes, and he opened his mouth; but then he closed it, as if he'd thought better of whatever answer he'd been planning to give. The light died. He shrugged, and a muscle jumped in his jaw. "They thought I... well, honestly, they took me to the bus station, handed me a ticket, and told me to keep in touch."

Bridget's spoon dropped from her hand into her bowl.

Daed gasped. "I heard you were a black sheep. But so bad that your family—"

"I was *not* a black sheep." Gabe's voice had a sharp edge. "I was simply in the wrong place at the wrong time, and hung out with the wrong people. My so-called friends were brought in for vandalism and thefts, and I was questioned along with them. And then released. Because I was innocent." He set his mouth.

It was gut to know he wasn't a criminal. Still, his family had sent him away, so there had to be some truth to the black sheep part. Bridget studied him. Pain filled his eyes, along with what looked to be a tinge of regret.

Noah frowned and cast a concerned glance at Daed. As if he worried—as Bridget did—that Daed would put a stop to Gabe's coming around because he believed him to be a bad influence.

Daed stabbed a dumpling with his fork and said nothing.

"So, do you like it up here? What do you like to do?" Mamm was clearly attempting to smooth the sudden tension.

"Jah, I like it. It's…cold. Freezing. But there's a lot to see and do, and it's…educational. I'm glad I found a job right away."

"I need a job." Noah frowned. "So does Daed."

Bridget shifted. Maybe she could try to get a job, too, to help out. Would she be allowed to paint nature scenes to sell to tourists?

Gabe straightened. "What did you do in Ohio?"

"Farming. Not much gut up here." Noah glanced at Daed, as if waiting for him to mention their other business.

Except Daed remained silent. He went on eating, and ignoring them.

"Maybe the sawmill is hiring." Gabe frowned. "Or a lumber camp."

Bridget refused to keep quiet about their past occupations. If Gabe was going to help them find jobs, he needed all the facts. "They also catered to the tourists. We ran a bed-and-breakfast, and Daed and Noah took the guests on horse-and-buggy tours."

Gabe grunted, then took a final bite, emptying his bowl. He set the dish aside, his forehead furrowing.

"Don't guess that'd do us much gut around here," Noah muttered.

Daed gave him a sharp look.

"Feel free to go back for seconds," Mamm hurriedly told Gabe. "We have plenty."

Gabe set his spoon in his empty bowl, then stood and carried his dish over to the stove. He ladled in a second helping. "I don't see much need for a bed-and-breakfast here when there are several less than twenty miles away, and most visitors who cross the bridge are hunters, fishermen, or tourists headed to Mackinac Island."

Bridget had finished her meal, but she remained seated, unable to tear her gaze away from Gabe. Daed called him a "youngie," his voice filled with derision. But he was gorgeous, and seemed super smart. Gott had certainly smiled on her family when He'd led them to the haus where Gabe was staying.

Daed couldn't deny Gabe's intelligence, even though he seemed determined to keep on treating Gabe as a dummchen. Maybe he was just taking his cue from the other men in the district.

After everyone had finished eating and all the dishes were washed, Bridget set up the Monopoly board on the table, while the younger kids settled in the back bedroom playing Sorry! Shiloh went with them, probably to keep the peace, because Jonah didn't handle certain parts of the game very well. Mamm took out a pail of cookie dough one of the men had brought, courtesy of his frau, and began scooping spoonfuls onto a cookie sheet while the oven preheated.

Baking and cooking were certainly easier with the modern conveniences of the RV, despite the cramped quarters.

Daed counted out the Monopoly money, while Noah, seated beside him on the bench seat, made sure all the property cards were in the correct order. Bridget sorted the homes and hotels. Gabe had gone outside to empty a slop pail for the hog. Mamm didn't like for it to sit out over-nacht. Not that flies were a problem at this time of year.

The wind howled around the edge of the barn, its noise louder than Bridget had ever heard it before. She shivered.

The door opened, and Gabe came back inside. He handed the pail to Mamm and exhaled a weary sigh. "I've heard about the gales of November. Decided to bring my borrowed horse and buggy in from the cold. Hope you don't mind."

"It's fine, bu," Daed said. "Gut of you to treat the Zooks' animals with such care."

Gabe settled next to Bridget, and a surge of heat seared a path up Bridget's neck to her cheeks as his body filled the minimal space next to her. His thigh wasn't pressing against hers, but they were closer than a Bible's width. Personal space was definitely compromised. She scooted closer to the outer wall but still wasn't far enough away from him to catch a proper breath.

Instead, she inhaled a piney scent that came either from the soap he used or from working with wood all day.

He swallowed, his Adam's apple moving with the effort, and stretched out his arm along the back of the seat. He didn't touch Bridget, but his warmth filled the space, making it even harder to breathe.

Why was she so aware of this man? He affected her in ways she never would have expected. Nothing like Isaac. Her nerve endings came to life around Gabe.

"What are the 'gales of November'?" Noah asked.

"According to my boss, Patrick, the 'gales of November' refers to the peak of the Great Lakes storm season." Gabe shrugged. "I don't know for sure this is it, but if those aren't gales out there, I don't know what are. And it is November." He chuckled. "Might be the start of a blizzard. It is still spitting snow. Sleeting, mainly."

"Maybe you should go home, then." Noah drew his eyebrows together. "Though we'd enjoy it if you stayed. I suppose we could even put you up for the nacht, if need be."

Daed nodded. Not exactly encouraging, but probably because it was expected to be hospitable during natural disasters.

Bridget sucked in a breath. *Jah. Say jah.* Her mind darted back to the first time she saw Gabe, emerging shirtless from his bedroom—

"We probably could fit three up in the bunk." Noah jerked his thumb toward the ladder behind the driver's seat.

Gabe snorted. "Too close quarters, I'm thinking. Danki, but I'll be fine."

It'd probably be better for Bridget not to see his sleep-tousled hair, his sleepy eyes, and the lime-green pajama pants, anyway. Though he probably hadn't brought his pajamas along. As it was, the image was hard to forget. Forever seared on her brain. Making her imagine things she shouldn't.

A shiver raced up her spine. Her stomach clenched.

Gabe cast her a puzzled glance.

"Roll to see who goes first." Daed tossed the dice on the board. Mamm pulled the first tray of cookies out of the oven, their warm oatmeal-raisin scent filling the enclosed space.

Bridget's stomach rumbled in anticipation of the sweets, even though she truly wasn't hungry. She reached for one of the dice at the same time

Noah and Gabe did. Gabe's calloused fingers brushed against hers as she picked up the die. She fumbled as Gabe jerked away. The die spun on its corner, finally landing with the five facing upward.

Noah chuckled when he rolled a one. "I go first."

"Not if I match that," Gabe countered, leaning forward as Bridget withdrew her arm.

"Buwe. Competitive even in the rolling of dice." Daed grinned, winking at Bridget.

Daed and Noah could get quite competitive with this game. Bridget usually didn't fare very well, posing nein real threat, which was probably why they liked her to play. Gabe, with his current attitude, would be just as aggressive as her family. Maybe she should sit out and watch Jonah and Roseanna so that Shiloh could read.

But she was pinned into the booth. And she really didn't want to leave. Not with Gabe in such deliciously close proximity. He rolled, and his die tumbled toward the edge of the table. He leaned forward to grab it.

As he did, his other arm bumped against her, sending imaginary sparks flying. She froze.

He cleared his throat. "Sorry about that." And pulled his arm to his side.

She missed his warmth.

Her entire being throbbed with awareness. Even her tingling lips got in on the action.

Gabe Lapp equaled dangerous.

Very dangerous indeed.

⁓

Gabe reached for a cookie, still soft and warm from the oven. Mrs. Behr had filled a plate and set it on the table before disappearing down the short hallway to the bedroom with a tray filled with more of the same. Steaming mugs of hot chocolate cheered the tiny space.

Noah placed another haus on a property, then smirked as he leaned back.

Gabe surveyed the board. Bridget didn't have many properties, but income from her four railroads had enabled her to place hotels on Boardwalk and Park Place. The rest of the board was filled with green and red buildings belonging to the rest of them. Gabe mentally calculated what he needed to roll in order to avoid the railroad and the dark blue properties.

"Curious, Gabe." Hosea interrupted his roll. "Why do they call you 'Young Gabe'?"

Gabe chuckled. "Apparently there's another Gabe Lapp living here, now dubbed 'Old Gabe.' Nein relation that I know of. Nor do I know how old he is. I haven't actually met the man." He just felt sorry for him, having to share his name with someone of Gabe's reputation.

Gabe moved his game piece and landed on Boardwalk.

Bridget held out her hand. "Pay up."

Gabe eyed his pitiful cash supply. Considerably fewer bills on the table than in real life, but even that pile was skimpy. He probably could pay her if he started liquidating the property he owned, but it was late, and he needed to get home.

"I *could* pay…." He darted a teasing glance in her direction. "But a tornado hits, blowing your hotel away." He imitated the sound of a tornado as he scooped his hand over the building and made it disappear. Then he stood. "Seriously, I'm calling it a game, pun intended, and heading out. Early day tomorrow."

"Sure you don't want to spend the nacht?" Noah asked. "The wind is picking up."

"I'm sure." Gabe replaced the hotel and moved his game piece in front of Bridget. "But danki for offering. You're already crowded. It'd be worse with one more. And I really need to check on the Zooks' animals." He searched his mind for another logical excuse, in case they'd forgotten the excuses he'd already given. Even though he was seriously tempted to spend more time with this family and their cute dochter.

Bridget scooted out after him. "Let me send some of the cookies home with you."

"Nein, danki."

"Mei frau would insist." Hosea looked up. "Take them. She didn't bake the whole pail of dough. She can make more. Or one of the girls can."

Gabe grinned. "If you insist, then. Danki. I'll see you tomorrow, after I get off work."

Hosea shrugged. "I know what the bishop said, but others are coming by. Nein need to stop by every day. Unless you want to discuss something or you finalize the plans for the haus." He cast a sideways glance toward Gabe as if to gauge his reaction.

So, he wasn't wanted? Gut thing he'd declined the invitation to spend the nacht. Gabe scratched his jaw, feeling the prickles of his whiskers.

Hadn't Hosea taken care of talking to Patrick about the blueprints?

"I think that is your responsibility, Hosea. Talk to the builder."

Hosea glowered.

Gabe sighed. It was more evidence the man was incompetent when it came to construction. Driving tourists around in a buggy and watching corn grow certainly hadn't prepared the man for building a haus. He only wanted Gabe around to fix his problems, then leave.

"You're the builder. The bishop already said." Hosea's voice shook with frustration.

Gabe shut his eyes. Counted to ten. Twenty. Thirty. Then opened his eyelids. "Okay, then." He'd take on the job of getting the blueprints done…and make time to talk to the bishop, because he didn't like having his life dictated without being told why. "My boss does have someone on staff. I'll have Patrick kum by to talk to you, and arrange for the blueprints. Then he can schedule when I should start. In the meantime, order a dumpster so you can get rid of the old haus. I'll see you Sunday." He included Bridget in his sweeping glance.

She held out a bread bag full of cookies. "Gut nacht."

Flirting wouldn't earn him any points with Hosea, but Gabe was already on the outside, and he couldn't help himself. He deliberately let his fingers brush hers again, and waited for the satisfying blush to stain her cheeks. "Dream about me to-nacht, Green Eyes."

She lowered her gaze. Her blush deepened.

He would dream about her. Dream about marrying her someday. Dream about building his own home to share with her someday. Dream about the kinner they'd have someday. Even if this "someday" happened in a frozen tundra too far from his family.

He would build Hosea's haus—not because the bishop said so, but because it would give him a chance to be near Bridget and work on changing her mind. A chance to prove himself so he could build a future for himself.

Bridget sat beside Mamm in the buggy seat as they headed for town to do some grocery shopping. Piles of plowed snow filled the sides of the road, including their own lane, which Gabe's boss, Patrick, had cleared for Daed. They had been having long talks in town—Bridget didn't know where or about what—and Patrick came to the build site almost every day.

As they passed the haus where Gabe was living, she leaned forward, hoping for a glimpse of him. Nothing. The place seemed quiet, even though the Zooks were back. She'd met them at a church meeting, and the frau had stopped by with a meal and a Mason jar full of homemade candy made by the family's oldest dochter, Agnes.

Bridget hated that Daed had basically told Gabe to stay away. Four weeks had gone by with nein sight of him, except on church Sundays. Gabe stood in the lineup of single men and waited while the girls walked into the barn where services were held, always meeting Bridget's eyes with a steady, appreciative gaze, broken only by a wink.

It was just enough to keep her hoping and praying he was still interested in her. *If* he had been interested those two times he'd asked her out. It also kept her praying that, if he was the one, he would ask her out again. Sometime. Nein way would she reject him a third time. The unusual nature of her family's arrival in town must have colored her initial reactions to Gabe. If she could do it over again, she would say jah.

But he didn't seek her out to talk to her after services. And when it came to singings, he took another girl home afterward. A different girl every time. Or so Bridget was told by the women who came to visit with her and Mamm. Bridget hadn't gone to any singings, so she didn't know. Daed kept her and Noah close to home. Rather, in the RV-in-a-barn that now served as their home. After the New Year, he said, they could go, weather permitting.

Judging by the weather patterns they'd had thus far, Bridget didn't feel too confident.

Not a single note from Gabe had appeared in their rusty mailbox.

The blueprint designer had given Daed the finalized haus plans yesterday, so Bridget hoped that meant Gabe would show up on Monday—just two days away. But a week from Friday would be Christmas Day. Saturday, Second Christmas. And the ground was already covered in foot upon foot of snow. Bridget had never seen so much accumulation at one time.

When Patrick had kum to deliver the blueprints for Daed to approve, Bridget had worried aloud they wouldn't have a haus until spring. Patrick assured her it was possible to build a haus in adverse weather conditions, particularly in the Upper Peninsula, where there were "nine months of winter and three months of bad sledding."

Daed gave Patrick a confused look, but repeated it. Then he laughed and repeated it again.

By the third repetition, Bridget understood it.

Most of the construction would be done off-site and then transported to their lot. The process was expected to go quickly, since there was already a solid foundation, and they didn't need to keep the ground from freezing. Considering how cold it was, that last part seemed an impossible task.

Except, with the existing foundation, they needed to take into consideration the existing plumbing as they decided how to arrange the kitchen and bathrooms.

Mamm drove the buggy into the parking lot of the lone grocery store in town, then parked at a hitching post. Bridget hopped out, her shoes sliding a bit on the icy ground before she found traction.

"Careful, Mamm. It's slippery." She cautiously made her way to Mamm and grasped her arm. Maybe they could keep each other upright.

When they entered the store, Mamm got out the list. "Patrick said the construction workers would provide their own lunches, but I'm so used to our way. I'm at least going to have plenty of soups and sandwich fixings and hot koffee for them."

"Can we bake cookies, too? Gabe seemed to enjoy the oatmeal-raisin ones the nacht we played Monopoly." Bridget could have them ready for him in case he showed up on Monday, even though Daed didn't think he would.

Mamm smiled. "Jah. Your daed is surely disappointed Gabe hasn't kum around for weeks. But he's the one who told him not to."

"Why'd he do that if he wanted Gabe to kum?" Bridget mentally reviewed the list of ingredients she would need for cookies.

Mamm snagged a cart and then tore the list in two, handing the bottom half to Bridget. "It was a case of lose-lose for Gabe. If he came around, he'd prove he was incapable of following directions. But if he didn't, then your daed figured it meant the two of you wouldn't be spark-ing on the front porch, because he clearly wasn't interested."

"And he didn't kum." Bridget's shoulders sagged. But she would make cookies, anyway, because Gabe had winked at her last church Sunday. Her body heated just thinking about the look he'd given her.

But on Monday, the aroma of fresh-baked oatmeal-raisin cookies dis-appeared with the daylight, and nein sign of Gabe.

The cookie jar was empty by Tuesday nacht, and still he hadn't kum.

With the arrival of Wednesday, minutes after the three youngest had left for school, a flatbed truck pulled into the driveway, carrying assem-bled walls. With a whoop, Noah grabbed his coat and ran outside to help. Daed was a little slower, and not nearly as noisy, but, judging by his grin, he was just as excited. Mamm burst into tears, murmured something about finally having a workable kitchen, and went to clean the back part of the RV. In between removing pans of cookies from the oven—because Gabe was there!—and getting a pot of stew big enough to feed the whole construction crew simmering on the stove, Bridget sat in the passenger seat of the RV and watched the workers—particularly Gabe.

Hopefully, the haus would be habitable soon, because all seven of them living in a cramped RV had become a pain. Space would be nice. More than one bathroom would be a luxury. And dependable wood heat…ah, heavenly.

The buzzer rang. Bridget spun the seat around and went to remove the final pan of cookies from the oven. She stirred the stew while the cookies cooled a bit, then transferred the treats to a baker's rack.

In the distance, the downtown fire station's siren wailed, signaling lunchtime.

She quickly got out as many bowls and spoons as she could find. Sliced the bread she'd baked earlier, then set out the butter as the door opened.

"Leave your boots out here," Daed said. "Mei frau doesn't like the RV getting tracked up."

"Coats, too, since they're a bit dirty," Noah added.

Bridget stilled, watching the door until Gabe appeared. She quickly looked away, but her heart pitter-pattered out of control as Gabe stopped next to her to wash his hands at the sink.

As others crowded in at the sink, Gabe nodded toward the hall. Bridget moved that direction, and he followed. Once they were semi-alone, he leaned a bit nearer and lowered his voice to a whisper. "You holding up okay?"

She found a smile and nodded, not trusting herself to speak. Because, really, she wanted to throw herself into his arms, cling to his broad shoulders, and cry. She'd missed him so much. But that would be overly dramatic, and she'd only end up hurting herself. Better to play it cool and then write her thoughts in her journal when she had a private moment.

"Are you coming to the school's Christmas program on Wednesday?"

"I'll try. Depends on my schedule. Danki for inviting me."

"Jonah and Roseanna have small roles."

"I'll try." Gabe's shoulder brushed hers. "The fire department is having a fund-raiser on New Year's Day. You'll need a change of clothes."

Bridget stared. At least he was pleasant to gawk at.

He turned in her direction and leaned nearer so his breath feathered against her ear. "You're my date. Remember? You promised, and I said I'd hold you to it. And your daed gave his permission."

She'd promised?

Daed had given permission?

That was almost as gut as his blessing.

Bridget's mouth dried.

"If the haus is almost done." Gabe winked. "With that as incentive, it will be."

Never mind her heart pitter-pattering out of control. Now it thudded, like the bass music the Englisch teens played way too loud in their fancy cars. *Boom. Boom. Boom.*

She fought for each breath.

Gabe's finger grazed her arm.

A date. With Gabe.

Her and Gabe on a date.

Together.

Wait. She would need a change of clothes?

10

Gabe ended up missing the Christmas program at the school Wednesday morgen, due to his work schedule. But the only students he knew were Jonah Behr and his sisters, and since they just moved to town, he doubted they'd have major roles. He did, however, regret missing an opportunity to flirt with green-eyed Bridget.

That evening, he went by the bishop's haus. As Gabe drove in, Bishop Brunstetter was coming out of the barn, and he walked over to meet him. "Gut to see you, Young Gabe Lapp. What brings you by?"

"Questions."

"Care to kum in and sit a spell?"

"Nein, danki. I can't stay. It's just that my boss said something to me a few weeks ago.... I meant to ask earlier, but we're both busy, and I couldn't seem to catch you."

"What'd he say?"

"Something about how I'd be staying in the area. Made me curious...was I swapped for new blood? Or am I free to leave and go back to Florida?"

Bishop Brunstetter tugged at his beard. "What do you think?"

What did he think? Gabe squirmed, then decided to blurt out his thoughts. If the bishop wouldn't be forthcoming, the man deserved bluntness. "I think that this district in the Upper Peninsula started after several Amish communities failed, and this is another trial run, so why bother with fresh blood? I think the Amish who came here originally were from different areas—either that, or all related." He really wasn't sure on that point.

The bishop shrugged. "You know what the old proverb says. Bloom where you are planted."

"As if I'm a flower?" Okay, maybe that was a bit snarky. And flowers weren't likely to survive amid piles of snow.

Bishop Brunstetter chuckled. "It means you should take advantage of the opportunities you have in your life, and be grateful for the present situation."

Jah, he got that. But with such a noncommittal answer from the bishop, Gabe decided to write home to ask Daed that nacht, in the meantime avoiding the Zooks' dochter.

It would take a while to get an answer, so Gabe immersed himself in his job and tried to ignore that he was alone for Christmas, just as he'd been for Thanksgiving, since the Zooks had left for Mio again for a few days. On Christmas, a day filled with lonely hours and peanut-butter-and-jelly sandwiches, Gabe worked on designing his own dream home—a home he dreamed of sharing with Bridget someday.

Arriving at work on Monday, he stopped Cherry Blossom in the middle of the driveway and stared at the haus. Never in his wildest imaginings would he have expected the Behrs' haus to kum together so fast. His crew was gut, and they all wanted the exterior done quickly—but for different reasons from him. Okay, maybe the frigid temperatures did factor into his own work ethic, too. The quicker the walls were up, the sooner they'd have some protection from the elements—which currently threatened a full-blown blizzard. As if they didn't have enough snow already. So much for being out of this town before the first snowfall. But that goal had changed with the arrival of Bridget.

Another two days of work, and they could get a tarp over the roof, even if they had to wait for warmer temperatures before shingling. Gabe needed to talk to Patrick about that process. One of the guys said they had done it before, but it'd been an emergency situation.

As New Year's Day approached, they were at the point of finishing the interior. Hosea's frau and Bridget had started painting the walls as fast as his crew finished the drywall. They'd chosen a nondescript eggshell color. Not one of the vivid, warm hues preferred by many Englischers living in cold climates. It was probably one of the many unwritten rules. Plain walls for plain people—in this area, at least. At home, Mamm had painted the walls in pastel blues and greens.

The heat from the newly installed woodstove would help the paint dry. At least the working conditions had improved, even if he couldn't tease Bridget. Well, he supposed he could tease her, but he didn't want to have a bucket of paint dumped over his head. Something his sister would do in a heartbeat.

And then Hosea would blame him for making a mess in the haus.

As if the place wasn't messy enough with the process of installing bathroom fixtures and hooking them up to the existing plumbing.

Things were already awkward, considering Hosea tailed his every step, asking question after question. As if he didn't quite trust Gabe to know what he was doing. Or maybe he was trying to learn the trade so he could get a job.

On New Year's Eve, as Gabe cleaned up his own mess after the other guys left for the long weekend, Hosea approached him. "Mei frau wonders if you'll join us for supper. We have a tradition. Shrimp, crackers, and crab dip. Summer sausage and cheese. And fudge."

Hosea didn't say they'd missed his company, so it was probably too much to hope they had. Gabe had missed them, though. At least the Zooks were back from their Christmas vacation in Mio. Their presence eased his loneliness some, even if he did have to put up with Agnes's making cow eyes at him again. Her interest in him was flattering, even if it wasn't reciprocated. Just another gut reason to spend time working at the Behrs' haus.

"A tradition, eh? What's the occasion?"

Hosea hesitated a second. "New Year's Eve." It was said with a touch of annoyance, as if it should have been obvious. "We also play board games until the mid-nacht hour. You'd be welkum to spend the nacht, of course."

And kiss a cute girl at the midnight hour? Gabe didn't ask. Hosea probably wouldn't find any humor in it. Especially since he'd basically forbidden Gabe to visit once he'd witnessed his mild flirting the nacht they'd played Monopoly.

Besides, Gabe knew when to obey the rules. And when the rules were made to be broken. Like the Ordnung. Sure, he got into trouble; but when the rules varied from place to place, district to district, and hardly any of them had a scriptural basis—well, maybe most of them did, depending on how one interpreted the passage. Still. What happened to grace? Free will? Freedom of expression?

"Well?" Hosea's brow hitched up. "You'd already be here to take Bridget and Noah out tomorrow. Besides, Noah wanted me to invite you."

Ach, so it was Noah's idea. And neither Hosea nor Noah had factored Bridget into the equation. They just thought Gabe was fun to be around and would make things lively.

Inevitably, his enlivening efforts would get him into trouble at some point or another. After Hosea's cold shoulder and constant questioning, Gabe wasn't convinced the man would keep his word and let Bridget go to the fund-raiser. Another reason not to rock the boat and risk getting tomorrow's "date" cancelled.

He had plans to get into trouble on New Year's Day by stripping down to his swim trunks with the rest of the fire department for the annual polar plunge. Gut thing tomorrow was Saturday. He'd be in bigger trouble if the event were held on a Sunday. There was nein point in testing limits to-nacht. Unless a kiss at mid-nacht might happen. Tomorrow would be soon enough.

"Danki for offering, but I think the Zooks have something planned. Agnes has been making all kinds of different candies. Really can't miss it." He tried to force some can't-wait excitement into his voice. But he wasn't sure the candy was for New Year's Day. Only that he got his fingers slapped if he so much as reached for a piece. He hoped that, cow eyes aside, Agnes had made the candy for a different bu and would let him off the hook.

Still, that didn't stop him from snatching a couple pieces when nobody else was in the kitchen.

Hosea's mouth flattened. His expression darkened. "You courting Agnes?"

Did it matter? But that was another thing—Gabe wasn't certain of his role regarding Agnes. Just that he wasn't interested in her.

The letter he'd sent home just over a week ago had resulted in a long, newsy missive from Mamm and his sisters—all of whom reported missing him—but nein reply from Daed. But he might've been busy. In that case, the answer would kum when Gabe broke the rules and a preacher here complained to Daed about his wayward sohn.

With the polar bear plunge tomorrow, that complaint was sure to be on its way in a matter of days. Well, gut. Gabe was tired of waiting for an answer, even if it would take breaking the rules to get one. At least he would be having fun, and supporting a gut cause.

It wouldn't be a true date, since Hosea had refused to let Bridget attend without Noah as chaperone. A moot point, really, since Bridget didn't date. Still, Gabe held on to hope. He'd seen the pretty blush on her cheeks every time he winked at her on Sundays. Had caught her seeking him out at church.

Gabe glanced back at Hosea. The man's eyebrows rose higher than Gabe thought humanly possible. And Gabe mentally replayed their conversation to see what he might have missed.

Ach, Agnes. Courting Agnes.

He sucked in a breath of air, then released it with a whoosh. "Nein. At this point, I am not courting Agnes. But she does make ser gut candy. And since I'm staying in their haus—"

"At this point," Hosea repeated. "You mean, the idea's under consideration?"

"Nein. I don't mean that, either. I mean, I don't know what is expected of me. As if it matters, because I'll do what I want, regardless." He muttered the last part. He was his own man and could make his own decisions. If he was going to bloom anywhere, he should get a say in where and how. And he didn't want to stay in an overcrowded RV or in an unfinished haus to-nacht. Not without the possibility of a kiss.

Hosea's eyebrows drew together in frustration. "You are the *most* annoying bu."

Gabe forced a smile. "So I've been told." And on that note…, "I appreciate the invitation, but I'll see you tomorrow." He turned away.

Hosea muttered something Gabe didn't quite catch. It sounded like, "I expect you to properly court my dochter." But that couldn't be right. Gabe shook his head as he strode out of the unfinished haus and crossed the yard to the barn. He retrieved his borrowed horse from the stall, hitched him to the buggy, and climbed inside the vehicle.

He clicked his tongue, and Cherry Blossom started forward through the crunchy snow. Out of the corner of Gabe's eye, a moving figure caught his attention. "Whoa."

Bridget approached carrying a plate covered with tinfoil. "Mamm said to give this to you. If you aren't staying."

"Danki." Gabe glanced underneath the foil cover. He saw a few pieces of shrimp; a dollop of something cream-colored, presumably the crab dip

Hosea had mentioned; a pile of crackers, and a few slices of summer sausage and cheese. "Appreciate it."

"Sure you won't reconsider? It's always fun." She peered up at him through her long eyelashes.

He glanced around to see if Hosea was in sight. Nein sign of him. He must still be in the haus.

Gabe decided to say something with high shock value. "Any chance of a kiss at mid-nacht?"

Bridget's eyes widened. Her lips parted. Her face flamed red.

A moment passed. Two. Three. Then, "You have any mistletoe?"

⌒

The next morgen, gusts of wind off Lake Michigan numbed Bridget's cheeks as she rode with Noah and Gabe to the lakefront. When Gabe stopped the buggy, she saw a group of people standing on the shore. Some were dressed in swimsuits. Were they insane? The cold was brutal, especially with the windchill.

Bridget cast a startled glance at Gabe as he jumped out of the buggy and stripped off his coat. "What are you doing?" She watched him remove his shirt and suspenders, then start to unhook his pants. Surely, he didn't expect her and Noah to follow suit.

She averted her eyes, pulled her coat tighter around her body, and climbed out of the other side of the buggy after Noah. She shivered as she surveyed the ice-flecked water of Lake Michigan. Already freezing, and she hadn't even gone into the water yet. Wasn't sure she would, even. How could Gabe ask this of her?

"This is going to be so much fun!" Gabe came around the buggy, wearing nothing but a pair of bright-red swim trunks, and bounced on his toes. "Just awesome!"

Of course, he would say that. He lived for this kind of craziness. For feats that stretched the limits of the human body and all gut sense alike. Bridget tried not to look at him. Tried, and failed. As was often the case.

"Here, I brought you some flip-flops. They're Agnes's, so we'll need to return them." Gabe handed her some hot-pink thong sandals. He wore similar-looking, green ones on his feet.

Flip-flops. On a snow-covered beach. Nevertheless, Bridget took off her sensible tennis shoes and socks, then slid her feet into the plastic footwear.

Her toes immediately protested.

She reluctantly shrugged off her coat and walked with Gabe toward the lake. Nearing the taunting, ice-crusted water.

"Fun? Do I need to remind you that cold water killed all those people on the *Titanic?*"

He frowned at her. "Was that confirmed? Because I'm pretty sure they drowned."

Noah ran to catch up with them, still sensibly dressed in his work clothes. He slid to a stop next to Bridget in his stocking-covered feet. "It is seriously cold out here."

Bridget hugged herself, wishing she'd worn a heavier dress. But that would have made things worse once she got wet. Maybe she could turn back. Retreat to the buggy to wait out this foolishness. She looked around, wondering about the plans for changing into something dry. She'd left her extra clothes, along with her coat and shoes, in the buggy. She didn't intend to undress behind a clump of frozen grass or a pile of sand, and she didn't see any buildings nearby.

Of course, if the alternative was freezing to death....

And nobody had brought a towel. Or maybe Gabe had. She wasn't sure about that detail.

She certainly hadn't expected to spend New Year's Day doing something so crazy. Nor had she expected to see Gabe wearing only swimming trunks. She cast another sidelong glance at his bare chest. The muscles, the....

She sucked in a breath and forced herself to look away.

An Englisch man, sensibly dressed in clothes as well as a heavy coat, raised a bullhorn. Surrounding him was a group of equally well-covered men and women. "Welcome, all polar bears!" he began. "We are here to raise funds for the local volunteer fire department. A worthy cause, I'm sure you agree."

"That's the mayor," Gabe said quietly. "And those standing around him are other bigwigs in town. The media's here, too." He pointed to a woman in professional dress, standing with a man holding a giant camera on his shoulder. "We should try to make a quick getaway after, because they're sure to hunt down the two of you for a comment."

Bridget frowned and glanced at Noah. He shook his head.

"Me...." Gabe waved a hand downward, gesturing at his scantily clothed body. Drawing Bridget's all-too-willing attention again. "They won't know I'm Amish unless one of the firefighters tells them."

Noah shifted. "Won't we get in trouble with the bishop?"

Bridget felt a flare of hope. Maybe Noah would put his foot down. Decide they couldn't participate in this crazy event. He was her chaperone, after all. Gabe would understand her deferring to his authority.

Gabe shrugged. "I get in trouble whatever I do. This is just one more thing. Sure, they'll talk to me about it, and someone will write or call Daed, and he'll write me, but...." He sighed. "It's time."

Noah grabbed Bridget's hand. "We're in this together."

We are? Wait.

Gabe's fingers closed around hers, too, as the mayor counted down through the bullhorn: "Five, four, three, two, one—"

A loud cry broke forth from the group. Gabe whooped as he surged forward with everyone else running toward the lake, pulling Bridget with him.

Nein chance of getting out of this now. Not even when she dug her heels into the ground at the first frigid touch of the icy lake to her bare toes.

The two men on either side of her made sure she went into the water. All the way in. And under.

Bridget gasped for air when she surfaced. Alone. Even the borrowed flip-flops had abandoned her. She glanced around but didn't see Gabe or Noah. She fought the waves as she headed back to shore.

Someone tapped her shoulder.

She turned—and fell into Gabe's arms. Her heart pounded.

Then, with his gaze holding hers, he leaned forward.

She caught her breath.

And then Noah surfaced beside them. "That was fun!"

If only he could've waited a few seconds.

⌒

The polar bear plunge was more than fun. It was *almost* as awesome as Gabe had imagined it would be. But his lips ached, mourning a lost opportunity to kiss Bridget.

Or maybe they hurt from contact with the icy water. The rest of him had almost gone numb.

"They have hot chocolate ready and waiting for us," Gabe told Bridget and Noah. "That'll help warm us a bit, at least."

As he helped Bridget out of the lake, he caught a glimpse of the news reporter zeroing in on them. So much for the hot chocolate.

"Kum on." He kept hold of Bridget and ran toward the buggy. "We've got to go. Now."

Noah charged past them and jumped into the vehicle with an almost admirable leap, considering he must have been as frozen as Gabe.

"A word?" the reporter called as she approached, the photographer on her heels.

Gabe helped Bridget inside, then untethered Cherry Blossom before climbing in, himself.

"Sir!"

The reporter and the photographer were too close.

Gabe ducked his head to hide his face. "No pictures." He clicked his tongue and drove off. He scanned the shoreline for a bath-haus. There had to be one somewhere on this beach. The beaches in Florida always had one.

Of course, the polar bear plunge in Florida wasn't nearly as shock-inducing.

In the distance, he spied a small building. That must be a beach-haus. He drove over and parked in front of it. Gut, a men's side and a women's side. He helped Bridget out of the buggy and made sure she made it safely to the door. She was shivering so hard, her teeth knocked together.

"Hurry and get changed," Gabe told her. "There's a blanket under the buggy seat." Then he headed over to the men's side.

The building's interior was only slightly warmer than the outside air. It had nein heat, and the vents were open, ushering in the frigid air. But at least it offered relative privacy for them to put on dry clothes.

"I'm a bit hesitant to go back to the beach for hot chocolate," Noah said, his back toward Gabe as he slid his suspenders over his shoulders. "Is there someplace nearby we could go? McDonald's, maybe?"

"I wish." Gabe bent over to tie his boots.

"I'm just not ready to go home yet. It's worth any bit of trouble we might get into."

Gabe nodded. But…. Jah, Noah thought that now. But Noah didn't know what it was like to get into trouble. To have coals heaped on his head for minor infractions. And since it was after New Year's, he and Bridget had permission to go to singings in the community. Did they realize that being friends with Gabe might negate their permission to attend the youth outings?

Gabe—make that all three of them—had better get every bit of fun as possible out of this day before Hosea clamped down.

Still, Gabe needed to warn them.

"Obviously, you've never really gotten in trouble." Gabe slapped his black hat down on his head. "It means getting a scolding from the preachers and, if it's bad enough, the bishop. It means your daed getting angry at you. And, in some cases, it means getting sent from your home to Siberia. But…I agree. It is."

"Siberia?" Noah slid his coat on and turned.

"Here. Cold enough to be Siberia, ain't so?"

"Um, not sure. I think I read once that temperatures there can reach about eighty degrees below zero—"

"I wasn't being serious." Almost serious, though. Patrick had told him the coldest temperature ever recorded in the Upper Peninsula was 51 degrees below zero. Nein point in mentioning that information to Noah. It might scare him and his family back to Ohio. And until Gabe had a chance to steal that kiss from Bridget, he didn't want them to go.

They bagged their wet clothes and left the men's room. Bridget was already snuggled beneath the blanket in the backseat of the buggy. Except that she was still shivering. She looked up as they climbed in. "What next? I could make hot chocolate back at the RV." At least that's what Gabe thought she said. Her teeth were chattering so severely, it was hard to understand her.

Staring at her cheeks, pink from the cold, Gabe considered the suggestion. Going to the Behrs' temporary residence would mean having to share her with her younger siblings and her parents. One chaperone was more than sufficient.

Still, perhaps he'd have a chance to snuggle next to her. Help warm her up. And maybe snag a kiss.

He turned to her. Winked. "That sounds gut."

He enjoyed the pretty pink that flooded her cheeks.

11

Bridget had stopped shivering, but she struggled to focus and to stay awake. In the front seat of the buggy, Gabe and Noah discussed something, but she couldn't comprehend any of their words. Nor could she make herself move when the buggy stopped and she spied the RV through blurry eyes. Why was she so tired and dizzy? Nothing made sense.

The men climbed out of the buggy, and Gabe turned back to help her. He said something she couldn't understand as another wave of blackness washed over her.

She roused in Gabe's arms as he maneuvered her through the door of the RV, up the few stairs, and past the chairs. She wanted to wrap one of her arms around his neck but couldn't make her muscles cooperate.

Why was he carrying her? And why did he look so worried?

Blackness threatened again, only to recede when he lowered her onto her bed and tugged the covers over her. "I told your mamm to heat some blankets." His voice cracked. He trailed his fingertips over her cheek.

What'd she need Mamm for? She needed him. Needed the kiss she'd been denied earlier.

The mattress dipped as he climbed beside her, on top of the covers, and pulled her comforter-cocooned body into his arms. His warm breath fanned her face. His soft lips brushed a kiss across her forehead. "I'm so sorry," he whispered.

He was sorry they'd gotten interrupted before he could kiss her?

She sighed, closed her eyes again, and relaxed against him.

And then Mamm was there, wrapping a warm and wunderbaar blanket around Bridget. Lifting Bridget's head and helping her drink a couple sips of hot tea.

And Gabe was gone.

Maybe she'd merely dreamed him.

~

Hosea threw down the rag he'd been using to stain the kitchen cabinets. "I gave you permission to take my sohn and dochter on an outing, not to freeze them to death!"

Gabe winced at the anger in Hosea's voice, the darkness in his eyes, the implications of his clenched fists.

"I'm fine, Daed." Noah stood beside Gabe, facing his daed's wrath. "And he made sure Bridget got taken care of right away."

It was the first time anyone—other than Gabe's grossdaedi—had ever stood up for him. And Gabe appreciated the effort, even if it didn't seem to be helping.

"What'd you do, push her into Lake Michigan?" Hosea unfurled one fist to flap a forefinger in Gabe's face. "Why'd you go to the lake, anyway? It's not summer!"

Gabe resisted the urge to withdraw. He realized the concept of the plunge was probably dumb, but it *was* for a gut cause. He'd known it would get him in trouble with Daed. But he shouldn't have involved Bridget. Or Noah. But especially not Bridget. He was haunted by the deathly pale color of her skin. The sound of her shallow breathing. The panic when he noticed the eerie quiet in the back seat of the buggy. He'd pushed Cherry Blossom hard to get them back here as quickly as possible.

Gabe opened his mouth.

"It was a polar bear plunge, and it wasn't a push," Noah spoke up. "We held hands and ran into the water together."

Gabe frowned and put his hand on Noah's arm to stop him. Gabe deserved the scolding.

"Bridget did dig in her heels and try to resist going in," Gabe added. He should've let go of her. Let her stay safe and dry on the shore.

Hosea's eyebrows drew together as he glared at Gabe. His face turned an alarming shade of red. Did Gabe need to worry about Papa Behr having a heart attack or a stroke?

Noah raked a hand through his hair. "How could we have known she'd get hypothermia? We were just having fun!"

Gabe wished his friend—probably former friend, now that Hosea was gut and riled—would just shut his mouth and stop trying to defend him. Didn't Noah realize that what he'd just said could be considered talking back? Gabe's insides clenched with fear for his friend. What if he were sent away, as Gabe was?

"I lost a brother to hypothermia. You could've killed my dochter. You are stupider than they say!" Hosea shoved Gabe in the chest, knocking him back against a wall.

The shock of the blow was nothing compared to the impact of what he'd shared. Nein wonder Hosea was so sensitive about what had happened to Bridget. Gabe didn't try to move out of range of the older man's fists. He knew he deserved every blow he was given.

At least he'd had sense enough to realize Bridget was losing consciousness, and to get her home and call for her mamm to heat blankets and give her hot liquids.

"And Patrick said you were smart. The bishop called you 'more intelligent than most.'" Hosea sneered. "And to think I considered allowing you to court my dochter!" He gave Gabe's chest another shove.

Noah shook his head. "But, Daed—"

"He obviously influenced your gut sense." Hosea turned on his sohn. "I need you to think about this…this stupidity. You are not permitted to spend time with Gabe Lapp again. Period." He returned his attention to Gabe. "And you—you're fired."

Fired? Gabe blinked. Hosea was only hurting himself, since everything would need to be put on hold until Patrick could find someone else to oversee the work. But Gabe wouldn't argue. He'd expected to be banished from the Behrs' home. He managed a nod. "I'll collect my tools."

"Daed!" Noah almost shouted. "Listen to yourself. You can't do that—"

"I am sorry, for what it's worth." Gabe headed for the corner where he'd been storing his toolbox, keeping his back stiff, his posture strong. He would slump when he was alone. Maybe vent his emotions in another way.

"I can do this. My company, my decision." Hosea ignored Gabe, turning his wrath on his sohn again. Poor Noah.

Hosea's temper was worse than the preachers'. And the bishop never got loud at all. He scolded gently, with an almost bemused expression, as if to acknowledge he was doing what was expected of him, even if he didn't agree with it. Of course, this time, it might be different. The bishop might kum by the Zooks' to-nacht, ranting and raving. Maybe Gabe should stop by the bishop's haus to confess before he—wait. "My company"? He didn't mean—

"My company, too, Daed," Noah shouted back. "Even if you don't want him, I do. He's my friend, and you can't take that away."

"I am the owner, and what I say, goes. He's fired." Hosea's tone had changed, clearly communicating that nobody was to argue with him. "Don't talk to me that way, bu."

Nein, nein, nein. How could Patrick have sold his thriving business to two men who knew nothing about construction? But that would explain why Hosea had trailed Gabe for the past couple of weeks, asking question after question, and eagle-eyeing everything Gabe did.

But why hadn't anyone told Gabe?

He wouldn't ask Hosea. He'd go straight to Patrick.

He gathered his stuff, loaded it into his borrowed buggy, then went inside the RV. The middle girl—Shiloh?—stirred something on the stove. Mrs. Behr took another blanket out of the dryer.

"How is she?" Gabe's voice cracked.

"She's starting to warm up. Shivering again, which is a gut sign. She should be fine, thanks to your quick thinking." She brushed a tear away.

Another pang of guilt stabbed at Gabe's conscience. "I'll keep praying for her."

"Appreciate it, Gabe. Do you want to peek in on her now?"

Jah, he did, but he should get out of here before Hosea came in and resumed shouting. And he needed to visit Patrick to find out what was going on. And the bishop, to confess. He shook his head. "Danki, but I have errands."

Mrs. Behr nodded. "Feel free to kum by and check on her when you get here in the morgen for work."

Gabe nodded. He couldn't really answer because he didn't know for sure whether Hosea could fire him. Yet, even if he wasn't officially fired, he certainly wasn't welkum anywhere near Bridget. He bowed his head as he exited the RV, descended the steps, and trudged out to the waiting horse and buggy.

Ten minutes later, he pulled into Patrick's driveway. Patrick's wife, Sylvia, came to the door and waved him inside. Gabe took off his boots, then shed his coat, draping it over the back of a chair.

Patrick looked up from his recliner in front of the television, where a football game was playing, and turned down the volume. "Gabe! Have a seat."

"Do you want something to drink?" Sylvia asked him.

"Koffee would be great, if you have any." Gabe was still chilled to the bone and trying not to shiver.

"Sure. I'll be right back." She left the room.

Gabe wasn't really in the mood for chitchat, but he sat on the couch. "Sorry for barging in on a holiday. I just needed to talk something over with you."

"Not a problem. What can I do for you?"

"I just came from the Behrs'. I did the polar bear plunge with Noah and Bridget—"

Patrick laughed. "You actually went in?"

"I did. Had to prove myself to all you Yoopers who think I'm too soft for this climate." Even if their impression was correct.

Sylvia returned and handed him a mug of black coffee. Patrick had a thing about not polluting coffee with sugar and cream.

"Thanks." Gabe suppressed another shiver and wrapped his hands tightly around the hot mug as Sylvia left once more.

Patrick chuckled again. "You'll do, boy. You'll do."

"Jah, well…." Gabe swallowed. "Bridget got hypothermia. And Hosea is downright furious with me. Told me I was fired."

Patrick sobered.

"I figured he meant from working on his haus, but then he said some things that confused me. Referred to 'his' company."

Patrick gave a slow nod. "Yep. Finalized the details yesterday. Probably will make it official tomorrow."

"Why? He knows nothing about construction." Speak any higher, or louder, and Gabe would sound like one of the Englisch cheerleaders jumping around and shouting on the TV. He jumped to his feet and strode to the window. Now would be a gut time to have a cord of wood to chop. He was in big trouble.

"He does know something about running a business. And he had you to work there and teach his boy." His voice cracked.

Gabe turned.

A muscle jumped in Patrick's jaw. "See, the thing is, son, I have colon cancer. I've maybe six months to live, and that's if I go through their treatments. Three months if I don't. I needed to sell the business. Still need to sell the RV, and other things Sylvia won't need, so she won't have to deal with them. And since Hosea had you...." Patrick swallowed hard.

"You have cancer?" Gabe's eyes burned. "My grandfather had that." And died from it. The only man who understood Gabe. He listened to him when Daed wouldn't. And Patrick was the same way. Another "grandfather" of Gabe's, about to be lost.

Gabe's shoulders sagged. This was worse news than the loss of his job. He caught a glimpse of Sylvia's teary face in the doorway to the kitchen.

"Hosea has the right to fire you *tomorrow* after he takes over, but I can't believe he did such a fool thing. He needs you, and he knows it."

Gabe sighed. "Is there anything I can do to help?" His job was unimportant in light of this news.

Patrick nodded. "Come by every now and again to clear the driveway. I have a snowblower. And keep me company. Let me know how things are going."

Gabe nodded.

Patrick picked up his own mug of coffee. "So, the girl went in the water, too? She must really like you."

If only.

⟳

By suppertime, Bridget felt almost normal again. She was still a bit weak and wobbly, and her muscles were cramped, but her head was clearer. She dressed—who had undressed her?—and came out of the bedroom, sliding her hand along the wall to keep her balance.

Mamm must've heard her, for she spun around, wooden spoon dripping liquid onto the floor. "What are you doing up?"

"Better question is, what was I doing in bed?"

"Daed was so worried about you. That's how your onkel Eli died. I really wish your daed hadn't lashed out at Gabe as he did. Admittedly, Gabe might've been at fault, but he was truly upset. Worried."

That didn't answer her question. Bridget sank down on the couch, her spaghetti legs unable to support her any longer. She knew she had gone to the polar bear plunge with Gabe and Noah. The water was unbelievably cold. She'd shivered into her dry dress, but without any towel or dry underclothes, her dress had quickly gotten soaked. The rest of the details were foggy. Had Gabe carried her inside? Put her to bed? Crawled in with her? Kissed her forehead? If only she could separate reality from dream.

She certainly couldn't remember Daed lashing out at Gabe.

Mamm handed her a mug of hot tea. "Danki." The hot mug felt good on her hands. She wiggled her still-cold toes. She should've grabbed another pair of socks. She shivered and took a sip of the steaming liquid, then looked around. "Where is Daed?"

"He went to talk to the bishop about Gabe's behavior."

"Ach." He got into trouble nein matter what, he'd said. Did he enjoy stirring things up the way he did? So unlike Bridget. She was always careful to obey all the rules. To color inside the lines. To do what was expected.

The polar bear plunge was the closest she'd kum to rebelling, and there had been a surge of exhilaration when she bobbed to the top of the water and saw Gabe's grin so close to her. Even Noah seemed to enjoy himself.

"Where's Noah?"

"He went with your daed. Jonah and your sisters are out sledding until supper's ready."

Supper. Bridget straightened. "Can I help?" She tried to find the strength to stand.

"Nein. Just rest. I'm making bean soup and corn bread. The soup just needs to simmer. Should be done when your daed and Noah get home." Mamm poured herself a mug of tea and sat next to Bridget. "So, a polar bear plunge. I've heard of those. Stripping down to nothing, and jumping into icy water. You three did that?"

"Nein, not exactly. Noah and I were fully dressed. Everyone was. Well, some wore only swimsuits." Like Gabe. An image of his well-defined chest flashed through her memory. Another inappropriate thought for her to entertain, along with the memory of him dressed only in lime-green pajama pants.

Those images would jockey for position with her daydreams of him carrying her across the threshold of the RV. Putting her to bed. Kissing her forehead.

If only those memories were authentic.

But if they were, and if Daed found out, Gabe would be in even more trouble than he already was.

12

As Gabe pulled the buggy into the bishop's driveway, he noticed a familiar-looking horse and buggy already parked in front of the barn. It figured that Gabe would decide to visit when the man had other company. But maybe he would give Gabe a minute of his time, just long enough for Gabe to confess to having participated in the polar bear plunge and causing a grave condition to befall Bridget.

He'd wanted to get himself in trouble because he needed Daed's attention. He hadn't wanted to hurt his friends in the process. In fact, he'd really hoped nobody else would find out about Bridget and Noah's participation in his personal sin.

The Bible said nothing against polar bear plunges, as far as he knew. But maybe his behavior fell into the category of foolishness decried by so many passages in Proverbs. What was that quote—not from the Bible, he knew—about fools rushing in where angels feared to tread? He'd certainly rushed. And dragged his friends along with him. He should be more cautious. Daed's attention aside, he really needed to grow up and set aside foolish things.

Nobody came out of the barn to greet him. He slid the doors open and peeked inside. The buggy was there. "Bishop Brunstetter?"

Nein response.

He hated to go to the haus, but…. Wait. Was it the supper hour? A bad time to visit. But he didn't regret visiting Patrick and spending time watching football with him, even if that was the reason for his later-than-planned arrival at the bishop's. Maybe he would be better off just confessing to Preacher Zook. That would save the bishop some legwork, because Preacher Zook would kum down on him, anyway, as soon as his frau told him about the bag she'd found containing a pair of cold, wet, sandy swim trunks and an equally cold, wet, sandy towel.

Not to mention the missing pink flip-flops. Gabe hadn't been able to find them when he'd dug through the plastic bag containing Bridget's soaking-wet yet neatly folded dress. She hadn't brought a towel or a change of underclothes. Granted, he hadn't thought to mention those necessities. He hadn't even told her where they were going until they were already on their way. With wet underwear, nein wonder she didn't warm up even after putting on dry clothes.

Maybe he shouldn't bother confessing to anyone. Someone would confront him soon enough. Ranting and raving and gnashing teeth. Something to look forward to.

Not.

He turned to head back to his borrowed buggy.

Movement caught his eye. He glanced up as the bishop started down the porch steps. "Wasn't expecting you to kum by, Young Gabe."

"I didn't realize you had company. I just needed a moment of your time."

"Want to kum in?" The bishop pressed his lips into a flat line.

"I don't want to intrude. Just came to confess something. But it'll wait."

"Hosea Behr is here."

Ach. He'd made it there a lot quicker than Gabe had expected. But then, Gabe hadn't expected to stay so long with Patrick. Talking. Praying. Trying not to cry.

Gabe looked away. Kicked at a clump of frozen snow.

Was Daed aware that he'd sent his sohn to an icy tundra? About as opposite from Florida's climate as he could get? Or maybe that was the point—to make Gabe's brain too frozen to think about getting into trouble. Of course, that line of thinking would imply that being gut came naturally. It didn't.

"I guess I have nothing to say, then. Except for, 'I'm sorry.' I didn't mean to drag them into it, and I didn't mean to almost kill Bridget."

"But you're not sorry for doing it." A statement, not a question, with a long-suffering sigh tacked on. Bishop Brunstetter descended another step. And another. Until he stood on the snow-covered sidewalk.

"Honestly? Nein, I'm not sorry for doing it. Just for involving them."

"Take a walk with me, Young Gabe."

Gabe glanced toward the haus. Noticed the man silhouetted in the window. Hosea? He couldn't tell. "I really shouldn't take time away from your visitor."

"What he has to say will be heard. Right now, I feel you need to talk to someone. Why did you do it?"

Gabe sighed. Rolled his eyes. "Other than the obvious reasons—supporting a worthy cause, raising funds for the fire department? And for some fun?"

"Jah, other than those." A smile quirked the older man's lips.

"And other than my need to prove I'm just as tough as the Yoopers?"

The slight smile grew a notch. "You shouldn't feel the need to prove it. Der Herr knows your heart. But, jah, other than that."

Gabe sighed again. "My daed. Remember when I came by, wanting to know if I'd been swapped for new blood? It's been a while. You gave me a nonanswer about blooming where I was planted, so I wrote my daed. But I wasn't in trouble, so he couldn't be bothered to take the time to write back or talk to me. And I got tired of waiting. So, I chose to do something I'd get into trouble for, so he'd make time to talk to me." His voice broke, and he clenched his fists, hating himself for so candidly admitting to his pain. He sounded like a small child, complaining about his father's not having time for him.

The bishop remained silent as he studied Gabe, moisture filling his eyes. After a long moment, he shook his head. "We'll kum back to that. You do realize you've leaped from the frying pan into the fire."

"She'll be fine." He thought so. He hoped so. He prayed so.

"Jah. But will you?"

"I don't have any side effects." Gabe kicked at the chunk of icy snow again.

"Ach, I'd say the effects are still rippling. They may have only begun."

Gabe didn't have patience for the bishop's confusing nonanswers. Not today. His head pounded with a tension headache. "Speak plainly, please."

"Hosea says you dishonored his dochter."

Gabe raised his eyebrows. And waited for an explanation. He couldn't recall doing any such thing. He definitely would've remembered.

"You crawled in bed with her, he says."

Gabe frowned. "To warm her, jah. She was wrapped in a heavy comforter, and I was lying on top of the covers. It was just until her mamm could get there with more warm blankets and some hot tea."

"He's insisting you marry Bridget in two or three weeks' time."

Gabe reared back. *Wow.* That was quite a change from shoving Gabe around, calling him stupid, and ranting about the foolishness of the notion of Gabe's courting his dochter. The idea of belonging to a family, of being married to Bridget and having the right to kiss her—and more—tempted him. But.... *Marry Bridget? For trying to warm her?* As appealing as the idea was, Gabe had nein intention of falling into this trap. He snorted. "He doesn't think very highly of his dochter, then. The man fired me, leaving me unemployed, and he wants me to marry her? Where would we live? Under Mackinac Bridge? I have nein money for a haus."

"I suppose he thinks you'll live with them." The bishop shoved his hands inside his coat pockets and produced a pair of gloves. He tugged them over his fingers. "In which case, you'd still have a job, because—"

"Nein. Because I'd also be subject to Hosea's fierce temper, which is worse than my daed's. Because the man has nein respect for me. I might fall in love with Bridget, given time, but I can't live tiptoeing around and owing her daed for everything. I want to be respected as a man on my own two feet rather than be forced to accept handouts from a bully."

Bishop Brunstetter blinked. "What?"

"*Nein,* I won't marry her. I will *not* allow Hosea Behr to use me to do whatever it is he wants. To earn a gut reputation in the community for saving a poor, homeless bu? Or maybe so he doesn't have to look like a fool for firing me when he knows gut and well he needs me. *Of course,* his sohn-in-law would work for him. I'm not sure what his reasons are, but nein. I will *not* jump into this trap. I don't trust him not to change his mind about me again. Besides, Bridget and I hardly know each other. We haven't courted. Hosea would never allow it. Not to mention, she doesn't even date!" Not that he wasn't willing to date her. Maybe even court her. He was definitely willing to flirt with her and steal a kiss or two.

The bishop raised an eyebrow. "You refuse."

"That's what I said." Gabe shifted enough to glare at the man whose figure was still framed in the bishop's window. "If he wants to rehire me, he knows where to find me. But that's not saying I'll accept an offer. I reserve the right to make my decision *when* he comes to apologize." He returned his gaze to the bishop and assumed a more respectful stance. "I've made my confession. I'll confess to Preacher Zook, too, so you won't have to tell him, saving time and effort. Just call my daed and complain, please."

"*When* he comes. Huh. Cocky much?" The bishop chuckled. But he quickly smothered his mirth with a cough. "I'll call your daed, for sure. And then I'll kum find you, and we'll talk more."

⌒

The RV door slammed shut, startling Bridget where she sat on the sofa. She dropped the romance novel she'd borrowed from Mamm. The mug of hot tea in her other hand wobbled, its contents sloshing to the brim, but she steadied it on her knee before any spills could occur.

Daed stomped inside angrily, if not as loud as he could, since he was shoeless. Followed by Noah.

"That bu is going to be the death of me yet." Daed glowered at Bridget as if whatever had him riled was somehow her fault, and dropped down on a chair.

Noah calmly strode past, peeked into the kettle on the stove, and then lowered himself onto a bench at the table.

Mamm glanced at Daed. "Would you like some tea, dear?" She didn't ask "What bu?" or why or how. Or even what Daed would do now. But there was only one bu who could upset Daed this way.

Bridget held her tongue. She didn't understand Daed's reaction to Gabe. Sure, Gabe was a bit cocky and flirty, but—

"He refused to marry Bridget!"

She yelped and lost control of the mug of hot tea. The liquid sloshed over the edge of the mug, soaking her dress and scalding her skin. She jumped to her feet as Mamm rushed toward her with a damp dishrag.

"What did you say, dear? I misheard, for sure." Mamm took the mug and the book from Bridget. "Go get changed."

Bridget ignored Mamm and glared at Daed. "Why would the idea of his marrying me even kum up?"

"He…he…I…he…." Daed's face grew redder.

"Daed fired him for taking us to the polar bear plunge," Noah put in. "But he's too stubborn to apologize, so he figured he'd force him to marry you, thereby getting Gabe back in his employ without having to humble himself. Ain't so, Daed?" There was a challenge in Noah's tone.

Daed frowned and slumped his shoulders in a show of defeat, as if he had realized his manipulations weren't working. "I thought the bu was smitten with Bridget. The way he looks at her, the way he speaks her name…." He glanced at Mamm. "You said he was in bed with her."

So, Bridget *hadn't* dreamed that up. Was the tiny kiss real, too? The tender touch of his fingers sliding across her cheek?

"I said he was on top of the covers, trying to warm her." Mamm set the mug in the sink. "Go get changed, Bridget."

"Disregardless," Daed muttered. "He was still in bed with her."

"Regardless," Mamm corrected him. "Pride goes before destruction, and a haughty spirit before a fall."

Daed huffed, then turned to Bridget. "Go do what your mamm says."

Bridget slowly shuffled to the bedroom. Once inside, she slid the door partway closed, then stood there, peeking out.

"Disregardless," Daed repeated firmly, "he said nein to the bishop. And everyone knows that you *have* to obey the bishop. *Everyone*. Except for him, apparently. Worse, the bishop *accepted* his refusal."

"*Regardless*. The bishop might've thought you were in the wrong." Mamm leaned against the counter.

"Jah, he pretty much said the same thing. Sent Noah to the kitchen for cookies and gave *me* a talking-to about treating people with respect." He huffed again.

Bridget turned away from the half-open door. She wanted to keep listening but didn't want to get caught and punished. She hurriedly unpinned the dress, then grabbed her last clean one and slipped it on.

"Maybe Gabe refused, or maybe the bishop didn't state it as an order," Noah mused. "Maybe he said something like, 'Hosea insists you marry Bridget.'"

Bridget stabbed her finger with a pin in her haste to fasten the dress. She shoved the injured fingertip into her mouth. How could Daed do such a thing? Insist Gabe marry her over something so silly. Not to mention, fire him. Refuse to apologize. Well, it didn't matter. She shouldn't think badly of Daed. But how could he do this to her? Assuming Daed humbled himself and asked Gabe for forgiveness and help, and assuming Gabe granted him both, Gabe would have nothing to do with Bridget.

Unless…. The Mason jar of candy made by Agnes Zook and brought over by her mamm had gotten a lot of attention from Gabe. The man did love his sweets. Worse, he lived with Agnes and her family. If it was true that the way to a man's heart is through his stomach, then Bridget would bake cookies. Brownies. Other goodies. And somehow get them delivered to him.

Maybe some edible gifts would help make up for Daed's lack of appreciation. Because the memory of that gentle kiss had Bridget dreaming of a wedding.

Just not a forced one.

⌒

Gabe shuffled into the Zooks' kitchen where the family sat around the table, heads bowed for prayer. He stopped just inside the doorway and bowed his own head. But his thoughts were jumbled. Did Gott hear his prayers? Or only his confessions when he'd done something wrong, resulting in a harsh punishment, as from Daed? Maybe He would banish Gabe from His kingdom. Just like Hosea from his family. Harsh words and banishment. Gabe should be used to it by now, but being separated from Bridget somehow felt worse than when he'd had to leave Florida.

Still. Praying was an act of obedience, whether Gott heard or not.

Danki for the meal I'm about to receive. Whatever it is.

He sniffed the air, picking up the aromas of sauerkraut and sausages. Right. It was New Year's Day, and eating those foods was a tradition with his family. Apparently with the Zooks, too.

Help me to not ruin this day for this family. Help me to know what to do. He blew out a breath of frustration. *To find a job.*

To know You care.

Maybe Gott would hear him if he confessed.

Forgive me for dragging the Behrs into trouble with me. For—

"Amen." Preacher Zook cleared his voice. "Glad you could join us, Gabe."

The rest of his prayer would have to wait.

Gabe dropped his bag of laundry on the floor and took his usual seat. "Sorry I'm late. Stopped by to visit my boss." *Former boss.* "And the bishop. Had something to confess."

"Hmm," Preacher Zook murmured. And he sliced a piece of sausage. A clear indication the conversation would wait until later.

But there was nein way Gabe would talk to Agnes privately. He forced himself to look in her direction. Her eyes were on him and filled with longing. As usual. He met her gaze and held it. "I'm sorry. I lost your flip-flops."

Her brow furrowed in confusion. "My flip-flops?"

Oops. He'd forgotten he'd borrowed them without asking. The plan had been to return them without her ever knowing they were gone.

Daed would accuse him of stealing.

"Uh, jah. I…uh…well…." What a well-worded explanation. He grimaced.

Preacher Zook looked at him sharply. "Gabe Lapp, do you have a strange shoe fetish we need to address?"

"What? Nein!"

"Then why would you need to borrow Agnes's flip-flops on the first day of January? Might I remind you the high temperature today, factoring in the windchill, was fifteen below?"

"Wow. A real heat wave," Gabe said dryly.

Agnes giggled.

Preacher Zook's mouth quivered as if the man couldn't decide whether to frown or smile. Then he sighed. "Do the flip-flops have anything to do with your confession?"

"They do." Gabe smothered a slice of sausage in a mound of sauerkraut, then shoveled the bite into his mouth.

"Then perhaps we'd better hear it now."

Gabe nodded. Swallowed. "This morgen was the fire department's biggest annual fund-raiser, the polar bear plunge. As a volunteer firefighter, I felt I needed to be there. And I took Noah and Bridget Behr with me." He glanced at Agnes. "Bridget wore your flip-flops. They're somewhere in Lake Michigan now. Some fisherman will probably catch one of them. Both, if he's lucky."

The preacher made a choking sound. Hopefully, from trying not to laugh at the idea of a fisherman catching a pink flip-flop.

Gabe glanced back at Preacher Zook. "Bridget had a mild case of hypothermia afterward. I already confessed to the bishop, and he's going to call my daed. I'm sorry for my part in the disaster."

The preacher rubbed his hand over his mouth, obviously trying to hide a smile. "We'll talk later."

Gut. Gabe wouldn't get yelled at now, in front of the family. But he'd really just as soon get it over with. The part he wanted—needed—was Daed.

After dinner, Gabe carried his dishes over to the sink, then headed upstairs to his room. To hide from Agnes until Preacher Zook called for him.

"Gabe?" Her voice carried up from the bottom of the stairs.

He hadn't been quick enough to escape. With a grimace, he stopped and turned around.

Agnes came toward him, gliding upward with one hand on the banister. She stopped three steps below where he stood. Took a deep breath. "I need to know…." Her face contorted.

Unspoken, but hanging in the air between them, was her question: *Do I have a chance?*

He winced. Did this conversation have to happen? Best to be honest. "I…I don't know. There's someone else I'm interested in. But it's likely I'll go home before I would start courting anyone."

At least going home would give him a place to thaw out.

"I don't want to be in second place."

"When you meet the right man, you won't be." He tried to be kind. Maybe if Gabe found the right woman, Daed's rejection wouldn't hurt so badly, either.

"Bridget?" Agnes whispered. Tears beaded on her lashes.

He exhaled, hating to hurt her. "I think you know."

Her smile was sad. She turned and walked back downstairs.

Jah. She knew.

But the possibility of actually dating Bridget had dipped well below zero.

13

Bridget's stomach knotted as she entered the barn and surveyed the unfamiliar faces of those who had gathered for the first singing of the New Year. Bridget leaned in close to Noah. "I never realized how hard it is to attend youth functions where you don't know anyone." She pulled her coat closer around her, warding off the chill but doing nothing for the discomfort churning in her stomach.

"Jah. Makes me wish I'd been friendlier to newcomers in Ohio." Noah scratched his jaw. "Really wish Gabe were here."

Bridget craned her neck to get a better view of the other attendees. Gabe had to kum. She longed to see his familiar face, even if the men and women would be separated for the singing. Maybe he would wink at her. At least, she hoped he would.

It'd be too much to hope he'd ask to give her a ride home. Not when a week had gone by without a single sign of him—physically. Mentally, signs were everywhere. His absence left a huge hole that nothing seemed to fill. Work on the haus had screeched to a sudden stop. The only people working were Mamm and Bridget. Painting walls.

Bridget missed the construction workers. Missed Gabe. But January temperatures in the 90s were more likely than the prospect of Gabe's caving in to Daed's passive-aggressive attempts at manipulation. Soon, someone else would jump at the chance to hire him, and he'd be off the market. He might be already. She hadn't heard.

Besides, she didn't want a man who was *forced* to marry her. Didn't Daed get that? She was tired of being nobody. A voice unheard. Unimportant.

Tired.

Yet so fascinated by the man who would rule over her if Daed had his way.

She scanned the room again from their position near the door. Nein sign of either Gabe or Agnes Zook. But a group of giggling girls stared at Noah. Bridget nudged him and then nodded in their direction. She didn't want him to leave her side, though.

"Hey! You're here!"

Bridget turned and watched Gabe plant one of his hands on Noah's shoulder. A second later, his other hand landed on her shoulder. Warm. Firm. Welcomed.

She stilled as tingles worked from the source of heat to every cell of her body. She didn't want to move. Didn't want to dislodge his hand.

"Gabe." Noah turned.

Gabe pulled away, leaving her shoulder bereft.

Bridget pressed a hand against her stomach to tame the butterflies that had taken over before she forced herself to turn slowly, sedately, and calmly, when she really wanted to whirl.

Gabe winked at her. "Hey, Green Eyes."

Forget calm. Her pitiful attempt went right out the open barn doors. She burst into tears. Her face heated as she realized people were staring. *Gabe* was staring. She tried to regain control of her runaway emotions, but they refused to be tamed. She sucked in a noisy gasp of air, pushed past Gabe, and ran outside. She would go home and hide. She couldn't do this. Seeing Gabe after so long, and in a room full of strangers…. She wanted the familiar faces of her hometown. The people she'd grown up with. Plus Gabe.

Jah, she would go home. Well, to the RV, anyway.

Her legs had a different idea and slid out from under her. She flailed her arms and landed hard on her backside in the driveway between the barn and the haus. She cried harder and pulled the front of her coat over her face.

Bridget heard the crunch of gravel, snow, or ice as someone approached. She peeked out.

"I didn't know I was that scary." Gabe reached down, tucked his hands under her arms, and pulled her up. Her feet hunted for purchase on the frozen ground. Finding none, she clutched his shoulders. "Easy, there." He tugged her against his chest in a loose hug. "I missed you, too. Nein need to cry. Though it does make your green eyes greener."

She found her footing and reluctantly released Gabe. Being in his arms, touching him like that, was wrong. And word would get out. Gabe would be in even more trouble. She pulled away slowly, too insecure to tell him how much she'd missed him. She tried to let her expression do the talking.

"How's the haus coming?" His eyes darkened with a look of what might have been pain. He stepped away, his hands falling to his sides, as Noah joined them.

Noah snorted. "Daed bought a thriving business. And now it's going under. All work came to a standstill because of his stubborn pride."

"You mean mine." Gabe's eyes swept over Bridget's coat-covered body, not lingering anywhere but heating.

A gust of wind whipped at the hem of Bridget's dress. She pressed her arms against her sides to hold it down. But her breath hitched. The look in Gabe's eyes...would he ask to give her a ride home from singing?

His gaze rose to meet hers, and held it. He stepped forward. Slightly invading her personal space.

Her heart rate increased with the anticipation of something she couldn't put into words.

But, nein. He moved between her and Noah as someone inside the barn called out a number from the Ausbund. "I'd like some hot cocoa. Want some?" Gabe asked.

Noah nodded. "Sounds gut. Bridget?"

Bridget tried to answer, but all that came out of her mouth was a croak as both men walked away. She swiveled and looked down at the icy spot where she'd fallen. She took a deep breath, wiped the tears off her cheeks, and cautiously made her way back inside.

So much for getting a ride home from Gabe.

Then again, he'd never ask in front of Noah.

He would probably take another girl home.

Bridget entered the dim interior of the barn. Someone seated on the girls' side waved at her. Bridget squinted to see better. Agnes Zook. And there was an empty seat next to her.

The old saying came to mind about keeping one's friends close and enemies closer. Was Agnes calling her over in an attempt at friendship? Or did she consider Bridget an enemy?

"Here's your hot cocoa." Noah handed Bridget a Styrofoam cup.

"Danki." She went to sit next to Agnes while Noah walked to the other side of the room. But the seats on either side of the chair he chose were occupied by men she didn't recognize, and she didn't see Gabe. She swallowed her frustration. "Danki for the candy you brought over," she said to Agnes. "It was ser gut."

Agnes beamed. "Gabe can hardly keep his fingers out of it."

Bridget nodded. That she knew. She'd seen him helping himself to liberal portions of the contents of the jar Agnes had given them. Though Mamm *had* told him to take as much as he wanted. Clearly, he sacrificed not to take the whole thing.

"He brought me here to-nacht," Agnes whispered.

Probably went without saying that he would take her home again. Agnes, or someone else besides Bridget, would be in the buggy with him.

Bridget nodded again. Forced a smile. And glanced around at all the girls staring at her. Whispering behind their hands.

She pulled her coat closer and hugged herself.

She shouldn't have kum.

~

Gabe wouldn't ask to give Bridget a ride. She didn't date, ain't so? Besides, he'd brought Agnes and her younger sister, Carolyn, and would likely need to take them back home afterward. Unless they found other rides. But it seemed likely they'd be riding along with the girl of the day— whoever she might be. He'd decide later. A different girl every two weeks.

He dated. Just not the one he wanted.

Bridget—if she stayed true to her decision not to date—would ride home with Noah. But it'd be interesting, and telling, to see what she did. Despite her having made a spectacle of herself, though the reason behind it baffled him, several guys near him elbowed one another and goofed off with frequent glances in her direction.

He couldn't blame them. He had trouble keeping himself from staring at her, too.

He took a deep breath and thumbed through the Ausbund, looking for a song that caught his fancy. At home in Florida, they sometimes sang folk songs or more modern tunes—country, rock, or pop—they heard on the radio. Nobody would ever tell. The rule was simple: What happens in Pinecraft stays in Pinecraft.

Though that wasn't completely true. After all, it was because of what had happened in Pinecraft that Gabe was judged, found guilty, and sent up here.

His breath fogged white in the cold air when he exhaled. Fascinating. He'd noticed that happening on previous occasions but was usually too busy to pay much attention to the strange occurrence. Now, watching it beat staring at Bridget, glaring at the youngies who were acting out in an effort to get her attention, or droning along with a song in German. Whoever led the singing that nacht had nein sense of timing or key.

Movement near the doors caught his attention. The youngies jerked to attention as the bishop strolled in.

Strolled. Not strode. Maybe he was a chaperone.

Someone followed him. Hosea. He strode. Mouth set. Fists balled.

Gabe's stomach clenched. *It's an ill wind that blows nein gut.*

They made a beeline for Gabe.

◡

Bridget straightened as Daed came into the barn and marched behind the bishop down the rows of young men. Daed's body language radiated irritation. Anger. Or maybe just frustration. Hard to tell without seeing his expression.

The men stopped in front of Gabe.

Neither man said a word that she could hear. But Gabe rose from his chair and followed them out.

Noah jumped up and trailed after them.

Bridget wanted to go, too. But she knew she would be sent back inside. Men's business. Noah might be sent back, as well. Depending. But if the issue was related to Daed and Noah's new business and Gabe's old job, maybe not.

She forced her attention back to the Ausbund she shared with Agnes, and found her place. But she couldn't sing. Nausea threatened. She looked after the men again.

Agnes leaned closer. "What do you think they needed Gabe for?"

With Daed involved? Bridget forced another smile. "My daed bought the company Gabe worked for."

"Jah, and fired him. I was there when Gabe confessed. Do you think your daed's here to apologize?"

Bridget shrugged. She wasn't sure Daed was quite desperate enough to apologize. But maybe he was, after a week of floundering, losing all his employees, and having long discussions with Noah and Patrick.

But then, why was the bishop involved? She hated to think what that might mean. The bishop might be trying to make Daed apologize, but she doubted Daed would make a public spectacle of himself just to humble himself. More likely, he'd argued with the bishop and talked him over to his way of thinking. *Marry Bridget.* And then he would get Gabe's guaranteed return to work. By default.

Why couldn't Daed let it go? There had to be other qualified men available who could step in and do the job.

But then, she didn't want anyone else. She wanted Gabe.

Daed and Noah did, too. At least, Noah did. And Daed wouldn't be so determined to have his way if he didn't want Gabe back. He just didn't want to confess that he was wrong.

Again. He had already done that once. *I'm wrong, and I say I'm wrong.* Maybe, by some miracle, he would manage to say it twice.

The song changed; now they sang a different one, printed near the front of the book. Four verses crawled by, the leader singing in monotone the whole time. It reminded Bridget of church services, both at home and here. It seemed tone-deafness was a requirement of ministers who led the singing. Some things never changed from location to location.

Bridget shifted in her seat, glancing outside. This was it. She was leaving. If she got caught, she'd use the excuse of needing to use the bathroom. But the nacht-time shadows were falling. With her black coat and bonnet, she might be able to scoot away unnoticed.

"Might" being the operative word. Probably wasn't dark enough. Yet. She would take her chances.

"I'll be right back," she whispered to Agnes. Then she rose to her feet and hurried outside.

All she saw outside the doors were two buggies. One was Daed's. The wind still whistled through the trees. She stopped, listening. Nein voices. Where had the men gone? Wherever Daed was, he likely wasn't staying quiet.

Still, Bridget heard nothing. Just the wind that accompanied the snow flurries that had started.

Maybe Daed would be reasonable. If he apologized.

Very carefully, she made her way across the ice and headed toward the hosts' haus. She would use the bathroom. And maybe she would see the men on her way out.

She went into the haus and wiped her feet on the mat in the entryway. From the living room came the low rumble of men's voices.

She crept closer to the door to the room and peeked around the corner. Noah stood there, his back to her, arms folded behind him.

Gabe stood in a loose circle with Daed, the bishop, and a man she didn't know.

Daed nodded, then stepped out of formation and turned toward Bridget.

She darted backward. Then realized she had nein choice but to go outside. She opened the door, closed it hard, and walked forward, pretending she'd just arrived.

Daed's eyebrows shot up when he saw her.

A woman came out of the kitchen and noticed her. "Hallo. Bathroom is that way." She pointed in the opposite direction of where the men stood. "Follow me."

"Danki." Bridget scurried after her. Hopefully, Daed would buy her charade.

When she came out of the bathroom, the men were gone, the haus quiet, except for the woman puttering in the kitchen.

Bridget went outside and descended the porch stairs. The bishop and the unfamiliar man climbed into one buggy, while Daed got in his own. Maybe Bridget could get a ride home with him. It'd be better than watching Gabe help another girl into his buggy.

Then again, there was still a chance he would ask her. She hesitated too long. The men headed toward the road.

Gabe stepped out of the shadows, and she gasped.

"Shh." He glanced around, then nodded toward the barn. "Kum. Hurry." He led her around the side to the back of the barn. "We won't have much time before the chaperones catch us." He stopped in the shadows, seeming oblivious to the tall weeds that, in spite of the weight of snow upon them, reached as high as his waist.

Bridget stomped down some of the weeds. "What did my daed want? And who was that other man?"

Gabe's mouth firmed. "My daed. Up from Florida. What do *you* think your daed wanted?"

14

Gabe shifted his weight on the frozen snow. He should've taken the time to grab his coat from the pile on his way out of the barn. A few of the youngies hadn't taken theirs off—Bridget included. He'd planned on warming up quickly, with all the body heat in the barn.

Though maybe he could warm up another way. He looked at Bridget.

The color had faded from her cheeks. "They're still insisting you marry me? That's *horrible*." She sounded shocked, upset.

He hadn't exactly expected her to jump up and down with glee, but "horrible"? "Wow. I didn't know I was as bad as all that." He tried not to let his bitterness show.

She backed away, until she bumped against the side of the barn. Stayed put. "You're not. It's just...I don't love you. You don't love me. Nein. Just...nein."

He sighed in frustration. "What's love got to do with it?" Okay, maybe quoting the title of an old pop song was a bit snarky. And he probably shouldn't tease her. Not right now. But he'd wanted to gauge her reaction. He'd seen her peeking in on him and the other men, spying on the final few minutes of their conversation.

"Ah...love? Nix. Apparently." Bridget squirmed.

He stepped closer, deliberately encroaching on her personal space. Planted his bare hands on the barn wall on either side of her, effectively pinning her in place. He allowed his eyes to focus on her lips.

Her breath caught. Her gaze dropped to his mouth. Then jerked upward, meeting his eyes. Her inhalations and exhalations became erratic. Her cheeks flamed red.

She wanted a kiss, too?

His stomach clenched.

"If we married, we'd have this." He leaned in and brushed his lips over hers. Teasing, not lingering. Because, really, one of the chaperones would check on them soon. And he didn't want to get caught and be accused of seducing Hosea's dochter.

Bridget sucked in air.

"That wasn't so *horrible*, was it?" He removed one hand from the wall and trailed a fingertip down her cheek, over her bottom lip.

She shivered. Her gaze lowered again. Jerked back up. Again. He thought he heard a whimper but wasn't quite sure. It might've been the wind.

He moved three steps backward, then hesitated. Maybe a second pass wouldn't hurt. Just as brief as the first. He looked in both directions to be certain nobody was there. Then he leaned in to touch his lips to the suppleness of hers again. She surged forward, meeting him halfway, her softness pressed against his chest. His arms slipped instinctively around her waist.

He hadn't expected this response, but he would take it, for sure. He kiss-walked her backward against the barn wall, cupped her face in both hands, and took firm possession. Her lips were parted, her response more than he'd dared to dream, and she kissed him with abandon.

He lost himself in the moment, taking full advantage of what she offered. Her arms encircled his neck, her fingers feathering through his hair. He moaned.

She gave an answering whimper.

This was…heaven.

She might not date, but she was sure willing to kiss him.

Then a foreign sound caught his attention. Not the wind, not their breaths, not— He disentangled her arms from his neck and moved away.

She made another whimpering sound.

Steps crunched through the frozen snow.

They had to go. Now.

"Someone's coming," he hissed. "Let's go." He grabbed her by the hand and tugged her in the opposite direction, around the corner of the barn, and out toward the pasture where the horses and buggies were parked.

She clambered into his buggy. He untied Cherry Blossom from the tree, then slid into the seat next to her.

His thigh pressed against hers.

Would the chaperones check the buggies? Probably not.

Of course, sitting in a parked buggy in the darkness offered another temptation. One Bridget probably hadn't thought of, the way she snuggled against his side without hesitation. A far cry from the behavior of a woman who didn't date.

He shouldn't have taken advantage of her. Shouldn't have kissed her. Shouldn't have—

"Take me home." Her voice was breathy. "I need to talk to my daed."

She was still under the impression they *had* to marry.

"So, two weeks, then?"

He blinked. Would she be so easily persuaded to marry him? Well, after kisses like those, few people would probably protest.

"Don't you have something to ask me?" Her tone held a teasing hint.

"Jah, but it kind of skips over that all-important first date." He hesitated. "And, before I ask, you need to know...I allowed you to believe a falsehood."

⌒

Bridget wished he would wrap his arm around her and cuddle her close. Maybe kiss her again. Whatever it was he'd allowed her to believe, it couldn't be all that bad. "What are you talking about?" She snuggled closer.

But he didn't move. Just stared straight ahead into the darkness, not even making a move to release the brake.

He sighed. "I shouldn't have kissed you. Shouldn't have taken advantage of you. I'm sorry. It won't happen again."

It wouldn't? But...she wanted it to.

"They aren't forcing us to get married."

She stiffened and sat up. Slid away from him. "Why did you lie?" Technically, he hadn't lied. She'd surmised what the men wanted, and he'd taken advantage of her incorrect assumption. But for what purpose? So he could kiss her?

He squirmed. "You said it was horrible. I don't like to think being married to me would be that bad. I mean, I realize I have faults, but...."

She frowned. "Being forced to marry is horrible. Not marrying you."

He gave a half-hearted laugh.

"So, what *did* the men want? I mean, it had to be serious, since your daed came up from Florida and everything."

"Your daed actually wanted to apologize. I guess he figured it would go over better if the bishop witnessed it. He said, 'I'm wrong, and I say I'm wrong,' just like he did before. And he asked if I would please consider coming back to work. I said I would."

"Gut, that's gut." Bridget smiled. "But your daed...?"

Gabe sighed. "I don't know yet. He'd just arrived and was visiting with the bishop when your daed came over, so he decided to tag along and witness the exchange. But he's probably here to yell at me about the polar bear plunge. I didn't think that would warrant an in-person visit. I thought maybe a phone call. Definitely a letter." He shrugged. "Maybe the way I almost killed you elevated the severity to the level of a more interactive scolding."

Bridget scoffed. "You didn't almost kill me."

He eyed her with a sober expression. "I could have. Your daed certainly thought so."

"Ach." She slid closer, cuddling against his side once more. "So, you're coming back to work?"

Gabe shrugged. "Told your daed I would, but he has this kind of love-hate relationship with me. Next time I mess something up, he'll fire me again. To be honest, I probably wouldn't have taken the job back if I hadn't had the bishop and Daed standing over me. I got a job at the sawmill. Next day, bam. So now I have to quit that job and go back to work for your daed. I'll have to make sure the sawmill bosses know I'll probably be back." He shifted. "Look. I'm sorry I kissed you. Do you want to go back to the singing? Or go home?"

"Home. Please." She probably wouldn't ever attend another singing. It was too stressful. "You're welkum to stay awhile, though. I could make cookies. We could play checkers." And maybe sneak out behind the RV and kiss again. Without his needing to feel sorry.

Gabe smiled. He released the brake, backed the buggy out of the field, and started down the road. Without his coat. Did he plan on returning to the singing later to retrieve it? Surely, he wouldn't abandon it.

He shook his head. "Danki, but I can't stay. Hosea will take one look at me—us—and assume I've been trying to seduce you—"

"What?" She shoved away from him. The idea of seduction put a whole different spin on things. She hadn't realized…wow. That hurt. He thought she was a loose woman he could just steal kisses from, serial dater that he was. She looked out her window. "Tell Noah you took me home, okay? Then I suppose you need to decide which girl to really take home. A different one every time, I heard."

She despised the bitterness in her voice.

He remained quiet.

"I suppose you know all the gut sparking places, too, ain't so? Or do you take every girl behind the barn?"

He maneuvered the buggy past the rusty mailbox marking her family's driveway.

"*Were* you trying to seduce me?"

"Not trying."

"What then, succeeding? Seriously?" Hopefully, he didn't hear the wail she struggled to keep contained. "Don't ask me out again."

"Wasn't planning on it." His voice was hard this time. "Believe me, you'll be begging me for a date before we go out again. Even as friends. Because we aren't friends, are we."

It wasn't a question.

He stopped in front of the barn and climbed out of the buggy. "But, just so you know, I wasn't seducing you. It was supposed to be just a kiss. Spur-of-the-moment."

Ach. She slid across the seat and allowed him to help her out. "Listen, Gabe…." She had to find the words to apologize. "I—"

"Gut nacht, Green Eyes. See you in a few days." He jumped back in the buggy and drove off.

A few days?

She stared after the dark form of the buggy.

"I was wrong, and I say I was wrong." She meant it.

But he didn't hear, because he was long gone.

〜

Gabe walked back into the barn. The group had ceased its poor attempt at singing and were now helping themselves to the snacks:

sandwiches cut into fourths; raw vegetables and chips with dip; grapes; and cookies, whoopee pies, and other baked goodies.

He scanned the crowd, looking for Noah, and finally found him talking with a girl in a corner. He walked over. "Hey. Sorry to interrupt, but I took your sister home early."

Noah grimaced. "She'd be a recluse if she was allowed. When we lived in Ohio, I had to force her to go to the frolics and to make her stay till the end. Of course, it got easier after Isaac noticed her."

She had a beau in Ohio? Gabe's stomach hurt. He'd kissed another man's girl. Flirted with her.

Noah must've sensed his anxiety, because he quickly added, "He broke up with her when he found out we were moving to Michigan."

Well, that was gut to know. It spared Gabe a little bit of guilt. Especially since he wanted to kiss Bridget again. He had nein desire to kiss another girl. Just her.

"I'm going to get some food," he announced. He wasn't hungry but wanted to give Noah a chance to talk to the girl standing with him. Gabe had taken her home once before. He'd called her Butterscotch because of her hair color, and she'd acted flattered.

With a wink in her direction and a gentle punch to Noah's arm, Gabe headed for the table full of food. He grabbed a can of soda from the ice chest—not that ice was needed in this weather—and turned toward the sweets. Helped himself to some fudge, made by Agnes. Hers was the best. A brownie, made by someone else. A stack of assorted homemade cookies. Gut thing Mamm wasn't here to nag him about eating too many sweets.

"Hiya, Gabe Lapp."

He spun around with his loaded plate and looked into the milk-chocolate-brown eyes of a girl he'd never taken home. The eagerness in her gaze stated clearly that she would be his company for the evening. He hid a grimace. *And here we go again. Another round. Different player.* It was almost enough to make him lose his appetite. Almost, but not quite. He searched his memory bank for a name and came up with nothing. "Hiya, Sweet Thang."

She giggled, her eyes lighting. "I love a southern drawl."

"You need a ride home later?" His stomach cramped at the memory of Bridget's bitter accusation—"*A different girl every time.*" Little did she know, she was the only one who caught his attention in *that* way.

Probably because she was hard to get. Or had been. He hadn't exactly expected her to fall into his arms, reciprocate his kisses, and snuggle against him. Though maybe she'd done all that because of her belief that they were being forced to marry.

Whatever the reason, her thawed affections had refrozen quickly on the ride home.

And he still wanted her.

Maybe he should've proposed. Waited until she accepted. Allowed her to continue in her incorrect belief.

But, nein. He might push the envelope where the Ordnung was concerned, but he didn't deliberately sin. Letting her believe they were being forced to marry would have been the same as telling a lie.

But then, maybe allowing Sweet Thang to believe she had a chance was akin to lying, too.

He looked down into her twinkling eyes.

His stomach hurt even more than before. He took a swig of soda, then nodded toward a couple empty benches. He'd figure it out later. Because, while he hadn't exactly heard anything she might have said, her body language indicated that she had accepted his offer of a ride. Had swallowed the Sweet Thang salutation, hook, line and sinker, and was open to a relationship.

And he wouldn't date Agnes because…why, again? Because she made cow eyes at him? Because she was so obvious in her affections? Because he knew it was wrong to lead her on?

At least she had candy-making skills in her favor. Including fudge, which nudged her upward by several notches.

He would give Sweet Thang a ride home, but they wouldn't take a trip behind the barn or stop at a sparking place.

Did this town even have sparking places? One could contract hypothermia just by making out in a buggy.

Or maybe not. Because he and Bridget had generated some serious heat.

15

Bridget had to do something. She just didn't know what.

She'd misjudged Gabe. Should've known better. He hadn't been trying to seduce her. A spur-of-the-moment kiss—that was so Gabe.

On the other hand, Noah had reported that Gabe returned to the singing and took another girl home. A girl Gabe had called "Sweet Thang."

Noah had laughed about it, saying Gabe called Noah's own date "Butterscotch." That Gabe had nicknames for all the girls.

And Bridget had thought "Green Eyes" meant something. As if she were special and important to him.

A noise outside the RV caught her attention. She looked out the front window and saw a horse and buggy coming up the driveway. It parked in front of the barn, close enough for her to identify the driver as Bishop Brunstetter, and his passenger as Gabe's daed. Why were they here? To verify that Gabe had almost killed her? To complain about Daed's treatment of Gabe in firing him and lashing out irrationally?

Either of those objectives could have been fulfilled last nacht when they interrupted the singing. And hadn't Gabe said that Daed apologized? So why would they need to complain about something that had been resolved? Perhaps they were truly here to check on her welfare, since they'd had other issues on their minds last nacht.

She felt a prick of guilt. She'd lashed out irrationally, too.

And she still didn't know what to do about it.

Gabe would probably never speak to her again, unless it was absolutely necessary.

But maybe it was better this way. They would have ended up hurting each other with careless, thoughtless, senseless words.

The two men climbed out of the buggy. They looked in the direction of the RV, and the bishop lifted a hand to wave at Bridget.

Daed and Noah weren't home. They'd gone to Patrick's to use his phone to call all their former employees and notify them of Gabe's imminent return to work. It was nice Gabe had so many people in his support system. Bridget should've been numbered among them.

She went down the few steps to open the door and greet the men. "Daed's not here, but please kum inside to wait for him, if you'd like. Would you care for some koffee?"

"That sounds gut." Bishop Brunstetter nodded at her, then turned to Gabe's daed. "Take off your shoes before entering, Gabriel."

Gabriel? So, Gabe was named after his daed. They definitely resembled each other.

Gabriel did as the bishop requested, and smiled at Bridget as he entered. "So, you must be the one my sohn calls 'Green Eyes.' He mentioned you in his most recent letter home. Hard to miss those eyes. Gut to meet you, Bridget."

Bridget smiled but couldn't think what to say. Probably better to remain silent than stutter and stammer like a dummchen.

"Who's here?" Mamm came out of the bedroom where she'd been folding a load of laundry.

"Gut to see you, Frau Behr," the bishop said. "This is Gabriel Lapp, from Pinecraft, Florida."

Mamm smiled. "Welkum. You're a long way from home. I don't know if you could've paid me enough to leave Florida to kum here." She shivered.

Both men chuckled. But Gabe's daed did gather his coat more closely around himself.

Bridget poured two mugs of koffee, which she set, along with a plate of cookies, on the table.

Gabe's daed picked up one of the mugs, gripping it with both hands.

Mamm eyed the men. "What brings you by, if I may ask? Hosea has gone to see Patrick about—"

"We're actually here to see Gabe," Gabe's daed said. "Zooks said he'd gone to work, and we figured it should be pretty near quitting time."

"Why do you need to see him?" A note of worry colored Mamm's voice. "It's not about the forced marriage, is it? Because I think they decided against it."

Gabe's daed gave her a long look. "I think that's best discussed with Gabe."

"He should be finished with work soon." Bishop Brunstetter glanced at the digital time display on the microwave as he slid into the bench seat. "We'll go on out to the haus after we finish our koffee."

"He's at the sawmill."

Both men swiveled to stare at Bridget.

Bridget shrank back. Maybe she shouldn't have blurted out that information. If only she could disappear.

"I wasn't aware he'd gotten a new job." The bishop adjusted his mug on the table, turning the handle to the left.

Gabe's daed frowned. "I'm pretty sure he didn't tell his mamm, either. She usually keeps me informed."

"He told me last nacht, when he brought me home from the singing."

"Hmm." Both men uttered the noise simultaneously, as their stares turned speculative.

If only she'd kept her mouth shut.

Then both men shook their heads, as if simultaneously dismissing the possibility that Gabe might have any interest in her. And they'd be right, of course. Gabe had freely admitted to having kissed her only because he wanted to show her that marrying him wouldn't be as horrible as she might think.

The kisses hadn't seemed to affect him at all. He was the one who'd heard the chaperones coming. She, on the other hand, needed to be dragged to the buggy, so overwhelmed with feeling she'd been.

Gabe's daed lowered himself into the seat across the table from the bishop. "When do you think he'll be back?"

Mamm glanced at Bridget, eyes wide, before saying, "Hosea? Or Gabe?"

"Both." He reached for a cookie.

"Gabe said a…a few days," Bridget managed to whisper. She glanced toward the door, wanting to run out and busy herself in the barn, even if it was freezing cold out there. But she couldn't leave Mamm alone with the men. That would be inappropriate.

The bishop raised his eyebrows. "A few days."

"Well, he had to give notice at the s-sawmill, and he…he wants to leave on gut terms, because…because he'll need a job again the next time

Daed gets angry at him." Why did she have to stutter like a preschooler trying to talk too fast?

Mamm gasped. "Bridget!"

"Well, it's true. Daed has a love-hate relationship with him. Gabe knows it, too. He said so."

Mamm glared, not with disapproval but to communicate that Bridget was saying too much.

Bridget clamped her lips shut.

"Sounds like my sohn talks to you." Gabriel patted the space next to him on the bench. "Have a seat, Bridget."

Bridget shook her head. She couldn't. When Gabe had sat next to her, their legs had touched. She wasn't going to sit that way with his daed.

"There's plenty of room." His daed quirked a brow.

The bishop nodded. "Sit, Bridget."

She swallowed her discomfort and obeyed. And...there was enough room. Ample space for not one but two Bibles aligned side by side. Which meant Gabe had crowded her on purpose.

Why would he have done that? Just to witness her discomfort? Or did she dare hope it might have meant something more? That maybe he'd wanted to sit near her, and not just to provoke a shocked reaction.

Her heart pounded, and she fisted her hands on her lap.

Perhaps he'd wanted to kiss her, too. And not just because he wanted to prove that marriage to him wouldn't be all that bad.

But then, if so, why had he apologized afterward?

Nothing made sense.

Still, the possible truth of this revised scenario made her heart race like a runaway horse.

She *had* to talk to Gabe. Even if she still didn't know what to say.

The RV door opened.

And *he* walked in.

⌒

"Preacher Zook said you were looking for me." Gabe set his jaw, padded across the floor in his stocking feet, and sat down next to the bishop without waiting for an invitation. He tried not to look at Bridget.

Well, other than to give her a quick, not-as-dismissive-as-he-would've-liked glance.

He forced himself to face Daed, expecting to see anger radiating from his pores. It'd be nice if Daed didn't yell at him here, but it wasn't as if much more damage could be done to Gabe's nonexistent relationship with Bridget. "Daed."

"Sohn." A seldom-seen dimple appeared on Daed's cheek. One that matched Gabe's. Or so he'd been told.

Gabe flicked a speck of something off his bare forearm. Probably sawdust. He hadn't taken the time to shower before coming here.

Bridget's mamm set a mug of koffee on the table in front of him as Bridget nudged a plate of oatmeal-raisin cookies—his favorite—closer. Tempting him. He helped himself to a cookie but didn't dare to take a bite. He knew that the second he did, the scolding would start, and it was preferable not to have a mouthful of a cookie he'd once thought delicious turning distasteful due to the yelling.

But both Daed and the bishop calmly drank their koffees as if nothing were more important. Bridget and her mamm fidgeted.

"What did you want?" Gabe asked of nobody in particular. Might as well get this over with.

"We'll talk later," Daed said calmly. Quietly. And his dimple flashed again.

Two flashes of the dimple in less than two minutes' time? Gabe was growing uncomfortable. "We'll talk now." He raised his chin slightly. There wasn't any truly private place to conduct the imminent discussion. Not here. Not at the Zooks'. Not at Bishop Brunstetter's. Because, despite his having lived in the area for several months, he had nein place to call home.

Daed's eyebrows twitched. "Fine. Do you know someone named Wyatt Johnson?"

That was the last question Gabe had expected. "Jah, I do, but not well." The man—believed by many to be homeless, judging by his ragged clothes and unkempt appearance—had sporadically worked construction jobs in Florida. Until he'd stopped showing up. Never collected his final paycheck. Gabe hadn't missed him.

The bishop shifted. Frowned. "We'll continue this discussion later." He nodded at Bridget's mamm. "Danki for your hospitality, but we need to go." Then his gaze fell to Gabe once more. "Gabe, kum by my haus. Have supper with us."

"Uh, sure." So that was where it would go down. Gabe repressed a sigh, then stood so that the bishop could get up from the bench. On the other side of the table, Bridget rose, too, as did Daed.

"Can we talk after that?" Bridget asked. Her gaze darted from her mamm to Gabe's daed.

Maybe she thought the presence of witnesses would make him likelier to answer affirmatively to her request. But he wasn't in the mood to coddle irritated Behrs. Not even cute, cuddly ones. The trouble was, how could he say nein without having even more wrath heaped upon his head?

He shook his head. "Not to-nacht. Probably not tomorrow, either." Maybe never. But he'd tell her the firm and final nein later.

"Soon?" She sounded hopeful.

"Might as well talk with Goldilocks now." Bishop Brunstetter gave him a smirking "I know young love" smile. "I think your daed and I have another visit to make before heading homeward. I'll see you in about an hour."

Bridget's mamm hurried toward the bedroom as the men exited. Leaving Gabe and Bridget alone.

Alone. But with nein privacy.

Nein matter. He had nothing to say. She could speak her piece; he would nod in agreement and then leave. Easy.

"Will you go over to the haus with me?"

He glanced down the short hallway. Inside the open bedroom door, her mamm worked on something, her back to them.

Bridget would probably feel more comfortable without a witness. Especially if she intended to lash out at him for kissing her and driving her home, only to return to the singing and offer a ride home to "Sweet Thang."

What she didn't know was that he'd gotten sick from downing too many desserts. After dropping Sweet Thang at home, he'd waited for his nausea to pass before sneaking into the Zooks' long after lights out.

He gave a half nod. It was more of a head bounce, side to side yet also up and down.

Even though he wasn't looking directly at Bridget, her hesitant smile lit the room.

And, suddenly, that smile became the most important thing in the world.

〜

Bridget's knees almost knocked together as she led the way to the unfinished haus. She opened the door and stepped inside. The interior was only slightly warmer than the outside temperature. A fire had been going while she and Mamm were working in the haus, but the embers had long been extinguished. She shouldn't have asked to talk to Gabe. Not when she didn't have the vaguest idea what to say. But she had asked. And now she was stuck.

Gabe followed her in but didn't shut the door behind him. Nor did he move past the entryway. Instead, he stood there. Silent. Surveying her as if she were some weird object dangling from the end of a fishing pole. Like a pink plastic flip-flop that'd put up a gut fight.

It was up to her.

She sucked in a breath and then choked on the air, coughing so hard she began gasping, with tears flowing down her cheeks. She could only imagine what Gabe must think as she fought to regain normal airflow through her lungs.

Even when she finally calmed, he still hadn't moved. The only difference was his expression. It had grown more confused.

Bridget turned away from him to lift the hem of her apron and wipe her eyes. Then she faced him again. "I'm sorry. It's just…." Might as well be honest and put it all out there. "Okay, I'll admit it. I was jealous. I get that you're a spur-of-the-moment guy. And, well, I'm a girl who overthinks things, and I wanted you to mean that kiss. I wanted you to mean it so much that you wouldn't want to return to the singing and take another girl home. I wanted you to be head over heels, can't-wait-to-kiss-her-again, please-Gott-let-her-feel-the-same in love with me." Her words tumbled out like a falling tower of children's alphabet blocks. "Unrealistic, ain't so?" Her laugh was bitter.

He blinked. Chuckled. "Well, I'm definitely at the 'can't-wait-to-kiss-you-again' stage. And possibly the 'head over heels' stage, because I can't seem to think straight around you. I have mixed-up emotions, for sure. But…." He shook his head.

"I didn't mean to react in a jealous rage," Bridget put in. "I want to be the one who's got your back, and supports you. I want—" She snapped her mouth shut. Her face burned. Had she really just admitted she wanted him to be in love with her?

He took a step farther into the room. "You don't date."

Her eyes stung. She shook her head.

"You're asking me to court you?"

"I'm not asking." But she nodded, then hung her head, ashamed of her uncontrolled dump of emotions.

"How about I tuck my can't-wait-to-kiss-you-again feelings away and focus on the head-over-heels part and stop seeing other girls. Maybe if we concentrate on becoming friends, I will get to the 'please-Gott-let-her-feel-the-same in love with me' stage." There was a twinkle in his eyes. A dimple flashed beside his kissable lips.

She nodded mutely. Inside, she was giddy with hope.

"You do realize, though, I don't know why my daed is here. He asked me about a guy I knew back home who's gone missing. I don't understand, though I'm sure he'll enlighten me. But whatever he says may change my plans. It's possible he's here to take me home to thaw out."

Her attempt at a smile failed. She turned away from him once more, focusing her gaze on the new windows. They'd been installed mere days before everyone had walked off the job. "All I wanted to do was say I was sorry. Not give a full-fledged confession I had nein control over."

He chuckled again. His boots clomped across the floor as he approached her from behind. His strong arms wrapped around her in a loose hug. "I forgive you."

Were there any sweeter words in the human language? A fresh round of tears burned her eyes.

He leaned over her shoulder and kissed her cheek. "If I thought there might be a chance of your getting out of the RV without being noticed, I'd throw a snowball at your window to-nacht."

But there wasn't any chance of that. They both knew it.

His arms slid away. "I'll see you in a few days, Green Eyes. End of the week, for sure. I need to go talk to the bishop and my daed before your daed gets home and detains me."

She nodded.

"I won't be starting work for your daed for another two weeks. I needed to give that much notice to the guys at the sawmill."

Daed wouldn't like that. Not one bit.

"And that's assuming I'm staying rather than returning to Florida."

Ach. Right. She twisted around to face him, but he'd already turned away and was moving toward the door.

At the exit, he stopped and glanced back. Winked. "That kiss might've been spur-of-the-moment, but I'm still reliving it, Liebling. Ach, jah. Head over heels, for sure."

And then he was gone. But the chilly haus felt a little bit warmer after his declaration. She wanted to burst into song and twirl through the rooms.

Instead, she stood in the doorway and watched him climb into the buggy. Watched him disappear into a nacht that seemed not to realize that the winter solstice had kum and gone, and the days were supposed to be getting longer.

He vanished like a pleasant dream shattered by the reality of life slamming into it.

Why *was* Gabe's daed in town?

16

The ache in Gabe's stomach felt like a stampeding herd of wild deer racing across it, bucking all the way. Why couldn't Daed have just called and saved him this drama? Gabe wanted attention, but not to the point of Daed's dropping everything and catching the first bus to Michigan.

This would be bad.

Very, very bad.

Gabe shivered into his coat, gripped the reins, and tried to focus on his latest kiss with Bridget instead of the upcoming talk with Daed.

It didn't work. *Bad, bad, bad.* The word beat a steady refrain in his head.

Never mind the flash of Daed's dimple in the RV. His civility was likely just a show for the bishop. The second Daed got Gabe alone behind the bishop's woodshed, fire and brimstone would rain down on Gabe in the form of words. Hard words.

But maybe, after Daed had gotten the scolding out of the way, he would answer Gabe's burning question: Had he been traded to the Mackinac County Amish for fresh blood back home?

Nein matter how long Gabe pondered the idea, it didn't seem possible. This community was too new. Amish youngies from the Sault Ste. Marie area, and the Amish "trolls" from under the bridge, joined them when the weather permitted. And Pinecraft, Florida, drew Amish visitors from all over the nation. Fresh blood came in regularly, almost on a daily basis.

As Gabe pulled the buggy to a stop at the bishop's haus, Daed came out of the barn.

Alone.

Carrying…a Thermos?

Gabe shook his head and looked again. It was a Thermos.

Daed approached the buggy and motioned with his head for Gabe to move down. "Slide over. I'll drive."

So, he had a specific destination in mind. A spot more private than the bishop's home. Someplace where there'd be nein witnesses. Nein impartial observers.

On a positive note, both of them would be removed from familiar territory, so neither one would have the upper hand from a location standpoint.

And Daed's expression was sober. Not angry.

Gott, please, let this go well. Help this to work out in my favor.

Suddenly, the stampeding deer in Gabe's stomach found a place to graze and settled down, as if they sensed the unexpectedly calm quality to Daed's mood.

Of course, that mood could change with a single wrong word from Gabe. It might help if Gabe took the time to think before speaking, instead of blurting out the first thing that came to mind.

Gott, help me to keep my mouth shut for once in my life.

Daed stashed the Thermos beneath the buggy seat, then climbed inside. He leaned forward and adjusted the dial on the battery-operated heater. "Pretty cold here."

An understatement of the obvious. Gabe nodded. Nein point in wasting words on trivial matters.

"Bishop Miah gave me directions to this place. Said it should be somewhat warm—at least warmer than the outdoors—and there are tables. One of the families recently purchased it for a business they plan to open, and, well, I'm not supposed to give anything away." Daed's dimple flashed for the third time that day.

Frightening. It meant Daed was in a gut mood.

Maybe he was merely looking forward to yelling at Gabe.

Gabe fought the urge to slump. He swiped his hand over his jaw, the prickles from his five-o'clock shadow scratching his palm.

Daed took the reins and drove away from Bishop Brunstetter's—odd that Daed was on a first-name basis with the man already—and headed into town. He stopped at a nondescript building on the square. A "sold" sign rested in the window. As many times as Gabe had been in town, he'd never noticed this place. It looked a bit run-down, but it was nothing some hard work and fresh paint wouldn't improve.

Daed grabbed the Thermos as he climbed out of the buggy, Gabe right behind him. Then Daed unlocked the door to the building and led the way inside. The room was chilly, but not nearly as frigid as the outdoors. The propane heat must've been running recently. A ladder leaned against a far wall, with some painting supplies nearby. The familiar odor of turpentine filled the room, prompting Gabe to wrinkle his nose.

In spite of the pungent smell, he was comforted to find himself on familiar footing. The building had undeniable potential. He tried to imagine what this place might become. Knowing who had bought it would help.

Daed looked around. "Bishop Miah said there were some disposable cups here. Let me see if I can find them." He grabbed a rag and handed it to Gabe. "You wipe off the table and chairs. I'll be right back." He disappeared through a door.

After a moment's hesitation, Gabe wiped off the chairs and the table. Then he looked around once more. Tools had been left in a messy jumble on the counter. He walked over and began to organize them.

This was strange. Daed didn't usually scold sitting down. And never over a hot beverage he shared with his sohn.

Never.

Daed came back into the room carrying two Styrofoam cups and a couple packages of peanut-butter sandwich crackers.

Snacks, too?

The world must be off its axis.

Bridget remained in the stillness of the new haus, reveling in the silence, the solitude. Relishing the rare chance for time alone to think. She walked through the quiet, half-finished space, seeing Gabe everywhere: giving directions to the men as they installed drywall. Kneeling on the floor as he matched the new plumbing to the old system. Making suggestions to Daed regarding the types of windows to purchase. Stopping beside her as she painted to say a few words—telling her she was doing an excellent job, leaving nein streaks—and to tease her about the bland color. *Why eggshell? What about pale blue? Or sea green?*

Her emotions had plenty of color. Jealousy's hue was jade. The same shade as one of her dresses. The same shade she'd seen when she spotted Agnes flirting with Gabe.

What she needed was something in red—guaranteed to knock a man dead. But wouldn't the preachers' eyebrows rise in horror and shock if she dared to wear something that screamed, "Look at me"?

She hadn't meant to spill to Gabe all her thoughts, emotions, and jade-infused jealousy, thoroughly mixed with silent pleas that he would return to her. But Gabe hadn't laughed at her. He'd listened.

And while he didn't seem ready to commit to courtship, he was willing to consider friendship. Though she'd thought they *were* friends. She'd considered him her only friend in this area. Noah's friend, too.

After all, Gabe talked to her. Flirted with her. Teased her. Comforted her. Helped her up when she fell—twice. Listened to her. And called her Green Eyes. Though nicknames apparently meant nothing, since he'd given one to just about every girl. All except for Agnes. She was the only girl he called by her actual name.

Did he even know Bridget's real name?

What made Agnes special? Was it her fudge?

What would it be like when Gabe finally whispered "Bridget" in her ear? Bridget shivered at the thought. She would probably tumble into his arms. Into his kiss…. She pressed her lips together with yearning, and wrapped her arms around herself as she remembered being so close to him. Remembered the tingles that had spread when his leg brushed against hers.

Gabe caused her to experience feelings she'd never known before. Not even when Isaac was courting her.

That kiss….

That kiss. It'd replaced the barely-there embers she'd gotten from Isaac's light kisses with a raging inferno that left her weak in the knees.

Her legs buckled at the mere thought of it.

And Gabe might not be allowed to stay here?

If he returned to Pinecraft, would she be permitted to follow him?

Hardly.

Hearing the front door open, she spun around and started for the entryway. Maybe it was Gabe, returning to give her a real kiss, instead of the light peck he'd placed on her cheek. To give her a tighter, closer, more passionate embrace than the gentle hug she'd gotten from behind. Surely, he was as dissatisfied as she with the brevity of that contact. She quickened her steps, then came to a sudden stop.

And they weren't already friends?

But it wasn't Gabe who'd entered. Instead, Daed and Noah stared at her with eyebrows raised, as if awaiting a response. One of them must have said something.

Disappointment flooded her. Exhaling loudly, she slumped her shoulders and lost her smile.

"I'm sorry. I didn't hear you."

"Obviously," Daed grumbled. "I said, I think that bu was put on earth for the sole purpose of giving me grief. After I called all those men and told them Gabe would return to work tomorrow, the bishop came by, accompanied by Gabe's daed, to tell me it'd be two weeks. *Two weeks!* He didn't even give me two weeks' notice before—"

"You fired him?" Noah added dryly.

Daed huffed. "Be that as it may, how dare he find another job when he knows I need him? And how in the world did that bu become so doggone important to the area's construction scene in the short time he was here before we arrived?" He glared at Bridget as if it were all her fault.

A surge of pride on Gabe's behalf welled up inside her. She'd known there was something special about him.

"I had to call back every one of those men and tell them work is suspended another two weeks. Now we have to wait that much longer to move into our home."

Noah rolled his eyes. "You did this to yourself, Daed."

Hopefully, Noah wouldn't get into trouble and end up fearing his daed as Gabe apparently did his own.

"Well, it seems to me Bridget could've done something about it, considering how smitten the bu is with her," Daed groused.

"Not smitten," Bridget murmured. "We aren't even friends." In Gabe's opinion.

But she was definitely smitten. As were half the single maidals in the district. Including Agnes Zook.

Daed snorted. "Smitten."

Noah shook his head. "He never said he was smitten. He takes other girls home from singings. A different one each time. And he flirts with them just as blatantly as he does with Bridget. I've seen him in action. The girls almost fall in his arms when his dimple flashes and he calls them by some endearment."

Daed's shoulders slumped. As did Bridget's heart.

She was nein better than the rest of them.

But then, Gabe had said he was head over heels for her. And that he planned to concentrate on friendship with her instead of serial dating.

And he had mentioned her in a letter home to his mamm.

That had to mean something.

⌒

In the vacant storefront, Daed sat down across from Gabe and reached for the Thermos. He unscrewed the lid and poured steaming koffee into one of the Styrofoam cups. "We need to see about getting you a horse and buggy of your own. Bishop Miah said there was an auction down in Mio in March. Think you can hold off that long?"

There was nein way Daed had made the trip north to discuss transportation for Gabe. Or an auction in March.

March? Evidently Gabe wouldn't be going home to thaw out, after all. The implied rejection stabbed his heart. Why couldn't Daed love him? Want him home again?

"I *was* traded for fresh blood, then." Gabe pressed his lips together so tightly, it hurt. The unexpected sting of tears pained his eyes, and a huge lump filled his throat, making it hard to breathe.

If only Bridget would let him date her. The next-best option was Agnes—probably the primary reason Preacher Zook had invited him to live with his family. Well, that, and the convenience his close proximity made for the preacher's scoldings.

Daed filled the other cup with koffee, then replaced the lid on the Thermos. "Nein, you weren't. I'd intended for you to kum home."

A wave of relief washed over Gabe. He straightened his posture.

"I only wanted to separate you from the unfortunate set of friends you'd found to hang out with when the construction business lagged and your days off outnumbered your working days."

Jah, those days were boring. They drove him to do things he normally wouldn't. Like the not-so-brilliant idea to go surfing when the ocean churned due to a hurricane. That'd been foolish and dangerous. But fun. At least, until someone had gotten caught in a current and drowned.

"When they arrested your friends for vandalism and theft, you were taken in and questioned. It hurt your reputation. Especially when your friends had drugs in their systems. The business that had hired us to remodel their storefront considered letting you go, because even though you were released after being questioned, they figured you must have been involved, somehow. Not only that, but they cancelled their contract with my company. Not right, but some people don't think things through. As I've said before, 'Idle hands are the devil's workshop.' I didn't want or need you getting into more trouble."

"I didn't mean to get into trouble," Gabe said quietly. "I'm sorry."

Daed waved his hand dismissively. "I know. You said that before. And while the incident was an important consideration in sending you here, that wasn't the deciding factor. Remember my asking if you knew Wyatt Johnson?"

"Jah, I remember. But I don't know him. Not really. I mean, I'd recognize him on the street, but I don't really *know* him." Gabe took a sip of the strong, bitter drink in his cup. The bishop's frau wasn't gut at making koffee. But at least it was hot. That mattered, with the chill of the room creeping under his skin.

"Jah, well…Wyatt Johnson was murdered."

Gabe spewed the koffee from his mouth, showering Daed's face and the tabletop. "What?"

Daed mopped his face with the paint rag Gabe had used on the chairs and table.

"Sorry." Gabe grabbed another rag from nearby and wiped up the mess on the table. "But really? That's awful." Then he frowned. "Wait. They think *I* did it? That I was somehow involved? They want me for questioning? Is that why you're here? Because I didn't do it. I was here."

"Nein." Daed shook his head. "My friend on the police force contacted me before the story hit the news, and I knew I had to protect you. That you had to leave."

He *had* been shipped out of town in a hurry. Nein warning.

"They arrested one of your friends for the murder about a month ago. But when I saw changes in your behavior and feared what you were becoming, I knew you had to leave. You hung around drug addicts, robbers, vandals, and a probable murderer. Like it or not, you become who you associate with. You might have intended to witness to those guys, but that's not usually the way it works, Sohn. It says in First Corinthians fifteen that bad company corrupts gut character." Daed's voice cracked.

Had he sent Gabe here out of a loving desire to protect Gabe from himself? He truly had made poor choices of friends.

"I was assured the preachers and the bishop here would keep you out of trouble."

"Well, they try to, anyway," Gabe muttered, attempting to lighten the mood. He took another sip of koffee.

"They are impressed with you, Sohn. With your service to the Amish and to the community, with your work ethic, and with your willingness to go the extra mile to help others and to forward the causes you believe in." The dimple on Daed's face danced. "Although they couldn't help but laugh at some of your antics. Jumping out at people in a haunted haus, and participating in a polar bear plunge." Daed's lips quirked. "Both of which will earn you a scolding from them, if you haven't already received it."

"I think I have." If Gabe counted Hosea's screaming in his face, and Preacher Zook's expressed concern over a shoe fetish. Besides, Bishop Brunstetter had said he would talk with him later.

Daed cleared his throat. His eyes misted. "That brings me to the important issue. The one I came up here to discuss with you. According to Bishop Miah, you deliberately misbehaved in order to get my attention." Pain filled Daed's voice.

Gabe squirmed, feeling guilty for having caused his daed distress. "Rather immature of me, ain't so?" He'd been foolish to interpret the bus ticket north as a sign of rejection rather than an act to save him.

He firmed his shoulders. He would move forward with a clean slate. Start acting the way Daed claimed the leaders of this community viewed him, antics aside.

"I didn't mean to make you feel unimportant," Daed went on. "You are very important to me. Bishop Miah reminded me that, oftentimes, people base their opinions of Gott—of who and what He is—on the behavior of their earthly daed, and other male authority figures in their lives. If that is true, then you probably see Gott as an unrelenting judge rather than a loving, concerned Father who wants the best for you." His voice cracked. He wiped his eyes.

Gabe swallowed. He stared at an unopened package of crackers on the table, his eyes barely registering anything beyond an orange blur. His impression of the character of der Herr did align closely with his perception of the men Gott had placed over him. Quick to judge, severe in scoldings, and slow to listen.

Daed sighed. "You've been searching for approval, for attention, from sinful men—including me—when you really need to focus your attention on serving Gott. You need Him more than you need anyone else. Gott spreads around forgiveness and grace like you used to spread jelly on toast. He gets it all over the place."

Gabe mustered a weak smile. Is that really what Gott was like? He hoped so. The grace he'd received from the bishop and now from Daed started seeping into the cracks of his heart like a healing balm. He wanted to believe Gott could really love him and forgive him.

"Ich liebe dich, Sohn, and I want the best for you." Daed smiled. "I'm also proud of you. Don't ever forget that. I'm sorry you believed I had nein time for you except for when you needed a scolding. I will try to do better going forward. You are my sohn, and you're more important to me than life itself. I want to see you succeed, not drive you away from Gott and family." Daed reached across the table and gave Gabe's shoulder a squeeze.

"Danki, Daed." The moment called for a hug. But Gabe sat there, staring at Daed and wishing he would dare to initiate such a move.

"As much as I've missed you, and as much as I realize this climate is a shock to your system, I strongly suggest you stay." Daed rubbed his hands together as if to warm them. "You have a gut, Gott-fearing bishop on your side, and a community of Amish and Englischers alike who embraced you with open arms, whether you see it or not. And then, of course, there's a certain young woman who seems to have caught your eye." Daed's dimple flashed again.

Gabe's face heated.

"It's time for me to be a positive factor in your life. Not always focusing on the negative." Daed reached for a package of crackers and tore open the plastic wrapper. "We have this time together to connect. Tell me about your life here. And don't leave out any details about your girl."

17

Bridget slid a baking sheet of drop biscuits into the oven and then set the timer. She wondered how hard it would be to forgo the conveniences of the RV and return to the usual way of doing things. Whether she liked it or not, that day would kum. Mamm, Daed, and Noah had already moved out of the RV into tents set up in the barn, claiming they were tired of the overcrowding. Bridget was thankful to have been given the option of staying in the big, comfy king-sized bed, even if she still had to share it with her two sisters.

Noah reached over her head, opened a cabinet door, and took out a mug. As he filled it with hot koffee, Bridget stepped away from the oh-so-convenient electric range, opened the refrigerator, took out a bottle of cream, and handed it to him.

"Danki." He grinned. "So, will you kum skating with us to-nacht? All the youngies will be there, and there'll be extra skates. There's bound to be a pair that fit you." Noah poured some cream into his mug, then added a spoonful of sugar.

Ice-skating did sound fun, but she wasn't in any hurry to be near frozen water. Not after what happened with the polar bear plunge. Though, surely nobody would skate unless the surface of the pond was solid enough.

But if she didn't go, she would have to wait another whole week to see Gabe. It had already been one week since she'd last seen him. Not that she was counting. And that assumed he was still around. She hadn't heard, one way or the other.

"Butterscotch said to invite you. Gabe and Agnes will be there. And her younger sister. What was her name?" Noah scratched his head.

A thrill surged through her. Gabe was still here. "Her name is Carolyn." Then Bridget frowned. "Gabe and Agnes. Why does everyone in the community now mention them as a pair?" She huffed, then rushed to change the subject before Noah could accuse her of jealousy. "And what is Butterscotch's real name, anyway?"

Noah wrinkled his nose. "She told me, but I can't remember. Butterscotch just seemed to stick when Gabe said it. Besides, she doesn't mind. She giggles every time she hears it."

Bridget raised her eyebrows. "Maybe so. But I think she'd really like it if her special guy called her by her real name." Or used a different pet name from the one coined by a big flirt.

Noah rolled his eyes. "Whatever. Every girl likes endearments. That's obvious, the way they all react to Gabe. Even you look all dreamy when he calls you 'Green Eyes.'"

Bridget couldn't think of a gut response. She rinsed out the mixing bowl and set it aside for a better scrubbing after supper.

"So. You coming?" Noah grabbed his koffee, scooted past her, and opened the bathroom door. "We'll need to leave as soon as I get ready. Shiloh can watch the biscuits. And whatever else you're making for supper."

She would have to go over to the haus and interrupt Shiloh's painting of an upstairs bedroom. Plus, she would need to get permission from Mamm and Daed.

She shook her head. "I'm not going. I'd be the one to fall through the ice."

Noah's mouth opened and closed. Then he shrugged. "Suit yourself." He ducked into the bathroom and shut the door.

Hearing a tapping sound toward the front of the RV, Bridget turned in that direction. She tossed the dishcloth into the sink and took a step toward the door as it door opened, and Gabe appeared.

"Hey, Green Eyes. Did Noah ask you about going ice-skating?" He paused at the top of the stairs.

Bridget floundered. It was one thing saying nein to Noah. But telling that to Gabe was quite different, because all she could think of was holding his hand and conversing quietly as they skated around the pond in the darkness. Maybe sneaking a kiss or two. Warming up by the bonfire afterward with hot cocoa and s'mores.

The ice cracking…another ice-cold dip…. She shuddered. "Jah."

Wait. That came out wrong.

She must've sounded unsure, because Gabe frowned as he paused between the two front seats of the RV. "I hear a 'but.'"

"I don't want to go." She bit her tongue before blurting out the reasons why.

Gabe studied her for a long, silent moment.

"I'm afraid." Okay, that was part of it. Well, all of it, but not all for the same reason. The fear of making a fool of herself in front of strangers trumped her fear of falling through the ice. Not to mention, she was afraid to watch Gabe flirt with the other girls, and to have them see her pain and distress while she tried to pretend it didn't matter.

"I get that, but I won't let anything happen to you."

A promise he couldn't keep. After all, he'd let go of her during the polar bear plunge. And other girls would want to skate with him. It wasn't as if the two of them were a couple.

"It'll be fun," he said quietly.

"Your definition of 'fun' seems a far cry from mine."

The light in his eyes faded. A look of weariness swept over his countenance. He seemed tired. Exhausted. Maybe he was.

The bathroom door opened, and Noah came out. "Hey, Gabe. You ready to go?"

Gabe's eyes skittered from her to Noah. "I think I'll skip to-nacht. Do you mind going by the Zooks' and picking up Agnes? She'll likely find another way home."

"Aw, Bridget. Don't ruin our fun." Noah pushed past her. He set his empty mug on the counter next to the mixing bowl.

Noah's definition of fun seemed to match Gabe's. Living life on the edge.

The timer chimed. Bridget grabbed two pot holders, opened the oven door, and lifted out the sheet of golden-brown biscuits.

Gabe eyed the baking sheet and made a noise. Was that a groan?

"I need to talk to your sister, anyway. Maybe here would be better. Those biscuits smell ser gut, Green Eyes."

Noah grunted. "Daed will be here. You'll have a better chance to talk in private while skating. Seriously. Daed will try to monopolize your time and guilt-trip you into working on the haus because you're courting Bridget. As a volunteer, not for pay."

Gabe's frown deepened. Was it because of the pressure to court her?

She would let him off the hook. "I'll send a biscuit with you, Gabe. Go and have fun." She glanced at Noah. "Besides, we aren't courting."

"We aren't?" Gabe's brow furrowed. "We agreed I would stop dating other girls, and focus on you. That is courting, last time I checked." He touched her hand briefly. Not long enough.

Bridget blinked. "But...we aren't friends, technically. And you don't even know my name." Noah had just mentioned it, but she needed to hear Gabe say it.

"Don't tell me you don't court, *Bridget*."

Her body warmed at hearing the way Gabe's voice softened when he said her name. He ignored her other comment. Or didn't refute it.

"Sure, but I thought we were focusing on friendship. That's what you said." She struggled to catch her breath as she searched his eyes for the truth. Was he actually smitten with her, after all?

Gabe gave her a half smile. "You could kum along and not skate. You could sit by the fire and toast marshmallows. But this may be the last chance for ice-skating for a while. I understand it's supposed to get warmer. At least, that's what Preacher Zook said. Temperatures are supposed to actually rise above freezing for a while. I'm not sure when. Maybe next week. I'm looking forward to thawing out."

Noah put on his coat and then grabbed Bridget's, thrusting it toward her. "You're going. You and Gabe aren't having your first date under Daed's surveillance."

Gabe raised one eyebrow.

Bridget opened her mouth to argue that it wasn't a date. But, apparently, it was. And Noah was right about what would happen if they stayed here. Daed would supervise, wanting to micromanage every single moment. Though that hadn't stopped Gabe from flirting before. Sitting too close on the bench seat, whispering in her ear, touching her....

He would have to be careful at the frolic, but not as careful, because couples would pair up to skate together. They'd be able to hold hands—even if they were wearing gloves—and talk. And on the ride home, they'd be alone. Unless Gabe had to drive Agnes or Carolyn.

"You're such a recluse." Noah withdrew the coat he'd held out to her.

Gabe glanced at Noah. "Not sure I like that term. Reminds me of a venomous spider." He looked back at Bridget with a soft smile. "But you *will* get a reputation for being unfriendly and stuck-up if you don't put yourself out there. I understand you're shy, but Noah will be there. Agnes will be there. And, if you go, I'll be there. Honestly, I'd rather spend the evening under the watchful eyes of your brother and the chaperones than your daed's."

Bridget exhaled a loud sigh. "All right, I'll go." She pressed her lips together and tried to push her fear back into its cubbyhole. Gabe was right. If she wanted to make friends, she needed to be friendly. Besides, what were the chances of her falling through the ice? As cold as it'd been for weeks on end, not very high. "Noah, go tell Shiloh she needs to finish supper. And let Mamm know where I'm going."

"Great. I'll see you there, then." The light in Gabe's eyes was back, but he still looked tired. At least they would have a chance to talk. She could learn why his daed had kum. "I've never been ice-skating before. Ponds in Florida don't freeze over. Maybe it'll be something like Rollerblading. I did that once. This is going to be fun."

Ponds in Ohio froze over only sometimes. Not every year. And not for long periods of time. Bridget wasn't all that gut at skating. Passable, maybe.

"Awesome." Noah laid Bridget's coat on the sofa. "I'll get the horse and buggy ready. We'll see you there, Gabe."

"Wait." Bridget frowned. "Aren't we riding together?"

"Nein, you'll ride with me. Gabe has to take Agnes and Carolyn. But you'll ride home with Gabe. Seriously, Bridget. You know how this works."

Jah, she did. But Gabe was already there. And groups could arrive together and leave together if they wanted.

It just seemed silly.

Her breath hitched as she realized what this meant. Noah had more than a passing interest in Butterscotch.

And Bridget might be alone with Gabe on the ride home.

∽

Gabe parked the buggy out by the road. All the space closer to the pond was taken. They were late in arriving, simply because Agnes and

Carolyn had nein sense of time. Half an hour ago, he'd told them they needed to leave immediately. They'd nodded and told him they were almost ready, then carried on with whatever it was they were doing. Then he'd reminded them five minutes later. And five minutes after that.

After the fourth reminder, a glowering Gabe had huffed before plopping down in a chair.

Preacher Zook had given him a sympathetic look. "Best get used to it, sohn. Maidals are naturally late."

That had seemed to Gabe a rather broad generalization, and inaccurate. Gabe's mamm, for example, always arrived at least half an hour early to church events and frolics to help set out the food and catch up on the "latest news." Gossip, Daed called it, though Mamm adamantly denied it.

Gabe smiled at the happy memory of home. It had been gut catching up with Daed. But he was a bit homesick now that they'd reconciled. His parents enjoyed a relationship in which they teased each other lovingly. Maybe he could have something similar with Bridget.

Music pulsed from somewhere near the pond. Someone must've brought a radio. It was playing so loud, the bass's rhythm seemed to shake the ground.

"Can't you get us any closer?" Carolyn whined. "I have to carry that big platter piled with sandwiches."

"And I have two containers of fudge, plus the big picnic jug full of hot water." Agnes looked over at him. "I know what you're thinking, Young Gabe Lapp, and it's not true."

Gabe hitched an eyebrow. "What am I thinking?"

"You're thinking it's our own fault, since we were running late. But we had a lot more to do to get ready than you did." She moved to pat his arm.

Gabe shifted out of reach. "Uh-huh. I'll carry the jug." It'd be his job, regardless. He went ahead and scanned the parking area once more. They couldn't get any closer unless they parked in an area that seemed to be a perpetual mud pit.

"You'd have less far to carry the jug if you parked closer," Carolyn grumbled.

"Less far? Is that even proper grammar?" Gabe got out of the Zooks' buggy and tied Cherry Blossom to a post. "The gut spots are all taken. You'll just have to walk."

"Couldn't you at least drive us nearer to the pond and let us get out before you park the buggy?"

Seriously? He rubbed his forehead. If he insisted they walk—even though it wasn't all that far to carry a tray of sandwiches or two pans of fudge—it would be unkind, and he might get scolded. But the suggestion that he drop them off smacked of wanting to make an entrance, to be noticed. Not to slip in, unheralded.

On the other hand, if he dropped them off closer before parking, he wouldn't have as far to carry the heavy jug full of hot water, and it would be easier to escape Agnes's clutches. Despite the conversation they'd had about his liking another girl, Agnes still watched his every move and stuck to him like the annoying layers of sawdust he couldn't seem to wash off.

He untied Cherry Blossom and climbed back into the buggy. "Fine. I'll drop you off closer."

Agnes leaned over and wrapped her arms around him in a too-close, too-personal hug, pressing her curves against him. From Bridget, it would've been a welkum gesture. Now, he wanted to escape.

"That is, if you'll let me go." He tried to keep his irritation out of his voice.

Agnes released him and settled back on her side of the buggy, wearing a smirk of satisfaction.

Gabe would not skate with her to-nacht. Not with her, or Butterscotch, or Sweet Thang, or any of the scores of other girls he'd given nicknames he nein longer recalled. He would focus on the one girl who fascinated him, the one he wanted to settle down with. But he wasn't sure about uniting with her family. Specifically, her daed. But he supposed that was the reason behind courtship. So one could be sure.

As Gabe drove closer to the bonfire some of the guys were trying to get going, he saw Noah park in the mud pit.

Gabe dropped off the sisters and the picnic jug, then located the blaring radio and turned down the volume before moving the buggy once more. His original parking spot was gone, taken by other latecomers. Judging by the size of the crowd, some youngies from the Sault, and maybe some Lower Peninsula "trolls," had joined them for this frolic. He parked farther down the road, then started hiking back. The road had been plowed, but patches of slushy snow and ice still remained. Probably due to the heavy traffic from the buggies and cars already there.

He stopped when he spotted Noah and Bridget driving toward him, and waved them down. Noah stopped next to him.

"I'll walk Bridget up, if you want. Parking is quite a hike from here."

Noah grunted. "Jah. I found out why that last 'conveniently located' spot was empty. I'll never get all the mud out of my shoes."

Gabe chuckled. "Hey, Green Eyes. Glad you could make it." He held out a hand to help her down, then reached for the plate she was carrying. "I'll take that for you. What'd you make?"

"Shortbread cookies."

"I'll make sure I get one later."

Walking beside him, Bridget gazed at the ground. "Agnes told me about your sweet tooth. I can't compete with her candy, though." She trembled slightly.

"Nein need. My sweet tooth doesn't discriminate." He winked when she looked up at him. "Just don't tell my mamm or daed if you see my plate piled high with goodies instead of bologna sandwiches and raw veggies."

"I'll make sure you get a carrot stick or two. And some broccoli."

He wrinkled his nose. "I like broccoli fine, if it's steamed and smothered in cheese sauce. Raw, not so much."

"It's healthier raw." A spark lit her eyes.

"Now that might be a deal breaker," he teased. "You can't go messing with my less-than-ideal diet." He reached for her gloved hand and squeezed just to show he was joking, in case she couldn't tell.

"Gabe's here," someone called out. "Hey, kum help us get the fire going."

He handed the plate back to Bridget. "There's a table for the food. Skates are supposed to be in a laundry basket nearby. I wear a men's size ten, if you happen to find a pair. Then wait for me. I'll help you put yours on."

Though, if she'd skated before, she was probably more proficient at that than he. But skates were really just shoes. Boots. How hard could it be?

⌒

Bridget found a pair of black skates in Gabe's size, and another identical pair for Noah. The skates were rather worn and scuffed, as if they'd gotten a lot of use.

But there weren't any skates her own size. Just one pair a size too small and another a size too big. Fearing the smaller ones would hurt and give her blisters, she carried the too-big ones, along with the two pairs of men's skates, over to a provisional bench made from a fallen log. She would lace hers extra tight.

Some girls were already out on the pond, holding hands and giggling as they skated in a line. Bridget looked around and didn't see either Agnes or Carolyn on the shore, so they were probably on the ice. Butterscotch approached the food table carrying a dish in one hand and a pair of skates in the other. She set the dish down and turned.

Bridget waved.

Butterscotch smiled and approached her. "Hiya. You're Noah's sister, ain't so?"

"Jah. I'm Bridget Behr." Bridget motioned to the space beside her on the log.

"I'm Arie Zimmerman."

"Nice to meet you." The name Arie was ever so much prettier than Butterscotch. Noah would have to learn her name if he hoped to have a serious relationship with her. Though it was too early to tell. After all, they'd just met last weekend.

"Nice to meet you, too. I've heard so much about you from Noah. And from Gabe and Agnes."

Really? She swallowed the comment she'd once heard an Englischer say. *I hope it was all good.* That would be begging for praise, and frowned upon.

"So, you moved here from Ohio? We came from Lancaster County. Daed wanted to escape the heavy traffic, and opted for this area. Little traffic, comparatively. He works for a logging company now."

Bridget nodded, not sure what to say. It sounded as if Noah had already filled Arie in on the condensed version of her own family's history.

"How is the construction process coming along? Everyone was shocked to hear an Amish family had bought the haunted haus. That anybody bought it, really."

"Noah did mention we're rebuilding from the ground up, didn't he?"

"Nein." Arie shook her head. "Just that things were going slower than planned due to some problems with management."

Technically true. And the kindest way of putting it, without disrespecting their daed publicly, since most of their problems had been a result of Daed's firing Gabe. Noah hadn't exactly misled Arie, though. Maybe he'd assumed she knew. After all, news traveled very fast via the Amish grapevine.

Arie worked at lacing her skates, taking frequent glances around, as if expecting Noah to join them. "I hope the ice holds. I heard the temperature's supposed to rise. Weird for this time of year. They're saying snowfall is going to be less than usual this year, and they're blaming it on global warming. Whatever that is." She shrugged. "I heard some Englishers talking about it at the grocery store the other day. But Mamm is happy the spring thaw is coming early. The vegetable seeds she ordered from an heirloom seed company in Missouri came in the mail today. We planted tomato seeds in our small green-haus this afternoon. That is Mamm's business, but she's hoping it'll grow enough so Daed can stay home. They had a lucrative nursery business in Lancaster before Daed decided to sell and move us here."

Mamm had remarked on the short growing season up here. Bridget hadn't thought much about it at the time. "I'll tell my mamm about your green-haus. As soon as our home is finished, we should probably start plants, too."

The wind blew smoke from the bonfire into Bridget's face, and she coughed.

"You okay?" Arie stood. "I need to get out there while I can. See you on the ice."

Just then, someone yelled, "Stay away from the far side of the pond. Ice is cracking over there."

The girls skating in a line moved toward the nearer shore, and Arie joined on at the end of the looping, weaving, laughing human chain.

Gabe dropped down beside Bridget, closer than a Bible's width, and reached for a pair of the black skates she'd found. "Size ten?"

"I think so, jah." Why was it so hard to think clearly when he was in such close proximity? "I got a pair for Noah, too." She looked around for her brother but didn't see him.

"He went with some of the other guys to check the ice. Probably should've been done before the girls went out there." Gabe lifted a shoulder. "I suppose the worst that can happen is an unintentional polar bear plunge, take two."

"Where is the closest hospital, just in case?" Bridget tugged off her shoes, then slid her feet into the too-big skates and began tightening the laces as much as possible.

"St. Ignace. A bit too far by horse and buggy, but I'm sure someone around here has a cell phone and could call for an ambulance, if needed. But don't worry. You'll be fine. I'll make sure of it. This is going to be fun."

Everything was fun to Gabe. Or seemed that way. If only she shared his optimism.

"Need help with those?" Gabe scooted off the log, his skates somehow already laced snugly, and knelt on the ground in front of her. Granted, she'd been sidetracked from her task, talking to Arie and then to Gabe.

Gabe grimaced. "This snow is slushy. I wonder if the temperature is already rising."

"It should refreeze as nacht comes." But Bridget immediately second-guessed her supposition. It was already evening. "Maybe it's melting because we're so close to the fire, and there were a lot of people sitting here to put their skates on."

"Maybe." Gabe gave the laces of her right boot a final tug, then started tying those of the left side. Seconds later, he rose and reached out a hand. The knees of his pants were wet. He furrowed his brow.

"What's wrong?" Bridget grasped his hand and allowed him to pull her up.

"Just...." He shook his head. Then his dimple flashed. "Borrowing trouble. Let's get out there before we can't."

"Arie said something about global warming and an early thaw."

Gabe nodded, then frowned. "Arie?"

Bridget sighed. "Butterscotch."

Gabe lifted his shoulder again. "Ach. I can't remember their names. And her hair color reminds me of butterscotch candy. Actually, the shade is probably closer to mustard, but that wouldn't make for a very becoming nickname, would it?" He winked.

Bridget giggled. Couldn't help it.

"Now, you...." He intertwined his fingers with hers as he led her onto the ice. "I remember your name."

Gabe stayed close to Bridget as they attempted to skate the perimeter of the pond, avoiding the section that Noah and some of the other guys had blocked off with orange cones. Bridget had nein idea where they'd found those.

Neither she nor Gabe was very steady on the single-blade boots, and she wobbled in her too-big skates while he clung tightly to her, as if he needed her help to remain upright. She was glad to be able to help him, for a change.

"Nobody ever told me it'd be this difficult," Gabe murmured. "Those girls make it look easy. Maybe it is—for girls. If I let go, promise you won't latch on to the tail of their snake while I tumble in an ungraceful heap on the ice."

Bridget laughed.

Gabe didn't. He tightened his grip on her, and nodded in the opposite direction from the group of girls. "Can we skate over there? I need to tell you—"

A loud crack. The line of girls shrieked.

A splash.

Someone shouted.

Gabe spun away, releasing Bridget's hand.

Bridget screamed as she went flying, somehow twisted into a spine-knotting turn that swung her halfway around, and then landed hard on her backend on the other side of the orange cones. Searing pain shot through her wrist.

The ice shattered beneath her. Water seeped into her dress. *Nein. Not again.* Despite the pain in her wrist, she tried to scoot forward. The ice cracked more, and the water level rose. She froze, not daring to move.

Then she saw Gabe. One of his legs went north, the other south. Or maybe it was east and west. She wasn't sure. Either way, he was doing a full split.

If she weren't so scared, she would've laughed to see him tumbling in an ungraceful heap.

There was another loud crack. Followed by a groan.

18

Sharp, throbbing pain sliced through Gabe. Blackness threatened to overtake his consciousness. He fought to remain awake.

That entire line of girls had fallen in the ice-cold pond water. It wasn't all that deep, but if they panicked....

They would panic.

Judging by the screams he heard, they had already begun.

He tried to move, but the pain escalated so much that tears filled his eyes. He sucked in a gasp.

He didn't know how to move. Not with his legs stuck in opposite directions. Wasn't even sure if he could move.

But those girls...they needed help. His girl needed help.

Pain seemed to radiate from every part of him, but he tried to pinpoint the origin. Seemed to be his right leg.

He attempted to move the left one. Another wave of dizziness overtook him, with nausea mixed in.

He shut his eyes, relaxed his arm muscles pressing against the ice, and allowed himself to lie flat. Water saturated his shirt.

But lying flat allowed him to slide his left leg closer to his right one.

He fought the nausea and opened his eyes. The world swam: a bunch of multicolored clothes surrounded by black....

He shut his eyes again.

Wait. Bridget.

He forced his eyes open and looked around. Still heard a lot of screaming and shouting. Loud wails.

This was not gut.

"Someone needs to get that girl," said a voice.

"I called nine-one-one," said someone else. "An ambulance is en route."

"I'm thinking we'll need more than one."

Gabe didn't recognize any of the voices. Just that they were male.

If he survived, it wouldn't be for long. Hosea would kill him.

⌒

Bridget grabbed the hands that reached for her, ignoring the jarring pain in her wrist. A man pulled her off the cracked ice, helped her to stand, and assisted her back toward the shore. Away from Gabe, who lay flat, his eyes shut. The thought that he might be unconscious sent tears streaming down her face. She cradled her arm close to her stomach. Ach, it hurt.

"Help him." She nodded at Gabe. "I'll be fine."

"Let me get you to safety first."

The man helping her looked vaguely familiar, but she couldn't place him. She sat on the log he led her to, near the fire. She would smell of ash, but at least the heat would help to dry her outfit. The stench was worth bearing to be off the weakening ice. "Danki." Cradling her swollen wrist in her lap, she nodded toward the pond. "Can you help Gabe now?"

The man didn't answer but headed back out on the ice. Other men were in the pond, helping the girls who had fallen though the ice climb out of the water to safety.

The stranger bypassed them and went to Gabe. He helped him straighten his legs, then got him to a sitting position, hooked him beneath the arms, and pulled him off the ice. Brought him to the log by the fire.

Bridget touched his shoulder.

He winced.

"Are you okay?" Kind of a stupid question. He obviously wasn't.

He swallowed hard—more like gulped, really—and nodded. "Fine."

"'Fine'? As in, freaked out, insecure, nervous, and emotional?" She nodded. "Me, too."

"Turn that 'insecure' into 'injured,' and you nailed it." He swallowed again. "Might be longer than a week before I get back to work." He coughed, from the smoke, probably. Gulped again. "Unless I get a walking cast. Or crutches."

Even then, his activity would be severely limited.

A pickup truck with a red light flashing on its roof pulled into the driveway.

"First responders," Gabe said.

As if she didn't know.

Noah rushed over, his pants wet to just above his hips. "Gut, you guys are safe. I worried when you weren't fished out of the pond. I pulled Butterscotch out. She's wrapped in someone's buggy blanket." He pointed to a small group of girls huddled together and shivering on the other side of the fire. Upwind, so they weren't breathing in smoke.

Bridget glared at her brother. "Her name is Arie."

"Right. Arie. Sorry." He turned to Gabe. "I'm going to get my buggy and take Arie home. Will you be leaving soon?"

Gabe coughed again. "Pretty sure I'm going to the hospital. Think I broke something. Just not sure what. It all hurts. Everything does."

Noah frowned, turning his gaze to Bridget. "You want to go with him?"

She looked at her swollen wrist. "Um, I think I need to go to the hospital anyway."

Noah's frown deepened. "Okay. I'll take Arie, Agnes, and Carolyn home, and let Preacher Zook know where you are, so he can get his horse and buggy. He can notify the bishop and your daed." He glanced at Bridget. "I'll tell Daed…I guess."

Jah. Daed wouldn't take this well. Bridget fidgeted. How would Gabe's daed react? Would it be the last straw?

"See ya later." Noah grimaced before walking off.

Gabe half-smiled as he reached for Bridget's uninjured hand. "This is going to be fun."

Fun. Right.

For once, he didn't sound convinced.

⌒

Gabe wasn't so sure that "fun" was an appropriate descriptor of his hospital experience. By the time the doctors were finished X-raying, poking, prodding, and pulling, they decided Gabe had only managed to sprain an ankle. *Only?* And they gave the sprain a score.

Grade three.

Gabe wanted to look at those X-rays himself. He was certain the doctors had missed something, for, surely, a sprained ankle couldn't hurt this much. He'd suffered a similar injury before and had been able to move the sprained part. A crutch for a few days, limited weight-bearing, and it was all gut.

Apparently, not the case this time.

Of course, this was the first time he'd gotten a grade for the sprain.

The doctors also informed Gabe he'd torn his groin muscles in his upper-inner thighs, which largely contributed to the acute pain.

Gabe was pretty sure he'd have severe bruising there, too. It hurt. Period.

He was given prescriptions for a painkiller, a wheelchair, a pair of crutches, and an ankle brace. How on earth would he manage getting into a buggy? Maybe the bishop would know of someone with a vehicle to drive Gabe where he needed to go.

A nurse assisted Gabe into a wheelchair and handed him an envelope full of discharge papers. "Do you have someone waiting for you?"

Gabe pulled in a breath. "I came in with a friend. Can I wait with her?"

"What's her name?" the nurse asked.

"Bridget Behr. She came into the emergency room, too."

"I'll check. Wait here." The nurse left the room. Minutes later, she returned. "I'll take you to the waiting room. I'm told there are quite a few Amish gathered there."

Hosea would undoubtedly be among them. Gabe grimaced.

The nurse didn't seem to notice, though. She cheerfully chattered about the unexpected, yet welcome, warm spell. And how the weathermen hadn't predicted it until that very day. Apparently, they'd thought it would track south. Way south.

Gabe didn't particularly care. He couldn't even find it in him to flirt with the nurse.

The waiting room was long and narrow, filled with chairs and end tables well-stocked with magazines. On the far wall was a flat-screen TV that was muted, and beneath it a table littered with pieces of an unfinished jigsaw puzzle.

"Quite a few" seemed to overstate the number of Amish in the room. Some he recognized from church Sundays, but he didn't know their names. He knew only three.

The bishop.

Daed.

And Hosea.

Fun?

Not even remotely.

Hosea was pacing. It might've been Gabe's imagination, but he thought he saw smoke steaming from the man's ears.

The nurse paused just inside the door. "Where do you want to go?"

"Is going back in time an option?"

She laughed and patted his shoulder. "If only."

Gabe sighed. "Over by the two men sitting near the windows."

Daed and the bishop were talking quietly, but they both fell silent as the nurse pushed Gabe's chair nearer. After a moment, Daed stood. The bishop followed suit a second later.

Hosea stopped his pacing, planted his fists on his hips, and glowered at Gabe.

The nurse must've decided—wisely—that she'd gotten close enough. She patted Gabe's shoulder again, then disappeared out the door, shutting it behind her.

Gabe firmed his shoulders, pivoted the borrowed wheelchair around, and faced Hosea head-on.

The man's face flushed. His eyes flashed. He strode forward, stopping three feet away from Gabe.

Gabe didn't like looking up at him. But his ankle wouldn't support him if he stood. He would crumple to the ground. And that was assuming his groin muscles would cooperate enough to get him vertical without another wave of nausea.

The bishop walked forward and put himself between them.

From behind, Daed clasped Gabe's shoulder. "What did the doctor say, Sohn?"

"Sprained ankle. Pulled muscles."

"Gut. A couple days, you'll be back to work." Hosea still glowered. "Bad enough you had to go and get Bridget hurt again. I just don't know if I could accept your hurting the building of my haus and, ultimately, my business."

Gabe swallowed. "Grade-three sprain. Non-weight-bearing."

Hosea sucked in a noisy breath. His face turned redder. "Gabe Lapp, so help me—"

The bishop stepped nearer to Hosea. "Forgiveness is better than revenge in the long run. And a lot cheaper."

"Do you have any idea what he's doing to me? To my business?" Hosea raised his hands. "I've lost customers. I've lost employees. My own haus is on hold."

"Because you fired me." Gabe immediately wished he could retract his words.

"If you're in a hole, stop digging deeper," the bishop said quietly, leaning closer to Hosea.

Gabe opened his mouth, but he wasn't sure what he planned to say. Maybe an apology for upsetting Hosea.

Daed patted his shoulder again, then stepped forward into Gabe's line of sight. "Hosea, there are plenty of things in life worth caring about. But there is nein need to get upset or lose your temper over matters with little significance in the long run. Your dochter will be okay. My sohn will heal. Your business will rebound as soon as you realize that Gott is ultimately the One in control. Not you. Let go of yourself, your pride, and your desires. Step back and give Him the reins. Things will go a lot smoother when you let Him handle your business, your life...everything."

Gabe swiped his hand over his jaw. Daed's calm, quiet statement cut him deeply. He bowed his head as the words planted themselves in his heart, in his mind.

"You need Gott more than anything else," Daed added. "Put Him first. It's not about you. It's about Him."

The door opened, and a nurse appeared. "Behr family?"

19

Bridget was loaded onto a gurney, pushed into an elevator, and taken to a different floor—the nurses didn't tell her which one—after the emergency-room doctor decided she needed to have her right wrist bones reset. An IV needle had been inserted in her arm, and the doctor had used a lot of technical words she hadn't understood; but the simple summary was, she had a badly broken wrist. In her dominant hand.

The emergency doctor said something about her needing to wear an air splint—whatever that was—until the swelling went down enough for her to get a plaster cast. He also said it would ultimately be up to the bone specialist to decide.

She should've stayed home instead of going skating. If she had, she wouldn't have broken her wrist. Gabe wouldn't have broken whatever bone he had, or endured excruciating pain, judging by his drawn expression, his unwillingness to even move a muscle, and the moisture filling his eyes. If only they could be together now, to comfort each other. Encourage each other. Pray for each other.

And he thought this was going to be fun?

When the elevator stopped and the doors opened, the nurse pushing the gurney made a stomach-churning turn and rapidly wheeled Bridget out. She shut her eyes but quickly decided that was worse than not seeing the rapidly passing ceiling tiles.

This was not fun.

The closest thing to fun that nacht had been when Gabe held her hand as they walked toward the bonfire, him teasing about broccoli, and pointing out the unsuitability of Mustard as a nickname. Even his holding tightly to her on the ice had been somewhat fun, in spite of his sarcasm and his poking "fun" at himself in the process.

A male nurse in maroon scrubs greeted Bridget and steered her gurney to a space separated from the rest of the room by mere curtains. He pulled the drapes shut, glanced at the screen of a computer mounted on a cart, then studied the hospital bracelet on her good arm. "Can you tell me your name?"

Bridget frowned. She was pretty sure it was printed on the bracelet. But maybe he didn't know how to pronounce her last name.

"Bridget Behr."

"And your birthdate?"

She peered at the bracelet. There was her birthdate, upside-down from her point of view. The nurse should have nein difficulties reading it. "It's on there," she said, nodding at the bracelet.

"I need you to tell me."

Bridget rolled her eyes before she fixed him with an annoyed stare.

"It's just to verify we have the correct patient."

"As if I would've found someone to switch bracelets with between the emergency room and here? Besides, that thing will have to be cut off."

"Humor me." He didn't react visibly to her frustration.

Once she had recited the rest of the information on the bracelet, the nurse retrieved a blanket and smoothed it over her. "Fresh from the warmer. The anesthesiologist will be here soon." He flipped a button to turn on the tiny TV set mounted in one corner, then disappeared through the curtain.

Was Gabe somewhere nearby, waiting for the anesthesiologist to visit him, too? If Bridget were to shout his name, would he answer from a bed on the other side of the curtain? It'd give her a sense of peace to know she wasn't alone, but she didn't have the courage to do such a thing.

Just then the curtain opened, and a hospital volunteer in yellow peeked in. "Bridget? I have someone to see you."

Hope infused her. "Gabe?"

Daed appeared.

She tried to swallow her disappointment.

Daed eased down into the chair beside her bed. "A broken wrist, jah?"

He seemed calm. That probably meant he hadn't seen Gabe yet.

"That's what they say." She looked down at her arm. "The anesthesiologist will be here soon."

Daed's mouth worked. "How bad is the break? Not just a fracture?"

"The bones need to be put back into place. I don't know…the doctor muttered a lot of stuff, then said it'd be up to the specialist. Why'd he bother telling me anything? Shouldn't he have just admitted not knowing what is going to be done?"

If only talking helped to take her mind off the pain.

Daed chuckled. "I don't know what I'm going to do with G—" He cut himself off and looked away.

She braced herself for hearing Daed say he forbade their courting again. She wanted to ask if he'd heard anything about Gabe's condition, but she feared doing so would position Gabe to bear the brunt of Daed's anger when Gabe was physically unable to handle such a thing. She bit back her words in an effort to protect Gabe.

The curtain moved, and a man in olive green scrubs entered. "Hi. I'm Dr. Camden, the anesthesiologist. If you'll excuse me, sir, this will just take a moment."

Daed nodded, stood, and stepped out.

The doctor attached a plastic bag full of clear liquid to an IV pole. "Someone will be by in a little bit to get you," he told Bridget before bustling out.

Daed came back into the room and sat next to her once more. "Thought you'd like to know, Gabe sprained his ankle and tore a few muscles. Quite badly, I guess, since he is not to put any weight on his foot. I'll need to see if he'll be able to kum back to work to supervise the crew. That is, if the crew agrees to return. I can't imagine the sawmill will have any use for him in a wheelchair." He sighed with evident frustration.

Bridget chewed her lip, considering her next words. Speaking quietly, lest someone overhear, she said, "Daed, don't take this wrong. I don't mean any disrespect. But maybe you should consider being a little nicer to Gabe. He knows you don't like him. And you know you'll be sunk without him."

Daed frowned. "I like Gabe fine. It's just that…well, he's young and foolish. But then, I guess I'm old and foolish. Gabe has saved my hide—our hides—many times already, and I guess my pride has issues with a reckless young man being wiser than an old man who should know better." He hesitated. "Do you want to see him?"

Bridget brightened. "Would I be allowed?"

"I don't see why not." Daed stood, awkwardly patted her gut arm, then turned away and disappeared out the curtained doorway.

Bridget couldn't wait to see Gabe. A visit would distract her from her pain and from the fear of whatever it is the doctors were going to do. Plus, she wanted to see for herself that he was okay.

After what seemed like an eternity had passed, the drapes moved again, and Gabe rode inside in a wheelchair pushed by a man dressed in pale yellow scrubs. Gabe still appeared wan, exhausted, and probably in extreme pain, but his dimple flashed—albeit in a somewhat muted version of his smile.

"Gabe." Bridget reached out her gut hand to him.

"Hey, Green Eyes. Having fun yet?" He took her hand.

"Fun. Ach, jah. Fun by the buggy load." She rolled her eyes.

He tugged her hand nearer. "I'd kiss it to make it better, but…." He hesitated and looked down at her hand for a moment before meeting her eyes once more.

Something in the depths of his gaze snagged her attention as he drew her fingers to his lips and kissed the tip of each one, then the palm, before moving to the sensitive skin of her wrist.

Bridget shivered. Never had she imagined a simple kiss of the hand could be so sexy.

Maybe she should return the favor. She lifted Gabe's hand to her mouth.

The curtain opened.

∼

Gabe jerked his hand away as a couple of female nurses peeked inside. His sudden movement sent shards of pain cutting through his body…and his heart. Another romantic moment ruined. Well, maybe not entirely ruined. He'd seen the unmistakable heat in Bridget's eyes in response to his kissing her fingers. Had sensed she wanted to return the gesture. And the lingering emotion in her expression intimated her desire to pick this up later.

He wanted to do the same. This, and more.

"We'll be taking you back to surgery in a moment," one of the nurses told Bridget. "Say your good-byes, hon."

"I'm scared," Bridget whispered.

Gabe cringed. Swallowed. Instead of kissing Bridget, he should've been praying with her. Helping her to find the peace she needed. But how could he help her when he himself lacked peace, when his relationship with Gott was in shambles?

But this wasn't about him. He reached for Bridget's hand again and bowed his head. "Dear Gott…." It was strange and awkward, praying out loud. His fingers trembled in Bridget's grasp. Or maybe hers were moving. "Please be with Bridget as she goes into surgery. Help the surgeon to be able to align the bones quickly and painlessly, and help her to heal without complications. Please give Bridget peace." Did his prayer sound as stilted to her as it did to him? Was she wondering why he bothered praying to Gott when it was clear his prayers usually went unanswered? He was a fraud, plain and simple. *And help me to be the man I should be.* "Amen."

Bridget's eyes were wide and slightly dazed when he looked at her again. Was it because of her pain? Her fear? Or shock at his praying out loud with her? Dare he hope that, between the kisses, the talk of courtship, and his calling her by name, she was totally in love with the man his prayer presumed him to be?

A yellow-clad woman waited in the opening of the curtains. Another volunteer. "Let me take you back to the waiting room, sir. We'll come and get you when she's in recovery."

Doubtful. They'd get Hosea, which was as it should be. Gabe was nobody. Just the guy she wasn't dating. He couldn't even state with confidence that they were courting. After all, they'd gone out only once.

Twice, if he counted the polar bear plunge.

And both dates had ended in disaster.

That didn't bode well for the future of their relationship, especially considering the way her daed felt about him.

He should end things now. Before they became even more emotionally attached.

The hospital volunteer backed his wheelchair out of the cubicle. More nurses, these ones dressed in patterned scrubs, waited to take Bridget to wherever she was going.

Gabe pulled in a breath. Let it out. Now would be a bad time.

"Gabe?" Bridget's voice was weak, drowsy.

His attention shot back to her.

Her eyes were shut. Her breathing even. "Ich liebe dich."

The volunteer paused, giving him an opportunity to respond.

He blinked. Opened his mouth. Then shut it.

Because he'd just decided he wasn't right for her.

Because her admission had just changed the rules of the game.

Because he wasn't sure of his feelings, other than strong attraction.

And because she was clearly sound asleep.

⌒

Sounds of moaning broke into Bridget's sleep. Bridget opened her eyes and looked around. A female nurse in pink sat beside her, writing something on a clipboard. It was quiet. And Bridget was extremely tired. She shut her eyes again.

Another moan.

She tried to ignore it, but the moaning continued until she opened her eyes again.

The woman in pink glanced at her, smiled, and reached for Bridget's hospital bracelet.

A loud groan. It was coming from the cubicle next to hers.

Bridget shifted. Her right arm felt weighted. She glanced down and saw an inflatable cast extending from the knuckles of her fingers to just below her elbow.

She looked back at the nurse in pink, whose gaze was on her wrist-watch while the fingers of her other hand grasped the place on Bridget's forearm where Gabe had kissed her. Something made a buzzing sound, and there was a viselike tightening around Bridget's upper arm.

"Blood pressure cuff." The woman must've sensed her alarm. "They're bringing your family back."

Daed, then.

Had she dreamed that Gabe had kum to sit with her before the surgery? She couldn't have. She remembered Daed saying he would get him. And Gabe had kissed her hand. Her wrist. Prayed with her.

Nein, she hadn't dreamed Gabe.

She shifted again when the nurse let go of her arm.

"Your pulse jumped. You must've been thinking about that handsome young man who was in here earlier." The nurse recorded something on her clipboard. "Your boyfriend?"

Would it be wrong to acknowledge their fledgling relationship? It was still so new.

Bridget found her courage. Her cheeks warmed as she nodded.

The nurse smiled. "It was so sweet when you told him you loved him."

She told him...what?!

20

With assistance from Daed and Bishop Brunstetter, Gabe managed to get into the backseat of the vehicle someone had sent to the hospital for the three of them.

It was a struggle for Gabe to keep his eyes open, likely the result of the strong narcotics the doctor had ordered to be injected before Gabe had left the emergency room. It was a wonder he'd stayed awake long enough to see Bridget.

Should he blame the kiss on the drugs?

Gabe fumbled with the seat belt, and Daed leaned over and secured it.

As the volunteer who'd escorted them outside reclaimed the hospital's wheelchair, Gabe gulped. How on earth would he manage to move around without a wheelchair or a set of crutches? How would he access his second-floor bedroom at the Zooks'?

He would figure that out later. Holding his eyes open for another second was impossible.

He jolted awake when the car came to a stop. He rubbed his eyes. "Where are we?"

"We're at the after-hours medical supply." From his seat up front, Daed peered over his shoulder. "We need to rent you some equipment."

Gabe sighed. One worry lifted.

After he'd been outfitted with a rented wheelchair and set of crutches, Gabe dozed again. The next time he awoke, the car was coming to a stop outside the bishop's haus.

The bishop turned to him. "You'll have an easier time getting around at my haus. We have an all-season room with a hide-a-bed."

Gabe managed a nod.

164 Laura V. Hilton

The bishop made a makeshift ramp out of several thin pieces of plywood propped on the three steps leading up to his porch, and somehow he and Daed managed to shove Gabe's wheelchair up the flimsy boards and into the haus.

The bishop's frau—Gabe didn't know her first name—clucked over Gabe before leading the way to the all-season room. The bed was open and made up. *Gut.* Gabe hoisted himself out of the chair and had to moan due to the pain it caused him. His legs buckled, and he fell across the mattress, his feet dangling off. He didn't care. He wasn't moving.

When he awoke, dawn had begun to color the sky. Someone must've turned his body so he would lie in the right position on the mattress. Gone were his soggy, smoky, wrinkly clothes from the nacht before. Now he wore a white undershirt and a pair of pants that were slightly too short and too loose. The aroma of koffee, along with the smell of something sweet and citrusy, teased his senses. He carefully sat up, fresh waves of pain shooting through him, and looked around. The crutches had been propped within easy reach, and the wheelchair also waited nearby.

He would use the crutches. He strapped on the ankle brace, which he should've worn yesterday. More pain. He needed to power through in order to reach the kitchen and get his prescription painkillers. He carefully stood.

Acute pain shot through him with the first hop. His legs buckled again, but he caught himself on the bedside table. One of the crutches fell to the floor with a clatter.

Maybe the wheelchair would be a better option, at least until his torn muscles healed. He tried to remember how long the recovery was expected to take. Maybe he should look over the sheets of instructions the nurses had given him, especially since the doctor's spoken words had jumbled into a confusing mass in his head. Where had he left his packet? Was it in the kitchen with his pain pills?

All he could clearly remember was Bridget's "Ich liebe dich." And the memory tore his heart wide open.

He wasn't worthy of her love. Wasn't worthy of anyone's love. He needed to somehow ground himself, to become the man he should be.

He vaguely remembered Daed's quiet comments to Hosea. Something in them had nudged him. He'd wanted to pray, to somehow move past the gap in his relationship with Gott, but he hadn't. And now he couldn't recall the conversation. He needed to talk with Daed.

He wheeled himself out to the kitchen just as Daed and the bishop came inside from doing the chores.

Daed set an armful of cut wood in the box near the stove. "Glad you're up, Gabe. How are you feeling today?" He moved to the doorway and removed his work coat, gloves, and hat, hanging the garments on a hook.

The bishop bent to pull off his work boots.

"Sore." Right now, Gabe envied the ease with which the two older men moved.

Frau Brunstetter reached into the cabinet and took down a prescription bottle. "Here you go, Young Gabe. You're supposed to take each pill with food, so you might want to hold off a moment. I need to ice the orange rolls, and then breakfast will be served."

"It smells delicious." Gabe's stomach rumbled loudly in agreement. Gabe glanced at the pill bottle and read the label to see how often he was to take the pills. Then he twisted the cap off, shook out a single pill, and set it near the full koffee cup that waited at the seat he presumed was his, since it was the only one without a chair.

"Do you take sugar and cream with your koffee?" The bishop's frau set the sugar bowl on the table. "Here is brown sugar for the oatmeal."

If this koffee was anything like the awful, bitter brew the bishop's frau had sent with Daed when he and Gabe had talked in the empty storefront, it would definitely need some improving with the addition of cream and sugar. "Um, sometimes I do. Usually not, but I drink it however my host does." Gabe glanced toward the bishop and raised an eyebrow.

The older man chuckled. "I know there are some strong opinions on how koffee is meant to be prepared and consumed, but in this haus, one is not judged by how one takes one's koffee—or whether he prefers tea or even hot cocoa."

"Well, in that case, I'd love some cream and sugar." He would try to limit himself to one spoonful of sugar so Daed wouldn't complain to Mamm of his overindulging in sweets.

Daed washed his hands at the sink. "Thought that if you felt up to it, we'd go by the sawmill to let them know about your accident and pick up your final paycheck, and then go by the Behrs' to see how we can help." He reached for a towel and turned to Gabe. "You could probably do some work from a wheelchair. Or at least supervise some of the crewmembers Hosea rounded up to return to work. And I know a thing or two about construction, so I'll help." He hung the towel back on the rack, then approached the table and sat next to Gabe. "I'm thinking, with this recent warm spell and the snowmelt, we should get the roof finished before the temperatures drop again. I could help with that—and teach Hosea and Noah, if they don't know how."

They most certainly didn't. Gabe felt another worry lift. With Daed there to teach, as well as to buffer the strained relationship between him and Hosea, things would go better.

And maybe Gabe would be able to see Bridget, if she'd been released from the hospital and felt up to crossing the yard to sit with him. He knew he wouldn't be able to visit her in the RV.

"The bishop is going to buy lumber to build portable wheelchair ramps to make it easier to get you in and out of here—and the Behrs'," Daed said.

"Danki," Gabe said to the bishop. "I plan to switch to crutches as soon as I'm able." His stomach rumbled again as the bishop's frau set a bowl of steaming oatmeal studded with raisins in front of him.

"Don't push it," Daed warned him. "You need to let your body heal."

"Shall we pray?" The bishop didn't wait for his frau to sit down before he bowed his head, so she remained standing, grasping the back of her seat, and bowed her head.

Gabe closed his eyes and lowered his head. *Gott, help me to be the man I need to be. Help me to heal quickly so I can get back to work, too.*

Daed had once told him that Gott sometimes allowed things to happen to people when He needed to get their attention. To give them time to read the Bible and pray, and become who Gott intended for them to be. To give them a chance to learn to walk according to His purpose.

Wasn't there a Bible verse that said something to that effect? It was in the book of Romans, if Gabe remembered correctly. He would take his Bible with him to Hosea's and try to find it.

Except, his Bible was at the Zooks'. Probably still buried at the bottom of his suitcase, since he hadn't read it once since coming here. Hadn't carried it to church. Hadn't even thought of it. Until now.

"Amen." The bishop lifted his spoon. His frau fetched the platter of rolls and a pitcher of orange juice.

"Daed, I need to get my Bible," Gabe said quietly. "It's at the Zooks'."

Bishop Brunstetter chuckled. "I'll need to go there to get your clothes and other belongings, anyway, since you'll be staying here for a time. At least until you're healed. Wouldn't do for those unmarried girls at the Zooks' to be attending to your personal needs, lest one or more of them fall in love with their patient. I have heard that one of them has her eye on you."

Gabe was glad to stay here as long as possible. The last thing he needed was Agnes hovering over him, nacht and day. Though maybe seeing him helpless would be enough to make her stop chasing him.

He doubted it. But he could hope.

With her left hand, Bridget awkwardly tossed handfuls of chicken feed on the floor of the smelly attached chicken coop. Daed had insisted she perform as many of her routine chores as possible using her nondominant hand, but it was hard making her left hand do things it wasn't used to doing. Feeding the chickens was usually Roseanna's job, but many of Bridget's daily chores, such as cooking and washing the dishes, were out of the question. So, Mamm was using the time before and after school to teach Roseanna some techniques of more advanced cooking—tasks such as cutting in butter, folding in ingredients instead of stirring, and beating egg whites until stiff peaks formed.

Bridget didn't get those steps perfect every time, but it would be a blessing when her wrist healed enough for her to return to the kitchen. She hadn't expected missing those jobs this much.

Hearing a horse whinny, she peeked out the front of the barn to see who'd kum. She doubted it was family, since Jonah, Shiloh, and Roseanna had taken one of the buggy horses to school so they wouldn't have to walk in the slushy mess that used to be snow.

The bishop pulled his wagon to a stop. "Hallo, Bridget. Hosea around? I brought some wood to make a ramp for Gabe to use to get in and out."

A ramp? How badly had Gabe been hurt? She caught her breath. *Wait.* Was Gabe coming?

"Daed and Noah are in the haus," she told him. "They wanted to see if there was anything they could do. A couple of guys might show up for work later, but we aren't sure."

"Gabe and his daed will kum by after they've been to the sawmill. They're probably there now. Had to wait for a driver."

Gabe was coming! The excitement worked through her like a flash of lightning, then faded into a fizzle. How had he reacted to her unintentional declaration of love? Her cheeks burned.

"We're going to see if there's any way Gabe can work while he's recuperating. I figure he could finish staining the cabinets, at least. And maybe supervise and instruct Hosea and Noah as they learn the business. They need hands-on training. Gabe's daed figures he can put in some time working, too."

"How long will he be here?"

The bishop arched an eyebrow. "Who?"

Bridget's face burned. "Gabe's daed." Her response wasn't much louder than a whisper.

Bishop Brunstetter shrugged. "I didn't ask. I suppose he'll be here for as long as it takes. Long enough to forge a relationship with his sohn, a bond that can't be broken. He said he'd prayed for an opportunity to reach out to Gabe this way, and it seems Gott has answered. Not only is Gabriel here, but Gabe is forced to be still and spend time with him. The way I see it, this is a gut thing."

The bishop was wordy today, and it wasn't even a sermon. Nor was there a proverb in the entire monologue. Or maybe there had been, and she simply hadn't caught it. Still, a lot of what he'd said confused her.

"I'll go talk to Hosea and Noah. Maybe, betwixt the three of us, we can get a simple ramp assembled right quick." The gray-haired man climbed out of the wagon, handed Bridget the reins, and trotted across the yard, disappearing inside the haus.

Bridget stared after him a moment. She glanced down at the reins and then up at the horse. The animal snorted and tossed its head. What was she supposed to do with it? She couldn't unhitch the wagon with only one hand. Though she could hear Daed insisting she try. *You're not handicapped*, he would say.

Nein, it just seemed that way. And she supposed that if she had to live the rest of her life with one hand, she would adapt. But that was a hypothetical situation, and not realistic. At least not now. She transferred the reins to her injured hand and used her left one to stroke the gelding's nose.

The door to the haus opened, and the bishop trekked back toward her across the muddy patch of yard. "I'll park closer to the haus to unload the lumber. Then I'll tether the horse to something over there. Danki for your help." The older man climbed into the wagon and moved closer to the haus.

Bridget finished the barn chores, clumsily removed her tennis shoes, and went inside the RV. Flour was scattered all over the floor, the counter, and the stove. Mamm stood at the kitchen counter, her mouth set, her forehead furrowed, and her eyes red, as if she'd been crying. "I told Roseanna that you and I would clean up. She needed to get to school, ain't so?"

Jah, but that'd been over an hour ago. They'd all eaten breakfast together, being careful to avoid tracking the mess. After the three youngest had left, Daed and Noah had crossed the yard to the haus, and Mamm had told Bridget to finish the chores while she cleaned up.

Except she hadn't cleaned up.

"Mamm, what's wrong?" Bridget stopped walking just shy of the mess.

"Nothing. Nix. I just need some time alone." Mamm huffed. "But first, I need to clean—"

"I'll take care of it, Mamm."

Mamm sighed. "Danki, Bridget. I appreciate it." Mamm firmed her shoulders and marched to the bedroom Bridget still shared with her two younger sisters. Everyone else had moved back into the tent, except for Jonah, who slept alone in the small bed above the cab.

Bridget found the broom and rather awkwardly cleaned up the flour Roseanna had spilled everywhere. She rinsed the dishes as best as she could, then set them to the side to be washed more thoroughly by someone else. The whole time she worked, she worried. What could have made Mamm cry? Was Mamm fighting with Daed over the way his stubbornness had delayed their moving into the haus? About everything that had gone wrong since they'd moved here, including Bridget's surgery? Was she sick? Pregnant? Or simply lonely because she hadn't made any friends here?

The pounding of construction began nearby. Bridget peeked outside and saw the bishop and Noah assembling a ramp for Gabe. It was so hard to imagine him using a wheelchair.

Bridget cringed. She should've insisted on staying home, and not given in to Noah and Gabe. Even if Gabe had ended up performing unpaid labor for Daed, at least he wouldn't have gotten seriously hurt. Neither would Bridget have, for that matter. They might've been able to spend some time together.

But it was too late now.

The sound of an engine had her turning her head to see an SUV pulling into the driveway. As the vehicle drove past, Gabe glanced up at the RV and raised his hand in a wave.

He was here!

Bridget finished cleaning up as best she could. After that, she would head over to the haus and see how he was doing.

And find out how he'd reacted to her declaration of love. If he even brought it up.

Because she certainly wouldn't.

⁓

As the driver parked the SUV behind Bishop Brunstetter's buggy, Gabe noticed the bishop and Noah hammering nails into a rough-looking ramp, of sorts, that had been fashioned in the front of his haus. It looked too steep for Gabe to wheel himself up without assistance. There were nein railings, so whoever handled the wheelchair would have to be careful not to accidentally—or purposely—push Gabe over the edge.

Judging by the hard stare Hosea aimed in his direction, Gabe would need to watch out for himself if Hosea were the one operating the wheelchair. Gabe sighed. What had he done to earn Papa Behr's ire this time? Or was Bridget's daed still upset over his dochter's broken wrist and Gabe's multiple injuries, albeit their being probably not as serious? Would he blame Gabe for the dunking Noah had taken in icy water, even though lots of young people from the area and beyond were at the pond?

Daed got out of the SUV and helped the driver unload the wheelchair. He then opened it and parked it outside Gabe's door.

Gabe's face burned with self-consciousness as both the bishop and Noah stopped what they were doing to watch him exit the vehicle with assistance. What was he, some freaky sideshow at the circus?

He slowly moved to a standing position and twisted his body enough to get into the wheelchair. Daed lowered the footrests and wheeled Gabe up to the ramp.

Gabe grinned at Noah. "Let's see how well you did." Hopefully, his teasing would take some of the attention off himself.

Noah raised his hands. "Hey, if anything goes wrong, it's Bishop Brunstetter's fault."

"Sure, blame the bishop," Gabe returned with a smile.

The bishop chuckled.

"Step aside, men." Daed pushed the wheelchair onto the ramp and maneuvered Gabe up onto the porch. "Gut job."

The heads of Behr Construction would need to adjust the angle if building a wheelchair ramp for a paying client, however.

Hosea opened the door wide for Daed to push the wheelchair inside. "We have a little fire going. Enough to take the chill off."

"It feels gut in here." Gabe leaned forward, took off his coat, and handed the garment to Daed. Then, to Hosea, he said, "What do you want me to do?"

Hosea added another log to the fire. "Whatever you can. Figured you could probably stain the kitchen cabinets."

"That shouldn't be too much of a problem."

Daed parked the wheelchair near the unfinished cabinets. "Noah, you kum with me, and we'll get started carrying tarpaper to the roof."

Hosea grabbed a few rags and spread them over Gabe's legs. Newspapers already covered the floor. "So you won't make a mess."

As if he would.

"Do you need help opening the varnish?" Hosea popped the lid open without waiting for an answer.

The man's inclination to be helpful made Gabe suspicious. Just then, the memory of Daed's words to Hosea in the hospital waiting room flooded back. Maybe Gabe should ask Daed to repeat it for him later, seeing as it seemed to have produced a dramatic change in Hosea. Maybe it would transform Gabe's heart, too.

"Think you have everything you need within reach. If you don't, just holler. We'll kum if you need us." Hosea started for the door, then hesitated. "You can still add wood to the fire, ain't so?"

Gabe sighed. "I'm not an invalid."

"Actually, you are." Hosea turned away and pulled on his jacket. "I'll be on the roof."

Gabe drew in a deep breath, adjusted the wheelchair to a better position, and got started. He worked steadily, finishing all the lower cabinets on one side, then rolled his chair around to the other side. He wasn't sure how much time had passed when the door opened and Bridget came in, carrying a basket in her left hand, with a Thermos tucked under her arm.

"Hey." Her face pinkened. "I made some cookies."

The delicious scent of his favorite cookie—oatmeal raisin—wafted out from under the cloth covering the basket.

He smiled. "Koffee, too?"

She dipped her head. "Listen. About what I said at the hospital...."

Gabe's stomach churned. He wasn't ready to address *that* issue.

But she was right.

They needed to talk.

21

Bridget's face burned. She hadn't meant to bring up her drug-induced declaration of love. Where was a hole to hide in when she needed one?

Gabe's smile faltered as he regarded her, the expression in his eyes turning serious.

"I was under the influence of whatever medicine they gave me. I didn't know what I was saying."

"Of course you were." The relief in his voice was almost palpable.

So, he didn't want her to be in love with him? Then what was she to make of his positive reaction to her statement several days prior, when she'd said she wanted him to be head over heels in love with her? She'd said those words in this very room. He hadn't objected then.

Nein, he'd said he was head over heels, and that he would stop flirting with other girls. Would start courting her.

What had changed?

And why was she stressing over it? He'd excused her blunder. She should let it go instead of insisting on arguing her worthiness of being loved.

"Have a seat." Gabe nodded toward a folding camp chair near the woodstove. "And I would love a cup of koffee."

She looked at the Thermos. "I didn't bring any cups."

"The Thermos lid doubles as one. I took my travel koffee mug home with me the last time I was fired."

She cringed. "I'm sorry about that." She sat down, set the Thermos on the table, and then, holding the Thermos steady with her casted hand, used her nondominant hand to unscrew the lid. The Thermos shook as she tipped it over to pour.

"Don't be sorry." He looked down. "Listen, Bridget. I've been doing some thinking. I like you. A whole lot. I might even love you." His voice trembled, and he hesitated. Then he firmed his jaw. "But I don't think it's going to work for us to be together."

She sucked in a breath, righted the Thermos, and stared at him. But what could she say? *Don't. Please, don't.*

"Both times we went out together, you ended up seriously hurt. I'm a danger to your well-being." He glanced pointedly at her cast.

And a danger to my heart. His words stung. Nein, they stabbed. With deep, wounding jabs that threatened to rip her to shreds.

"I'll end up killing you. Accidentally." He grimaced. "I'd hate for that to happen."

And so he would murder her hopes. Her dreams.

She swallowed the lump in her throat. Firmed her shoulders. Nodded quickly. "Of course. I understand."

Except that she didn't.

His smile flickered, fading quickly. "Right. Still friends?"

She raised her head, trying to control her wobbling chin. "We weren't friends to begin with."

"See? That's the thing. We need to be. That should be first and foremost in our relationship. Well, friendship, and faith in der Herr."

She wasn't sure she could be just friends with Gabe after giving him her heart. But he was right about the importance of putting Gott first in their relationship. He should be first in her life, too. She'd think more about that later, once her privately shed tears were spent.

He bowed his head and rubbed his forehead. "I'm not the man I need to be. I know that. Daed said something at the hospital…he was talking to your daed, but what he said hit me hard." He shook his head. "I wish I could remember his exact words. Also wish I had my Bible. I hope the bishop stopped by the Zooks' to pick it up."

"You aren't staying at the Zooks' any longer?" That news lightened her spirit.

"Nein, the bishop thought his haus would be easier for me to navigate." He shook his head. "And he made some nonsensical comments about nurses falling in love with patients. Or maybe it was reversed. I don't know." He rubbed his jaw.

Gut thing he was away from Agnes. Would Daed let Bridget take care of Gabe, instead? Maybe then she would have a fighting chance at winning his heart.

Gabe glanced at her. "He was right, though—it is easier to get around in his haus, since it's spacious and isn't cluttered with people. Plus, there aren't as many stairs. And Daed's there, so we'll have more chances to talk."

She set the cup of koffee near him and then awkwardly tightened the inner lid of the Thermos. "Do you want a cookie?" Maybe seeing him accept something she'd baked would temporarily soothe her wounded heart. Or he would decline, in which case she could beat a hasty retreat. She shouldn't have kum. If only she'd stayed away, she wouldn't be battling tears and a broken heart.

"I can't resist your cookies."

Or Agnes's fudge, huh? She withheld the bitter, envy-born words.

"Of course, there aren't too many sweets I don't like." He grinned.

Her smile wobbled. "I…I suppose I'd best get back to the RV and do…something." Doing just about anything would be better than fawning over him. Or behaving like a lovesick fool. *Just act normal.* Whatever "normal" would be in this situation.

"Don't go," Gabe pleaded, making a pouty face. "Unless you're truly busy, of course. I could use someone to talk to."

Bridget forced a laugh. "Okay, I'll stay. For a little while." But she had nothing to say. Nothing except to beg him to reconsider courting her.

Nein. She wouldn't go there.

She searched for a topic to talk about. Something to get her mind off the thick, cloying pain of her heart as it was ripped into shreds.

Hopefully, he would choose a sustainable conversation piece, because she had nothing.

⌒

Gabe took a sip of koffee, then snagged a cookie from the basket before offering it back to Bridget.

She shook her head. "Nein, those are all for you. My favorite cookie is chocolate chip with walnuts." Her voice sounded strangled, as if she were forcing the words past something unyielding in her throat.

The girl he'd fallen in love with had withdrawn behind the wall he'd worked so hard to draw her out from. He glanced at her cast again. Maybe the hospital drugs had diluted her sense of her true feelings for him.

But when he took another glance at her cast, he knew he'd done the right thing. He'd hurt her enough, physically. He couldn't risk hurting her more. Could he?

He'd figure it out later. Right now, they needed a "friendly" conversation to help salvage her pride and try to build a foundation of friendship.

A glint of sunlight coming through the window highlighted the wisps of hair that had fallen loose from her kapp. His fingers itched to touch those tresses, to smooth them back. And maybe to cup her jaw while he kissed away the tears that shimmered in her eyes.

Dangerous thoughts, those. He swallowed hard. Looked down at the treat he clasped in his trembling fingers. *Cookies.* They were making chitchat about cookies. Right.

"Those sound gut, but these are my favorites." He raised the cookie to his mouth. "What's for supper to-nacht in the Behr den?"

Bridget grinned. "Homemade pizza. And apple crisp for dessert, made by Roseanna. With lots of help from Mamm."

Gabe put his hand over his heart. "Tell me there's some way to get me up the stairs and into the RV for dinner. It's been ever so long since I had pizza. The bishop's frau is doing something with venison." He wrinkled his nose. "I haven't developed a taste for that yet."

"I could save you a slice of pizza," Bridget offered. "We're topping it with pepperoni, green peppers, onions, and mushrooms."

"Make it two, and I'll give you a kiss." He added a wink to indicate he was teasing, but she wasn't looking at him. Instead, she stared at the floor, her cheeks flaming red. She fidgeted the fingers of her uninjured hand, almost as if she imagined their tangling in his hair, the way they'd done when he'd kissed her behind the barn.

His stomach clenched.

He'd probably been too hasty in breaking off the relationship. He wanted to kiss her again. Wanted to feel her body pressed against his, her fingers in his hair. He imagined himself removing her kapp, pulling out her bobby pins one by one, and letting her hair fall to its full length.

He groaned.

"Are you okay?"

Nein. He would never be okay. Not if he had to go forever without....

He shut his eyes. He shouldn't even think of such things. Hadn't he broken up with her for her own gut, for her safety? He didn't want to accidentally kill her, like he'd killed the Englisch boy who'd gone surfing in the hurricane-tossed ocean just because Gabe had. Still, what he wanted was to ask her to kum to him, to sit in his lap, and to let him....

He groaned again.

"Gabe?" The chair squeaked as Bridget stood and crossed the space between them. She rested her hand on his shoulder. "Are you okay? Do you need a pain pill? Should I get your daed?"

"Nein. I'm fine." He firmed his shoulders, shrugged her hand off, and watched with regret as she retreated to her chair. Best to get his thoughts under control. He tried to think of something safe to discuss. Pizza was out, since it had been responsible for his mental side trip. He needed to walk according to the purpose of Gott.

That reminded him. "Do you have a Bible handy?"

"A Bible?" She frowned. "There's one in the RV, but—"

"Do you mind getting it? I need you to look something up."

Her frown deepened. "Should I get the bishop? Or your daed? He's a preacher."

"Nein, just the Bible. Please."

She rose, pulled her coat around her shoulders, and opened the door. "I'll be right back."

"Danki." He turned his attention to the cabinets waiting to be stained. Better than watching her skirts sway as she walked away.

Help me to find that verse, Lord.

He would find it, even if he had to read the entire book of Romans. And maybe another book or two, because he wasn't certain where that verse was located.

Maybe he should've asked for Daed.

In his peripheral vision, movement outside the window caught his attention. He turned his head and caught a glimpse of Bridget crossing the yard. Her skirts swayed with the gentle movements of her hips. He watched, his blood heating, until she disappeared into the barn.

Gott, please help me control my thoughts.

Bridget could hear loud banging as she approached the RV. She opened the door and, without removing her shoes, stepped inside, only to dodge a plastic tumbler. She picked it up as it clattered down the steps. "Mamm?"

Mamm gave her a tight-lipped smile. "It slipped out of my hand." Her voice broke, and she turned away, wiping her eyes with the back of her hand.

"What's wrong?"

"Nix," Mamm said sharply. "Why are you here?"

"I…Gabe asked for a Bible. Should I get Daed? Tell him you need him?"

"Nein! Don't bother your daed." Mamm bent to pick up something else from the floor. "This is his fault, anyway," she muttered, probably not intending for Bridget to hear. "Get your Bible and go see how you can help in the haus. I need to be alone for a while."

Bridget hesitated, but Mamm didn't look at her again. Instead, she started sorting through the stack of dirty laundry on the floor.

She grabbed her Bible off the dresser in the bedroom and returned to the haus. Gabe was rubbing varnish on a board when she entered.

"I got the Bible. Where do you want it?"

He looked up. "Would you mind reading to me? Holding a big, heavy book like that won't hurt your wrist, will it?"

"You want *me* to read it?" Her voice came out as a funny squeak. How could he ask such a thing? Men were supposed to be the spiritual leaders. Women didn't read Scripture aloud to them.

"Jah, I want you to read it, out loud. There's a verse I want to find, and I can't remember where it's located. Romans. I think."

"What chapter?" The pages fluttered through her fingers as she searched for the book of Romans. She rarely touched this tome, but if Gabe wanted her to read…. Hopefully, she wouldn't get into trouble. But if she did, it'd be worth it if it made Gabe happy.

"I should've said 'please.' And 'danki.' Actually, it'd be great if you could read as much of it as possible before you have to go."

"Doesn't your daed have one of those Bibles with a topical index that lets you look up the theme of the verse and then tells you where it's found?" Her lack of biblical knowledge shamed her.

Gabe appeared to concentrate on staining the board. "I don't know if he does. And I don't know the theme of the verse, either. Just that it talks about 'walking,' and if you look up 'walk,' it'll list about a hundred verses, more or less. Of course, it might not be about walking at all. I might be remembering wrong."

"It'd be easier to ask a preacher. He might know exactly where it's found."

Gabe looked up at her. "Do you have a problem with reading God's Word?"

She slumped. *Caught.* "It's confusing. And the bishop back home discouraged it. He had a list of approved passages. I'm pretty sure none of them was in the book of Romans."

"Gut reason to read it, then. To find out what he doesn't want you to know."

"What if he doesn't want us to know for a gut reason?" Her sense of curiosity warred with her fear of Daed's anger if he should find out.

Gabe frowned. "Bridget. There isn't a gut reason. Gott wants me to read Romans. I'm certain of it. And my daed reads whatever parts of the Bible he wants to."

"Jah, but he's a preacher. He's allowed."

Gabe grunted. "If you don't want to read, may I borrow your Bible? Unless Bishop Brunstetter remembered to pick mine up from the Zooks'."

"I'll read." But unease still slithered through her. Hopefully, she wouldn't get in trouble. Still, for Gabe, she'd do almost anything.

Or she would have, before he'd broken up with her. Now she needed to emotionally withdraw and protect her heart from further injury. She couldn't let him see how much his rejection hurt. It was even more painful than when Isaac had called off their relationship due to her impending move.

She found the book of Romans and began to read, all the while wondering why Gabe felt the need to know any of the confusing content.

As she concluded chapter one and was about to begin chapter two, Gabe cleared his throat, interrupting her. "I've a feeling there's going to be a lot in this book that we need to pay attention to. Something inside me is yearning for it, whatever it is." He put down the rag he was using. "We need to pray."

Bridget closed the Bible, keeping one finger in place to mark where she'd left off, and bowed her head.

Silence followed for one beat. Two.

Gabe cleared his throat again. "Gott, help us to understand what You want us to know. Help me—us—to walk according to Your purpose, whatever it is. Gott, my daed was right when he said I need You more than I need anything else. I feel like I need to ask You to give me another chance. I'll try to do better and to put You first. If You would help me understand, I'd really appreciate it. I don't know what to do."

A strange hunger filled Bridget. *I want to understand, too. Help me, Gott. Help us both.*

Something strong, almost palpable, filled the room. Bridget opened her eyes but saw nothing out of the ordinary.

And yet, there was something—or Someone—there.

22

Gabe pored over the Scriptures that evening before dinner, asking question after question of Daed and Bishop Brunstetter. The conversation carried on through the meal, though that hadn't been his intention. Gabe had always considered the Bible boring. How had he missed out on its excitement all these years? Never before had Gabe experienced such a consuming hunger for the Word of Gott. But both Daed and the bishop seemed to be in their element with the words of der Herr on their lips, wearing grins on their faces as they talked through every question Gabe asked.

At least talking helped him to swallow his stew, which he might've enjoyed, had he not known it was made from ground venison. At least he couldn't taste the gaminess of the meat.

Agnes had showed up just before dinner with a disposable aluminum dish of fudge, and she'd been invited to stay—likely her intention all along. While the men talked theology, Frau Brunstetter and Agnes puttered around the kitchen as they chattered about the weird, warm, windy weather that had settled over the straits.

When dessert was brought out, Gabe found himself feeling glad Agnes had kum. He didn't know what flavor fudge it was, only that it wasn't the traditional chocolate kind. Maybe white chocolate, since the color was creamy, studded with bits of chopped nuts. It tasted very sweet, almost like maple syrup. Unable to limit himself to just one piece, Gabe snatched a second helping when Daed and the bishop went in search of their Bibles.

Agnes served him a mug of a weak-looking brew of some sort. He couldn't identify the scent.

"Herbal tea." She smiled. "It'll help you relax so you can sleep. I made it myself from wildflowers and other plants growing near our haus."

She said "our haus" as if her home were his. The bishop's plan to keep Agnes away from Gabe while he healed wasn't working. Instead, she'd inserted herself into the Brunstetters' home as smoothly as if she had been born there.

Gabe turned his attention to the men when they came back to the kitchen. Agnes served them tea, too. Theirs smelled a bit more robust than the weak, odd-looking stuff she'd given him.

Bishop Brunstetter thumbed through the pages of his Bible as he sat down once more at the table. "I think the verse you referred to earlier, Gabe, was Romans eight, verse twenty-eight: *'And we know that all things work together for good to them that love God, to them that are the called according to his purpose.'* It says *'called,'* but I suppose that if you walk according to His purpose, then you are called." He flipped forward a few more pages. "Of course, you might've had in mind Ephesians four, verse one, where Paul says, *'Walk worthy of the vocation wherewith ye are called.'*"

"But first you need to know how you can be one of the called—and to become one." Daed opened his own Bible. "And then know for what reason you are called."

"Have you tried your tea, Gabe?" Agnes hovered nearby. "Do you want some sugar with it?"

Gabe eyed the drink dubiously before he took a hesitant sip of the foul-smelling stuff. It tasted like freshly mowed grass. "Would sugar make it better?"

Her expression fell. He hadn't meant to sound rude. He tried to think of a way to apologize without retracting what he'd said.

"You should probably get on home, Agnes." The bishop glanced at the wall clock. "Your daed will be worried."

She waved a hand dismissively. "Ach, nein, he knows where I am. Besides, I made some healing ointment to rub on Gabe's ankle."

"I'm perfectly capable of rubbing ointment on myself," Gabe said. Not that he had any intention of doing such a thing. Especially if the substance smelled as awful as her homemade tea.

Daed looked up. "If Gabe needs any help, I'm here to assist him."

Agnes sagged. "But I told Daed I'd be home late. Gabe needs me." She glanced at him, her expression begging him to agree.

Gabe looked away. He could think of a lot of things he needed more than Agnes. People he'd rather have caring for him. Such as Bridget. "Danki for your kindness, but I'll be fine. I don't need a nurse."

"Well, if you insist." Agnes bit her lip. "I'll kum back tomorrow to help."

Given the helpful forewarning, he vowed to be gone from the haus at daybreak and back at the Behrs' doing anything else.

Agnes fetched her purse, reached inside, and took out a small clear plastic container. An oily substance swirled around inside. She opened the lid, releasing the scent of peppermint. Or maybe menthol. "You need to rub this on, morgen and nacht."

Gabe wrinkled his nose. If the stuff worked to repel certain females, he'd gladly take a bath in it. Unfortunately, because Agnes had mixed the concoction, it probably wouldn't work on her the way he wished.

He cleared his throat. "You do remember the conversation we had not long ago, don't you?"

Her expression fell. "About your liking someone else?"

He didn't dare look at the bishop or Daed. If her boldness in blurting it out like that shocked him, it had probably produced the same effect on them. He nodded.

"You aren't married to her yet."

So, she still considered him fair game? His throat constricted.

The bishop coughed.

Gabe cleared his throat. "Danki for your kindness, Agnes. I appreciate it." He forced the words out, in spite of his fear that she might misinterpret them and believe he was thankful for her continued interest in him.

"Anytime, Gabe Lapp." She set the container on the table beside him and gave his shoulder a pat. A pat that turned into a rub, and ended with a squeeze. "See you tomorrow."

Once the door had closed behind her and the sound of her footsteps had faded away, the bishop grunted. "Can't abide pushy maidals."

"She has gut taste in young men, at least." Daed winked at Gabe. "And her fudge can't be beat."

Gabe nodded in agreement with Daed's compliment. But Agnes's most recent flirtations had turned those two small pieces of fudge he'd eaten into big, heavy boulders in his stomach. Mixed with the fresh-mowed-grass tea, they made his stomach churn like the ocean during a hurricane.

Time to refocus on Gott's Word.

"So, Daed. How can I know I'm one of the called? And how will I know what my purpose is?"

Daed's smile grew. "Let me show you."

⤸

After supper, Bridget set aside two slices of pizza for Gabe. Anything for another kiss from him.

Could that man ever kiss. If only she could somehow recreate the behind-the-barn experience. Replay the feelings, the emotions, at will.

Maybe a repeat performance would help.

She retreated to the bedroom in the RV and, after changing into her nacht-gown, curled up in the king-sized bed with her Bible. Gabe had expressed an intention to continue reading the book of Romans that evening, and she wanted to be up to speed just in case he wanted to discuss something with her. But the way the words drew her in went beyond Gabe. Curiosity filled her. That sense of the *Someone* from earlier, drew her.

Not that she'd be able to discuss anything knowledgeably. She may attend church every other Sunday, but she never listened all that closely. Being there was more of a compulsion, an obligation, than a desire. But then, she didn't know many people who were on fire for Gott.

That needed to change.

She jerked awake when she felt the Bible being pulled out of her arms, and blinked up at her two younger sisters.

"Lights out," Roseanna said. "Falling asleep while reading...." She frowned and shook her head at Bridget.

Bridget didn't usually do that. Then again, the Bible wasn't usually what she read.

But for Gabe....

Was it wrong to want to do the things he did?

It might be, because she wasn't entirely sure she was allowed to read Romans. And she hadn't wanted to ask Daed in case he forbade her to do so.

Of course, the rules varied from district to district. A practice that was outlawed back home in Ohio might be encouraged here. Other things had needed to change, after all, such as the kapp style she wore, and the colors of her garments.

Shiloh turned the light off as Bridget crawled under the covers. But now that her body had awakened, her mind didn't want to sleep. Her thoughts weren't focused on what she'd just read, however. Nein, she wanted to think about *that kiss*. And the logistics of kissing someone in a wheelchair. Would she have to lean over him instead of the other way around?

It wouldn't be the same.

The next morgen, after a restless sleep, she dragged herself out of bed to do the barn chores she could manage, and then helped Mamm get Shiloh, Jonah, and Roseanna off to school. By the time she finished, the skeleton construction crew of men who'd returned to work had arrived, along with Gabe and his father.

Daed took a couple sips of his koffee, then stood and gulped down the rest. "Haus should be move-in ready by the end of the week. That's what Preacher Gabriel says. Did you know he owns a construction company in Pinecraft? Guess that's where Gabe got all his know-how."

Bridget hadn't known that. She stored away the information in her heart. Every piece was a treasure.

Just before lunch, she went to the haus carrying a plate of the two big slices of pizza, a Thermos of hot koffee, and a mug. She found Gabe alone in the downstairs bedroom, sweeping awkwardly from his perch in the wheelchair.

She kicked the door shut behind her, then held out the dish to him. "I saved you two slices, as requested."

His glance skittered from her to the closed door, and he raised one eyebrow.

"I didn't want to make the rest of the crew jealous. About the pizza, I mean." She gave a nervous giggle.

"Danki. Frau Brunstetter packed me leftover stew." He wrinkled his nose. "I promised you a kiss."

Her face heated. She stared at her feet.

Gabe propped the broom against the wall, and rolled the wheelchair toward her. "Kum here."

Could this get any more awkward? "Look, Gabe, I know you were teasing. You don't need to…." But, oh, she wanted him to. She set the plate, Thermos, and mug on the top of a ladder standing nearby.

"When I said I couldn't wait to kiss you again? It was true. Besides, I promised. Unless you don't want me to."

Just like that, he'd put the ball firmly back in her court. She *wanted* him to, but…. She shuffled her feet.

Gabe moved closer. He put his hand on her left wrist and tugged her toward him. "Sit down." He patted his lap with his other hand.

Something inside her jumped. Her nerve endings sprang to attention. A shiver ran up her spine. "I don't want to hurt you."

He wrinkled his nose. "You don't weigh that much. I've carried you before. Don't worry about me."

Her cheeks more than heated. They burned. She glanced at the door to make sure it was firmly closed, then carefully lowered herself into Gabe's lap. His arms closed around her, gently pulling her nearer, holding her tight, yet doing so carefully, as if she were a valuable treasure.

His hand rose to grasp the back of her head, holding it in place. Then his lips were on hers. Warm. Inviting. Passionate. A whole world of emotions all wrapped into one.

She could never get enough of this. Never.

With a quick tug of his hand, he released her hair from its bun. The tresses tumbled down her back.

She sucked in a gasp. A mental alarm rang. He broke the kiss and combed both his hands through her hair, smoothing it, arranging it. "So beautiful." He kissed her again.

She silenced the mental alarm. *This* was right.

She wrapped her arms around his neck and ran her fingers through his hair as his kisses grew increasingly passionate. More demanding. Then his mouth roamed away from hers, over her cheek to her ear. He nibbled her earlobe for a moment, his breathing ragged.

She whimpered.

Then his lips trailed down her neck to her pulse. His hand shook as it found her waist. Her ribs. "Bridget." Her name came out as a groan.

"Ich liebe dich." She gasped the words. It seemed important he hear them. That he hear them when she wasn't under the influence of strong IV medication.

"Bridget." If anything, his hand trembled even more. "You make me crazy. I'm head over heels for you, for sure."

Head over heels was gut.

His attention returned to her lips, while his other hand grasped a handful of her hair.

A door slammed against a wall.

Gabe released her.

She wobbled to her feet, her vision failing to focus. She wanted to fall back into Gabe's arms. Finish what the two of them had started. Hear him declare his love for her.

Because, surely, he must feel the same, to kiss her like that. To touch her like that.

"What is the meaning of this?" Daed's voice growled. "Bridget Marie, for shame, letting your hair down like that in front of a man you aren't married to. Go fix yourself at once. And mind that you don't let anybody else see you."

She didn't bother looking at Daed. She could hear the scowl on his face. She raised her hands to touch her hair and didn't feel any pins. Looking for them now was unthinkable.

Plus, she wasn't about to run off and leave Gabe to face Daed's wrath on his own. She would stay and fight for him. She'd be his hero. Make that heroine.

She blinked, swallowed a sob, and rubbed her eyes. Her gaze focused on Daed.

And behind him, Gabe's daed.

And beside *him*, the bishop.

So much for not letting anyone else see her.

Gabe chanced a quick glance at Bridget. She gathered her hair with one hand, then somehow twisted it up in a bun and secured it without using a single pin. She bent to retrieve her kapp and put it on, her gaze lowered the entire time.

Hosea cleared his throat.

Gabe jerked his attention to the old man. Maybe he should've controlled himself better, but, Gott help him, he didn't regret kissing her or touching her hair. His only regret was getting caught.

But neither Daed nor the bishop appeared upset.

Hosea's face had turned an alarming shade of red, and Gabe could've sworn he saw smoke coming out of his ears. Hosea fixed a stare on Gabe, and his mouth worked, but nein sounds came out.

Should Gabe volunteer to quit before Hosea had a chance to formulate his heated rebuke and punishment? Or should he wait it out, since he knew what would follow?

If—not if, but when—Hosea fired him, he would *not* return to work for him again, even if the man got down on his knees and begged.

He hated looking up at the angry man from his perch in the wheelchair, but falling on his face before Hosea would be even worse.

Maybe now would be a gut time to exercise his fledgling faith. *Gott, please, step in and handle this situation. I'm sorry I sinned.* He wasn't sure if kissing Bridget was a sin or not. Some of the thoughts he'd had while kissing her likely qualified as sinful, though.

The bishop cleared his throat and studied Hosea. "If you find yourself in a hole, don't dig yourself deeper," he said. "Life is as uncertain as a grapefruit's squirt."

Daed made a sort of snorting sound, as if he were holding back his laughter, and his dimples flashed. He grasped Hosea's shoulder.

Hosea opened his mouth to speak, but the bishop interrupted him again: "Think twice, speak once."

Enough of the confusing proverbs. Gabe scratched his neck.

Bridget still stood in place, staring at the floor. Trembling, as if holding back sobs. Or maybe laughter? But, nein. There was nothing funny about this. Gabe wished he could encourage her that everything would be alright.

He wasn't sure if that were true, only that he felt a measure of peace about the situation.

Hosea raised his arms in surrender, turned around, and stalked from the room. As if the bishop's three proverbs had somehow made sense and changed his mind.

Gabe wouldn't hold his breath. As soon as Hosea found the opportunity to fire Gabe, he would. Again.

Neither Daed nor Bishop Brunstetter seemed upset. The bishop approached Gabe and stopped when he stood between him and Bridget. "And the truth shall set you free."

Would Gabe get in trouble for acting disrespectfully if he asked the bishop to speak plainly?

Or was the bishop asking Gabe to speak plainly about what was in his heart, and telling him to stop playing games?

Maybe Gabe should just stop pretending he understood.

"Life is as uncertain as a grapefruit's squirt? Really?" Gabe snapped. "What's that supposed to mean?"

Daed frowned. "Gabriel Andrew."

"Last nacht, you all but said you were in love with someone." The bishop looked from him to Bridget and then back.

Gabe was pretty sure he hadn't said that. But it was true. He glanced at Bridget.

"And I've suspected for months you liked Goldilocks, here. Now I know you feel something more."

Bridget's head jerked up, as if she was shocked by the nickname the bishop had used. Or by his declaration of Gabe's love.

Of course, the bishop's blunt speaking shocked Gabe, too.

"But I also remember some things you said before, about your perceived treatment by some men in the community," the bishop continued. "And I think this grapefruit is squirting in directions I never would've guessed. Ways that might wake up some people."

And there he went with his confusing talk again.

"There's going to be a revival in this land," the bishop said quietly. "I feel it. The Spirit of der Herr is blowing in."

The wind *was* howling, but Gabe was pretty sure it wasn't the Holy Spirit.

"This community will be shaken to its foundation." Bishop Brunstetter raised his hands and bowed his head. "Thrown to its knees. Gott help us all."

What?

23

Bridget stared at the bishop, not quite sure what to think about his statements. Was he making sense to Gabe or his daed? Both men were silent, their heads bowed.

The bishop lowered his arms to his sides again. "Guess we'd better get back to work."

Nobody was going to address their having been caught in a passionate embrace? Relief flooded her. And Gabe hadn't denied the bishop's observations about his being in love with her. That alone was cause for celebration.

But Daed…. She sighed heavily. As the two older men left the room, she crouched and began gathering her fallen bobby pins.

"Look. About what happened…." Gabe wheeled closer.

She didn't need to hear him tell her that it wouldn't happen again, that it was just a spur-of-the-moment thing. Such a statement would be untrue, because there was nein way this episode wasn't premeditated. At least on her part. And Gabe was the one who'd put the idea in her head. He'd brought it up when she arrived.

She closed her hand around the pins she'd collected. "Don't say it." She hadn't meant to snap. Or maybe she had.

"Don't say it?" He chuckled. "Okay, I won't tell you that he spoke the truth. I do love you. But I'm not ready to declare it to the world, and, quite frankly, I'm not sure I want to be Hosea's sohn-in-law." He sighed. "Unless we could live several hundred miles apart."

Jah, she got that. Daed's reaction to seeing her sitting on Gabe's lap, kissing him, was still questionable. He might have walked away after hearing the bishop's proverbs, but would those words cool his ire long enough to enable him to handle the situation rationally? Or was he a ticking time bomb?

"I guess I should find Daed, then." She finished collecting her pins, then stood and headed for the door.

"Bridget."

Her name hung there, suspended between them.

She turned. "What?"

"I'll handle him. Your daed, I mean. I'll talk to him."

Even if I'm fired in the process. He didn't have to say it.

"I'd rather take care of it." Because Bridget could turn on the tears to get her way, if need be. Daed might have a quick temper, but he did love her. She was sure of that much, even if he didn't let her have her way all the time.

"Let me be the man," Gabe said quietly. "Trust me, okay?"

She trusted him; she just didn't trust his ability to handle Daed. She squeezed the pins in her palm. They poked into her skin.

He rolled the wheelchair closer to her. "Please?"

"Sure." Her agreement was begrudging, but maybe she could do damage control later. What would Gabe say to Daed, anyway? That he hadn't meant to kiss her, but she'd crawled into his lap, and…. She stifled a wail as Gabe left the room.

She followed him out. Might as well go back to the RV and do something. Or not. She paused and went back into the bedroom. She needed to know how his discussion with Daed went. And there wasn't a better way to find out than by eavesdropping.

Assuming they would talk loudly enough for her to hear.

She was fairly confident Daed would, at least.

Gott, please help this to go well. Please? I love Gabe. And if he truly loves me….

"Hosea," Gabe said from somewhere near the front of the haus.

"State your piece, bu." Daed didn't sound loud. Or angry.

Just resigned.

⌒

Gabe took a deep breath and sent up a silent prayer. *Lord Gott, help this to go well.* Then he forced himself to look Hosea in the eyes.

Nein steam came from the older man's ears. And his face wasn't as red as before. Gut signs? Maybe.

"I...uh...I should first apologize for courting your dochter without asking your blessing." He'd finally manned up enough to admit that his purpose behind their outings was to court her.

Hosea shrugged off his apology. "In our home district, courting is kept secret, even from parents, until the wedding is announced."

"Right. But if that's the case, then why a porch swing for courting purposes?" Not that there was a swing, yet. But it was on the short list of things to finish.

"I want to make sure the guy is worthy of her. Will provide for her and take care of her the way he should." Hosea flushed. He avoided Gabe's eyes.

"I promise I'll do my best to take care of her the way I should." *And to keep her alive. To avoid such foolery as taking her surfing in the Atlantic Ocean right after a hurricane.* "I'll never invite her to do another polar bear plunge. And any future ice-skating will be done after I've checked to make sure the ice is frozen solid and not melting."

Hosea's grin—seldom seen—was welkum. But fleeting. "The thing is, you were touching her hair. It was down, and you were touching it. And that means you were thinking intimately about her. I wasn't prepared to see that. Especially so early on in the relationship."

"May I have permission to court your dochter?" He couldn't recall if he'd asked the question already, only that he'd apologized for moving ahead without Hosea's blessing. This courting business was confusing. Flirting was far easier. Nein strings attached.

But he liked these strings. And the kinder, gentler Hosea was a plus.

There was a long, drawn-out pause. Hosea studied him the way he might a horse at auction. To see how he measured up.

Gabe would probably be deemed lacking. Hosea had made nein effort to hide his irritation, annoyance, and temper in the past.

"I couldn't think of a better man for my dochter. I'd be proud to call you my sohn."

That was the last response Gabe had expected. If he'd been standing on his own two feet, his knees would've buckled. "Danki. I promise to try my best to be the man I should be."

"I have faith in you. The fact that you approached me just now says volumes." Hosea swiped his hand over his mouth. "I wonder where lunch is. I thought my frau would send Bridget over with it, but maybe she expected us to kum to the RV to get it, since the bishop is here. I'd invite you to join us, but…." He glanced at the wheelchair. "How long will you be in that thing?"

Gabe shrugged. He still hadn't read the doctor's notes. Studying the Bible had become a bigger priority. That, and his newfound relationship with Daed. Not to mention his relationship with his heavenly Father. "Daed said I need to take the time to let my body heal. I'm still in a lot of pain. It's hard to move. But I'd guess…I don't know, six weeks? Is that how long a sprained ankle takes to heal? The doctor said something about physical therapy, too, but I'm thinking resuming my normal activities will build me back up right quick."

"Praying so." Hosea glanced toward the door as it opened. The bishop and Daed came back in, followed by the few men who'd returned to work. Gabe wasn't sure where Noah had gone. Kum to think of it, he hadn't seen him all morgen.

"We went to round up the rest of the men." The bishop pulled out a pocket watch and glanced at it. "Lunch break. Roof should be finished by dark."

Hosea nodded, looking pleased. He glanced around. "Just a few finishing touches in here, some cleaning up, and we'll be ready to move in." He rubbed his hands together. "Then it's on to the next project. Patrick said something about signing a contract before Christmas for a remodeling job we're supposed to start next week. A new shop that's opening downtown."

Probably the place where Daed had taken Gabe to talk. But there were stairs leading up to the sidewalk, so it wasn't handicapped accessible. As a business, it would be legally required to add a wheelchair ramp. That addition would have to be first on the to-do list, for Gabe's sake.

Daed held up a Thermos. "Homemade stew, courtesy of Frau Brunstetter. Ready to eat, Sohn?"

Gabe frowned, remembering the pizza slices from Bridget. Those wouldn't be enough to fill him, though. "Sure. I'll be right back." He grinned and added, "Save me a seat." There wasn't a table, and they'd have to make space to sit on the floor.

Hosea frowned. "My frau made some sandwiches, she said, for anyone who may want them. But I thought she would send them over with my dochter. Where is Bridget?"

Gabe hadn't seen her slip past them, which meant she was still in the bedroom. He started to roll the wheelchair in that direction.

But nein sooner had Hosea asked than Bridget, cheeks stained red, gaze glued to the floor, appeared, carrying the two slices of pizza, the Thermos, and the mug she'd brought him. "I'll get the sandwiches, Daed."

"Eavesdropping, were you?" Hosea pursed his lips, but his eyes twinkled.

Her face flamed brighter.

"Go on with you. We're hungry." Her daed waved her past.

Bridget paused long enough to hand Gabe the pizza and set the Thermos and the mug near him on the floor before disappearing out the door.

"Shall we pray?" Hosea bowed his head. And after a moment, the rest of the crew, Amish and Englisch alike, did the same.

Gabe had much to be thankful for, for sure. But as he started to bow his head, he noticed the bishop frown as he glanced out the window, his gaze pointed skyward. As if he expected the fiery chariot of the Lord to appear then and there with the judgment he'd predicted.

A chill worked through Gabe.

Gott help us all.

24

B ridget!" Noah bellowed from downstairs. "The bishop's here!"
"Be right there." Bridget tied her black bonnet over her kapp, then
smoothed the skirt of her dress with her palms.

In the doorway of her new bedroom—the one she'd lived in for just
over a week—she stopped and glanced behind her to make sure everything was in place. A longtime habit. *Don't leave a mess.* All the drawers of
the antique dresser that was old back when Mamm was a little girl were
shut tight. The top was uncluttered, the only things on it being a kerosene
lantern and the book Bridget had been reading, her page saved with a
bookmark. A neatly pressed crocheted doily occupied the top of her book-
case in the corner, filled with her collection of much-loved novels. On the
bedside table was perched another lantern, this one battery operated; a
clock; a devotional book; and Bridget's Bible, with her lavender crocheted
cross bookmark peeking out from the bottom. Her tumbling-block quilt
in shades of purple covered her bed; her pillows were plumped, and her
neatly folded nightgown was draped over the mattress.

She missed the king-sized bed from the RV. Her old, familiar twin
bed seemed so narrow in comparison, even though she'd shared the bigger
bed with her two sisters and now she was alone.

What would it be like to share a bed with Gabe?

Her face heated at the inappropriate thought. Even so, she hoped
that day would kum. Maybe even this autumn. Assuming Gabe asked.

And with the bishop arriving now to pick her up and take her to his
haus for a date with Gabe, it could mean only one thing.

Gabe had asked the bishop to speak with her to see if she'd be willing
to marry him.

She forced a squeal into submission. It escaped as a quiet "eek," like a sneeze held in.

She couldn't wait.

Not after those heated minutes she'd spent on Gabe's lap. Such a moment was unlikely to happen again until after they married.

Since she'd been caught in a compromising position, with her hair down, on Gabe's lap, all parties involved had agreed that a chaperoned courtship would be best, lest their passions flare out of control.

Probably wise.

And it gave her something to look forward to on her wedding nacht, whenever that might be.

During her family's first week in their new home, Bridget and Gabe had spent time together every evening. And they'd discussed every topic under the sun. But he hadn't brought up the subject of marriage. She just assumed marriage was the plan. Daed believed marriage was on the horizon, to the point of calling him "Sohn." As for Mamm…. Bridget shook her head. Mamm still seemed depressed. Weepy. And disinclined to discuss anything. She just did as little as possible, and hid the rest of the time, either crying or sleeping. Daed said nothing, other than, "She'll adjust. Leave her be." Even moving into the new haus hadn't lifted Mamm's spirits.

"Bridget!" Noah yelled again. "Don't keep him waiting!"

Ach! She'd been daydreaming of Gabe and marriage. And worrying about Mamm.

"Coming!" She gave the room one last visual sweep. Everything was in place. If Daed came up here, he wouldn't find anything to complain about. And if her snoopy little sisters and brother poked around, she would know immediately.

She turned and ran downstairs to the kitchen. Shoved her feet into her tennis shoes, leaving the laces untied. Grabbed her coat and shrugged it on as she ran out the door, shoestrings flapping, and to the waiting buggy.

Daed stood with Bishop Brunstetter, conversing quietly.

"Have fun!" Shiloh yelled from her open bedroom window overlooking the driveway.

Bridget waved to her sister, then clambered into the buggy, sat down, and bent forward to tie her shoes.

"I'll bring her home later," the bishop told Daed. "Along with Agnes."

Agnes? Had Gabe also been spending time with Bridget's rival? When had he found the time, between working all day and passing his evening hours with Bridget?

Or had Agnes been inserting herself into Gabe's life with her efforts to nurse him, even though he'd graduated from the wheelchair and now got around on crutches? He'd told Bridget he felt better, that the pain in his thighs was mostly gone.

"Gabe is a gut man." Daed tugged his beard and glanced at Bridget. His eyes twinkled. "I think we could probably trust him to take Agnes home first. She lives only a half mile away. I can't think of any place between there and here to stop and park."

Bridget's face burned again. "Daed."

He chuckled.

"Except Gabe isn't bringing her home," the bishop said. "His ankle is still to be non-weight-bearing, and he hasn't managed to climb into a buggy yet. I'll bring her. If not me, then Gabe's daed."

"Gut enough." Daed smiled. "Have fun, Bridget."

She wasn't sure what had happened to make Daed accept Gabe. It didn't seem plausible for the bishop's softly spoken proverbs from over a week ago to have done the trick. Gabe's discussion with Daed after the fact didn't seem a likely cause for conversion, but maybe it had been effective.

Bishop Brunstetter drove in silence as they navigated the narrow driveway toward the main road. His mouth had settled into a slight frown, and he stole frequent glances at the woods on either side; whether he watched for bears or deer, he didn't say. Or maybe he searched the darkness, waiting for Gott Himself to appear and judge them, as he'd announced would happen one week ago. The day of *the kiss*.

Funny how Bridget now measured time in relation to that kiss.

She glanced at the older man. "Agnes is chaperoning?"

Bishop Brunstetter sighed. Frowned. Shook his head and pointed. "Some Englisch teens are having a party by the pond. Probably some alcohol involved."

Bridget twisted to peer at the ice-skating pond as they rode past. About three dozen vehicles were parked there, and the bonfire burned brightly. Laughter and loud music drifted on the air.

The bishop's observation had nothing to do with Agnes. Bridget waited for his next statement, which would, she hoped, have something to do with Gabe's wanting to marry her.

Unless he'd been courting both her *and* Agnes.

If that were the case....

Her heart hurt, weighed down by dread.

She shook off her pessimism. He'd said he would court her alone. He'd asked for Daed's permission.

She glanced at the bishop and tried to think of a way to shift the conversation to the only topic on her mind.

The miles passed in silence. Not even an owl hooted as they traveled through the small town to the outskirts on the other side where the bishop lived.

Would she have to initiate the conversation herself?

She tried to think of a way to do that, but couldn't. It boiled down to the fact that if Gabe hadn't asked the bishop, then he wasn't thinking about marriage the way she was.

Tears pricked at Bridget's eyes. That meant one thing.

Nein proposal.

Unless things were done differently in this district.

Hope flared again.

Bishop Brunstetter pulled into his driveway and parked in front of the haus.

The front door opened, and Gabe hobbled out onto the porch with his crutches, followed a second later by Agnes. She hovered close beside Gabe, the way a mamm spots a boppli just beginning to walk, looking ready to scoop him up and cuddle him close if he fell. Since Gabe had been working and moving around the haus for the better part of this week, Bridget didn't see the need for such solicitousness. But yesterday, the construction team led by Gabe and his daed had started working on a storefront in town that was being remodeled for a new business. Daed wouldn't say what type of business, or whose. Not to Bridget, anyway. And Noah was being just as closemouthed when he was home. He went to Arie's haus to spend time with her most evenings.

Bridget wanted to ask what Agnes was doing there, but felt that would be rude. She climbed down from the buggy.

"Hiya, Bridget." Agnes smiled at her. Bridget looked for signs of a smirk but didn't see any. Just friendliness. "I've been helping with Gabe's care while he's been laid up. I kum out every evening to help with meals and to make him some tea."

Gabe rolled his eyes. "I haven't been 'laid up.'" He stepped away from her.

Agnes followed him. "Frau Brunstetter said she couldn't have gotten along without me."

Bridget nodded. While Agnes's words sounded a bit prideful, the truth was, she needed to be useful. She had the gift of service, of mercy. Bridget got that.

Unfortunately, Bridget didn't have the gift of mercy. She was much too practical. Or maybe too selfish. "I'm sure everyone appreciates you."

Frau Brunstetter joined them on the porch. "Kum in, kum in. Dinner is almost ready. Agnes and I made pasties."

Gabe furrowed his forehead and glanced at Frau Brunstetter. "You still haven't told me what 'pasties' are."

The bishop's frau smiled. "They're meat and vegetable pies made with venison, potatoes, onions, and rutabagas. I'd never heard of them before we moved to Michigan. But now...." She shook her head. "Can't get enough of them."

"Rutabagas?" Gabe asked.

"A type of root vegetable," Frau Brunstetter said.

Gabe wrinkled his nose. "Vegetables. Ugh." He winked at Bridget.

The bishop's frau swatted his arm. "Oh, you." She glanced at Bridget. "You have to watch out for this one."

"Heard the pasties were popular with the miners up here," the bishop put in. "Easy to carry into the copper and iron ore mines. Little bit of trivia." He grinned. "I'll get the horse taken care of so we can eat." He drove toward the barn as his frau went back inside.

After a moment, and a somewhat sour glance at Bridget, Agnes did the same.

Bridget climbed the steps. When she reached the porch, Gabe gave her a quick hug, then brushed his lips over hers before releasing her. "This is beyond frustrating. I asked the bishop if he'd speak to you. I know it's too soon, but I'd like to write Mamm and tell her. He said to hold off. So, this is me holding off." He chuckled, then kissed her again.

He'd wanted to ask? Her heart lightened, and she smiled. "I'd best see how I can help with dinner."

"Ach, believe me, they've got it covered. Just beware if you are served weak tea that tastes like freshly mowed grass. I think Agnes is secretly trying to poison me. Or turn me into a milk cow. Those eat grass, right?"

Bridget laughed as she started inside. It was a relief to know that Gabe didn't welcome Agnes's presence.

"I'm serious." Gabe caught the door and held it open for her. "You've been warned."

The kitchen smelled tantalizingly of onion, garlic, and spices. Frau Brunstetter set two pies in the center of the table.

"Is there anything I can do to help?" Bridget took off her shoes and lined them up on the mat by the door, then hurried to the sink to wash up.

"Nein, just have a seat across from Gabe. Where the pink mug is."

Bridget did as she was told.

The door opened, and the bishop came in, a furrow in his brow. He glanced at his frau, then moved to the sink without a word.

"Should I tell Daed dinner's ready?" Gabe asked. He headed out of the room without waiting for an answer.

"Glad you could join us, Bridget." Agnes sat beside her. "We've been taking gut care of Gabe."

"Agnes has been a big help." Frau Brunstetter sat at the foot of the table. "I've enjoyed having her here."

Agnes smiled and wiggled a little in the seat.

Gabe and his daed came into the room and lowered themselves into their chairs. Gabe propped his crutches against the wall behind him as the bishop bowed his head and said, "Let's pray."

Bridget was about to close her eyes when the bishop jerked his head up and turned to stare out the window.

She followed his gaze.

There was nothing there.

⌒

The meat pasties turned out much better than Gabe had anticipated. And upon his first taste of a rutabaga, he decided it was somewhat like a turnip. A little milder, perhaps. Turnips, he knew. Too well. He wasn't a fan. The pasties, though—even with venison and rutabaga—he would eat again without complaint. And he wouldn't make a single sigh of discontentment over the cherry cobbler that had finished the meal, even if it was served with a mug of weak tea that smelled like freshly mowed grass. He struggled to resist the urge to moo.

In lieu of tea, Bridget was offered either warm apple cider or hot chocolate.

Totally unfair. He would have preferred the chocolatey goodness.

When dinner was finished, the bishop got out a checkerboard and placed it on the table between Bridget and Gabe.

Chaperoned dates were the pits. Gabe exhaled a sigh as he set out the pieces, giving Bridget the red ones, himself the black because his mood was dark. Frustrated. He wouldn't hope for a decent kiss, since the bishop would be taking Bridget home. The upside was, Agnes would leave at the same time rather than hover around him for the rest of the evening. The new work in town had gotten him off work earlier, and he'd spent as much of the afternoon as possible with the Behrs, returning to the bishop's haus to find Agnes waiting.

He should be grateful for her help. But what, exactly, had she helped with besides brewing awful-tasting tea? Or making more of the ointment he applied to himself? She was a bigger help to the bishop's frau than to him directly. But why didn't she go help Bridget, instead? With a broken wrist, couldn't Bridget use some assistance? And Agnes claimed Bridget was her best friend. Seemed to him a girl should rush to help her best friend. Not to mention respect her best friend's budding romance.

He realized his train of thought was immature, like that of a sulky child about to have a temper tantrum. And it was affecting his mood. If he wasn't careful, grumpy Gabe would scare Bridget off. Gabe dipped his head. *Gott, please help my attitude. Danki that Hosea softened enough to allow this date with Bridget. Danki also for Agnes's help, even if I don't appreciate her flirting.*

He forced his attention to the game, but a sense of restlessness still plagued him. His nerves were on edge, and his crankiness irritated himself. Being that Bridget, who wasn't known for her gaming prowess, won multiple matches in a row, she could probably tell that his focus wasn't on the game. Or on her.

When Agnes stepped out of the room, Bridget gave him a worried frown. "What's wrong?"

"Nothing." He shook his head. "I don't know. Just...." How could he put into words what even he could not identify? "Uneasy."

She nodded as if she understood. "He's been nicer lately."

Huh? Gabe frowned at the liquid grass in his mug.

"That's a plus, ain't so?"

He processed her comment another moment, until understanding dawned. "Your daed?"

"Jah. He's not what has you uneasy, is he?"

How could he answer when he really didn't know?

Her frown deepened. "Maybe it's whatever has the bishop on edge. He kept looking at the woods and acted worried all the way here. And when he came to pick me up, he and Daed were talking seriously about something."

Gabe shrugged. "It might be that fiery chariot thing coming with judgment that he predicted. I don't know." He glanced around. Agnes was nowhere in sight. He leaned closer and lowered his voice to add, "Or maybe it's that freshly mowed grass tea. I'm probably starting to grow horns." Then he grimaced. "Sorry. That wasn't nice. It's probably just my irritation at being limited in what I can do."

Limited in so many different ways. Not only physically, but also in his courtship efforts. To compound his discontent, he'd talked Noah into becoming a volunteer firefighter, and now Gabe couldn't even enjoy spending time with him at the station.

Kissing Bridget would definitely improve his mood.

He forced a smile and moved a piece. "King me."

⌒

An hour later, the bishop had gone outside to hitch up the buggy so he could take Agnes and Bridget home when, across the room, the battery-operated radio crackled to life. A broken voice, accompanied by static, broke the silence. "Fire reported out by"—*crackle, crackle, crackle*—"campfire"—*crackle, crackle*—"pond."

Gabe shot to his feet.

Alarm filled Bridget. Gabe couldn't seriously think he was up to firefighting. "Gabe, nein."

His daed looked up from the book he was reading. Or trying to read while keeping an eye on Gabe and Bridget. At least Agnes wasn't there shooting glares at them from across the room. "Nein, Gabe. You're a volunteer. You need to heal."

"I'm the one who talked Noah into volunteering, and I promised I'd be there for his first fire. Bridget is headed home, anyway."

Wait. Noah was a volunteer firefighter, too? When had that happened? A twinge of fear worked through Bridget. Gabe was still badly injured, and with his love of adventure and risk…. She opened her mouth to voice her own objection. "Nein—"

"Besides, this is just a campfire that's gotten a little out of control, from what I heard." Gabe gestured to the radio. "I'll do the easy stuff. Don't worry, Daed."

His daed opened his mouth but then shut it again as Gabe grabbed a large bag from the broom closet and then hobbled toward the door, the bag bouncing against his crutch.

"Gabe, nein." Bridget stood, reached out. "Listen to your daed."

Gabe hesitated a moment. "I'll be fine. Don't worry." The door slammed behind him.

Bridget pressed her fingers against her mouth and moved to the window. Her stomach roiled with nausea. Her heart clenched. Tears blurred her vision. It was hard to breathe through the pressure building in her chest.

Agnes ran into the room. "Where's he going? We've got to stop him!" She raced out the door and grabbed at Gabe's arm as a pickup truck pulled into the driveway.

Gabe shook Agnes off and climbed into the truck. The door slammed shut. And with a rev of the engine and a scatter of gravel, he was gone.

"Stubborn," his daed muttered. "He's going to hurt himself yet."

As if he wasn't already hurt.

What would Bridget do if he didn't kum back?

Agnes stomped back inside, tears pooling on her lashes. She reached for Bridget and drew her in for a hug. With Agnes sobbing on her shoulder, Bridget couldn't keep her own crying at bay. Her tears tumbled out, unwelkum yet unstoppable. She clung to Agnes just as tightly as Agnes clung to her.

"There, there. What's all this?" The bishop's frau made a tsking sound as she entered the room, then wrapped her arms around both of them. "One would think it was the end of the world."

Gabe's daed cleared his throat. "Gabe left to fight a fire."

"What?" The older woman spun around. "He's in nein shape to do that."

The bishop trudged into the room next, his face drawn. "Buggy is hitched and ready to go. Thought I'd better to get you girls on home, but now I feel it's best to keep you here over-nacht. Wind is starting to pick up." He pulled a cell phone out of his pocket and handed it to Bridget. "Call your folks and let them know."

25

As he maneuvered carefully out of Patrick's pickup, Gabe spotted flames licking the grass and brush surrounding the large fire pit. The logs positioned around the pit had ignited, with sparks billowing toward the nearby trees. The flickering fire illuminated the scared faces of the Englisch teens huddled safely to one side, their arms piled with blankets and the flotsam and jetsam of drinks and snacks. As he balanced his weight on the crutches, Gabe stepped on a discarded bag of marshmallows.

Since nein fire trucks had arrived, Gabe and Patrick joined some of the teens who were trying to douse the flames using buckets of water. Since there were only two buckets, their efforts weren't doing much gut, even though they'd formed a bucket brigade that stretched from the pond to the fire pit. Gabe positioned himself closest to the fire, tossed aside one of the crutches, and propped himself on the other while he awkwardly tossed water on the inferno before passing the bucket back down the line.

Soon Noah arrived with an Englisch volunteer firefighter and another pail. Not that a third one made any difference.

Fifteen minutes later, the situation hadn't improved. The howling, gusting wind had blown the fire into the nearby trees. Dead leaves on the ground ignited. And the teens had started leaving as more volunteer firemen showed up.

Where were the fire trucks?

One of the men pulled a shovel and a chainsaw from the back of his pickup. Another man brought a leaf blower. They ventured into the woods to do what they could with their tools to keep the fire from spreading.

Gabe pulled in a breath, coughing on the smoke, and threw another pailful of water on the flames. He tried putting some weight on his bad ankle, but the pain was unbearable.

By the time the first fire truck arrived, the surrounding forest was an inferno, the flames reaching their taunting fingers toward the heavens.

The fire chief barked out a series of orders to evacuate the nearby houses, call in reinforcements from local fire departments, and send the bystanders home—provided they didn't live in an area in danger of catching fire.

Gabe abandoned his bucket and hobbled to the fire truck to help with the hoses. The crutches got in his way as he tried to work, so he tossed them aside. His ankle screamed its objections, and the torn muscles in his thighs burned. By force of sheer grit, he shook off the pain that threatened to render him unconscious.

The wind howled, further fanning the blaze, as if Gott Himself sided with the fire, not against it. Or maybe it wasn't Gott but the evil one. Gabe could've sworn he saw faces in the flames, wearing expressions that mocked the firefighters' efforts. And the crackling of burning trees was like sinister laughter. One dead tree fell with a great shower of sparks. Choking clouds of noxious black smoke rose into the darkness. Fiery embers twinkled like stars in the hot, swirling air before cascading to the ground like gleeful fire fiends, setting the forest alight.

The fire chief glanced at the fire truck and swore under his breath. He grabbed his radio off his belt and strode away.

A few minutes later, the hose started spluttering as the water pressure dropped.

They could pump water from the pond, but unless more help arrived soon, their efforts would be doomed.

The nearest fire department was miles and miles away, and also staffed by volunteers.

Gabe groaned.

They were doomed.

⌒

The radio in the bishop's living room crackled to life again, and Bridget startled where she sat, slumped, at the kitchen table. There was still a lot of static, but it sounded as if they were asking for help from other townships.

The wind howled, and Bridget glanced toward the window. An orange glow filled the sky in the direction of the pond, and her home. Where was the fire? After the bishop had finished unharnessing the horse and taking care of the buggy, both he and Gabe's daed had gone outside, talking as they walked toward the road. About what, she hadn't a clue.

The bishop's frau had then said she needed to pray, so she'd left Bridget and Agnes staring at a plate of cookies, a pan of Agnes's fudge, and two mugs of hot chocolate—and nothing to say.

Agnes filled the silence with her sniffles. She had a rapidly emptying box of tissues on one side of her and a damp pile of wadded-up tissues on the other. Bridget bit back a growl of irritation, since, as far as she knew, Agnes's only reason for crying was *Gabe*.

Everything inside Bridget cried out, over and over and over, *Oh, Gott. Oh, Gott. Oh, Gott.* Hopefully, der Herr understood what she was trying to say, even if she didn't have the words to express it.

The fire was obviously more than just an "out-of-control campfire," as Gabe had claimed. The firefighters wouldn't have called for assistance unless the inferno was bigger. Badder. More dangerous.

Agnes blew her nose yet again, adding the used tissue to her growing stack before reaching for a fresh one. Was Bridget a heartless person for not crying over the man she claimed to be in love with while he performed a dangerous job?

Nein, she wasn't calloused and uncaring. Worry for Gabe, and for Noah, filled her. Along with worry for her family's home. For other families' homes.

Daed had spoken with tension in his voice when she'd called to say she would be spending the nacht at the bishop's. Had something else happened to upset him? Maybe knowing she would be sleeping in the same haus as Gabe? That was what she'd attributed it to, but maybe it was because of the fire—though she wasn't sure he would've known about the fire when they spoke. If Noah was truly a firefighter, maybe he had a radio Daed had overheard.

Bridget felt numb. Helpless. All she could do was pray for Gott to intervene somehow in whatever it was that had everyone—herself included—feeling so distressed and unsettled.

Gott? The refrain started again. *Oh, Gott. Oh, Gott. Oh, Gott....*

She glanced at Gabe's daed's Bible on the hutch in the kitchen. Would Gabriel mind if she looked through it for a promise to hold on to? Or was Bible reading by women taboo in this district? Bridget eyed Agnes. Would she tell and get Bridget into trouble? Or would Gabe's daed view her reading of the Scriptures as nein big deal, as Gabe had?

"Be still, and know that I am God: I will be exalted among the heathen, I will be exalted in the earth." The verse she'd memorized from the Psalms came to mind. And even though she still felt uneasy, she sensed something else beneath her anxiety—a peaceful assurance that Gott had this situation, and all her loved ones, completely in His hands.

The radio crackled with a response from a neighboring fire department. "Sending reinforcements," said a voice, sounding much clearer than the earlier messages.

The reply was a series of crackled, broken words.

An hour later, Frau Brunstetter came into the room and glanced at the clock. "We need to get to bed, ladies. Gabe will be here when you wake in the morgen, I'm sure. We have only one spare room, so you'll have to share a bed."

"Ach, I don't think I can sleep a wink," Agnes blubbered.

Bridget shook her head to show she felt the same. She wanted to go out there and do something.

"He'll need you in the morgen." The bishop's frau pointed toward the stairs. "Go on, now."

Agnes exhaled an exaggerated sigh and then plodded away, taking the tissue box with her. Bridget carried the empty mugs to the sink, then stared out the window at the orange glow in the sky. Was it her imagination, or had it grown bigger and brighter?

Her stomach knotted.

This was bad. Very, very bad. *Where are You, Gott?*

Wasn't there a verse somewhere in the Bible about Gott being in the fire with the men? She reached for the Bible.

⌇

Gabe's legs quivered and ached, and his ankle throbbed with every step. The initial evacuation orders had been delivered, but, as the fire burned out of control, moving ever closer to the homes in its path, he had nein recourse but to keep working.

With the fire's place of origin having been completely consumed, the firefighters refilled the truck with water from the pond and then moved to an area the fire hadn't yet reached, in hopes of halting its approach. But with the high winds, even the slightest shift in direction could alter the fire, too.

They were fighting a fire with so many unknown variables.

Gabe paused for a break, dropping down on a fallen log to drink from a chilled water bottle someone had been kind enough to bring. He stretched out his injured leg, hoping to ease the throbbing of his sprained ankle.

Stretching didn't help. And considering the pressure he felt as the splint pressed into his skin, his ankle had likely become badly swollen once again.

"Likely"? Make that "definitely." He'd been on it all nacht.

He shouldn't have sat down. Now he might not be able to get up again. Where were his crutches? He remembered seeing someone pick them up off the ground, but where had they gone? Into the back of someone's pickup?

Noah collapsed beside him with a water bottle of his own. His face was grimy. "Quite the introduction to my new position as a volunteer firefighter. Nothing like a trial by fire." He gave a wry laugh. "I'm kind of wondering where Gott is in this."

Gabe stared into the dark woods ahead of them. "I know what you mean." The little they'd managed to do on the ground seemed futile, with the fire spreading through the treetops, egged on by the relentless wind. *Gott, where are You?*

They needed help from above. A fire retardant was already being added to the ground to try to stop the fire from spreading, but an airplane spraying the same substance would be far more effective.

So would rain, heavy and long-lasting. Gabe glanced at the sky. The faint gray hue signaled the onset of dawn. Not that they would have a view of the sun. Not with all the smoke.

But with the limited view, it still was obvious that neither form of help was forthcoming.

Gabe drank the last bit of water in his bottle, then struggled to get to his feet. His injured parts screamed in protest. He shouldn't have taken that break. He handed the water bottle to Noah to dispose of, then grabbed the leaf blower to clear the dead leaves and needles in an effort to create another fire barrier. Not that it would do much gut with the wind, and the treetops aflame.

Another gust of wind carried the stench of smoke in his direction. Flames leaped into view.

"The fire jumped the barrier," announced the team captain. "We need to evacuate. Now!"

Noah jumped to his feet and ran.

Gabe tried to run after him, leaning on the leaf blower for support. After several steps, he stumbled, stepped into a hole with his bad ankle, and fell.

He tried to get to his feet but couldn't. And his team had abandoned him.

The roar of the approaching fire grew louder. The flames nein longer laughed. They shrieked.

Gabe sucked in a breath. "Gott, I'm sorry for my stubbornness, and for letting my frustration about being sidelined compel me to jump into danger before my body was ready to handle the task. Daed was right again. This fire was too much for me. If You still have a purpose for me and Bridget, give me another chance. Help me to know how to escape this fire." The words came without conscious thought, because he surely wouldn't be able to compose a prayer like that without Gott's help.

A glowing wave of flames, like a giant rug unfurling, came toward him. Its heat seared his skin like a blowtorch.

"Gott, help me!"

26

Bridget stifled a yawn and carefully slid out of the bed so she wouldn't wake Agnes. The poor girl had taken forever to fall asleep last nacht, with her nonstop wailing.

She tiptoed over to the window and peered out at the sun as it began to rise. The sky was gray and ashy, and the heavy odor of smoke hung low over the area. The bishop's haus was finally quiet.

Bridget had struggled to fall asleep, herself. For what felt like hours she'd lain awake, trying to ignore the unfamiliar creaks and groans of the dwelling, while praying and listening for Gabe to return.

She hadn't heard him, but she did hear men talking downstairs in low voices. At one point, she'd thought she heard Daed; but when she'd gotten out of bed, located her borrowed robe and socks, and padded out of the room, she'd seen a car's headlights disappearing down the driveway.

Now she dressed in her clothes from yesterday, being careful not to disturb Agnes, and went downstairs.

In the kitchen, the bishop's frau puttered around, removing the tea-kettle from the stove when it started to whistle. Oatmeal bubbled in a pan, but Bridget didn't notice anything else cooking. Nein toast, nein biscuits, nein eggs, nein breakfast meat. Nothing.

Of course, Bridget wasn't actually hungry. After a nacht of troubled sleep and frazzled nerves, all she wanted was a glass of cold water and a breath of air that was free of smoke.

And the safe return of Gabe and Noah.

"We're eating light these days." The older woman spoke as if she'd read Bridget's thoughts. "Hens aren't laying right now, and we used up the last of the bacon and sausage yesterday. I suppose I could fry up some venison steaks...."

"Oatmeal is fine." That beat the precooked bacon and powdered eggs Bridget's family had breakfasted on when they first moved to the area. "Did Gabe kum in last nacht?" She glanced around for clues. She didn't see either the bishop or Gabe's daed, but maybe they were outside doing chores. Or something.

"Heard the firemen were going to take shifts so they could sleep a few hours someplace. Probably at the station." Frau Brunstetter stirred the oatmeal, then lowered the heat. "So, nein, he didn't kum in. Miah and Gabriel did go to the station for a few hours to get the latest news. Your daed came by, sometime between ten or eleven last nacht. Your mamm was having trouble breathing with all the smoke, and he decided to take her and your younger siblings to the Lower Peninsula. He said he'd be back as soon as he'd gotten them temporarily settled somewhere. He asked if I would wake you so you could go with them, but I thought you'd rather be here for Gabe."

Bridget nodded. She *needed* to be here.

The bishop's frau didn't turn to look at her. "If you want to go, we'll find a ride for you. Other Amish are evacuating, too."

"I'd like to stay. Danki for understanding." How was Gabe? He'd barely been hobbling around on crutches when he'd gone out to fight the fire. Bridget sighed and breathed another prayer for him. Then she crossed the room, grabbed a glass from a cabinet, and went to the sink to fill it with water. "Mamm has asthma. The smoke would have made it extremely hard for her to breathe." At least her family was safe. But she hadn't heard that they were evacuating people.

Her stomach cramped when she realized that meant they expected loss of property. Loss of life. Was her family's new home okay? Were their neighbors' homes? "Has any—"

"I'm sure Gabe's fine. How's Agnes?" The bishop's wife gave her a sympathetic smile. "I doubt you got much sleep, with her sniffing and sniveling most of the nacht, but we didn't have anywhere else to put the two of you."

"I imagine she'll wake up rather stuffy in the head." At least that was what happened to Bridget on the rare occasion she cried herself to sleep— an activity the Amish frowned upon. *Big girls don't cry. Only a boppli cries.* She'd never say so to Agnes, but her behavior last nacht had seemed over- dramatic and unnecessary.

Maybe there was more to Agnes's actions than Bridget knew. Maybe it wasn't all about Gabe's leaving. Maybe Agnes was afraid of the fire and didn't know how else to express her fear. Whatever the reason, Bridget needed to show grace and pray for her.

Bridget's stomach cramped again, and she set down the water glass without drinking anything, afraid she might be sick. She needed to distract herself, somehow. She looked around for something to do. Some way to help. The table. She could set the table.

She went to the cupboard and got out a stack of bowls for the oatmeal. In the pantry, she found the crock of brown sugar, a box of raisins, an almost empty jar of maple syrup, and the cinnamon shaker. She set everything on the table, along with a pitcher of cream the bishop's frau handed to her.

The door opened, and Gabe's daed came in, followed by the bishop. Exhaustion shadowed the men's eyes, and the clothes they'd worn the day before hung limply from their frames, dampened, soiled, and smelling of smoke. Had the men spent the nacht in the barn? Or gone to assess the damage? She remembered the bishop's frau mentioning that they had gone to the fire station for firsthand news. They must've stayed there.

The bishop scanned the room, then went to his frau, his shoulders sagging. "We were just at the fire station, getting an update," he said quietly. "The Zooks' haus burned down. I hope the family evacuated, but if they left, they never came by here."

Bridget's breath hitched. Agnes really did have something to cry about—and nein place to go. *Lord, help her. Help us. Help the firefighters.* "What about my home?" It was located only a half mile from Agnes's.

Gabe's daed shook his head. "Nein word yet. Your home isn't visible from the road. But I won't lie to you…things aren't looking gut. The fire would've gone through that area before it reached the Zooks'."

A nauseating lump settled in the pit of Bridget's stomach. Her home was likely gone, but at least her family was safe. She pulled in a fortifying breath. She never thought she would thank der Herr for Mamm's asthma, but her condition might've saved her parents and younger siblings. *Danki, Lord, that my family is safe. Be with Gabe and Noah, wherever they are.*

"Probably shouldn't say anything to Agnes about her haus until we know for sure." The bishop's frau sent Bridget a pointed look. "I'd hate to distress the poor girl more, based only on rumor."

Jah. Bridget could only imagine another round of tears.

The bishop sighed. "It's not a rumor. If she asks, I won't lie to her. In fact, I think it'd be wiser to tell her sooner than later." He peered at the oatmeal. "Looks ready."

His frau nodded. "Get washed up, and we'll eat. Agnes can have breakfast when she gets up. Poor girl was an emotional wreck last nacht. Cried for hours." She shook her head.

"Hmm." Gabriel Lapp frowned. Probably figuring the same thing as Bridget had—that Agnes had been emotional over Gabe's leaving. But that supposition nein longer fit. Gabe had made it clear he courted Bridget. And what girl would behave as Agnes had around the girlfriend of a man she loved? Maybe it was the fire she'd been afraid of.

But that didn't seem to fit, either.

Gabe's daed peered at Bridget. "How are you holding up?"

Bridget squirmed. "I want to go out and help. See the damage for myself." Except she wouldn't be able to see everything. She wasn't Gott, after all. She had to have faith that He knew what was happening, and had control of the situation, even though the current reports were bad.

It was hard to believe what she couldn't see.

But she couldn't admit such a thing to the bishop and a preacher.

She forced a smile, though it probably looked more like a grimace. "I'm praying a lot."

Gabe's daed nodded. "There's nein such thing as a wasted prayer. It's human nature to struggle to have faith in the unseen. There's worry, for sure. I'm clinging to Hebrews eleven, verse one: '*Now faith is the substance of things hoped for, the evidence of things not seen.*' I'm choosing to trust that Gabe is all right, that Gott has this situation under control, and that '*all things work together for good to them that love God, to them who are the called according to his purpose,*' as it says in Romans eight, twenty-eight."

That must've been the verse Gabe was looking for when he'd asked Bridget to read aloud from the book of Romans. He should've asked his daed, after all. Bridget tried to smile but failed. She would try to remember the verse so she could repeat it for him later.

If he survived.

Her stomach cramped again. *Ach, Gott....*

"Stand strong. Have faith. Gott has a plan in this," the preacher told her.

Easier said than done. But Bridget nodded. And, honestly, beneath her fear, there was that quiet peace again—the assurance that, nein matter what, and even though she didn't know how, it would be okay. Even though her haus was likely burned to the ground, her family had gone far away, her brother's condition was unknown, along with Gabe's, and she wasn't actually engaged to be married...somehow she was being held in the middle of the firestorm.

"Breakfast is served." Frau Brunstetter set the pot of oatmeal on the table. "Please help yourselves." She leveled a look at her ehemann. "You do realize that with the Zooks homeless, we'll be putting Agnes and Gabe up for a while. The rest of the Zook family, too, when they return."

And the Brunstetters' cupboards were almost bare. Due to lack of money? Or nein time to go grocery shopping? A bad year for the garden?

The bishop merely nodded as he reached for a towel to dry his hands. "Gott will provide. He always does."

Except that it sometimes seemed He provided for the few and not the many. It seemed He ought to at least bless the bishop.

Bridget pushed the thought away. Gott *had* provided for her and her family. A place to stay when their home was uninhabitable. Casseroles brought by so they'd have food. Jobs for Daed and Noah. The innumerable things Gabe had done to help them out, despite Daed's initial treatment of him.

With that in mind, she would trust Gott with this.

"Let's pray." The bishop sat at the head of the table. "And let's remember the firefighters, too."

Bridget bowed her head. *Lord, be with Gabe and Noah. And help me to keep on trusting You.*

⌒

Gabe was going to die. Unless he somehow acquired superhuman strength and could scramble to his feet and outrun the flames. Though he tried multiple times to get to his feet, as slowly and as awkwardly as possible, escaping on his own didn't seem to be an option. He'd definitely undone any healing that might've occurred since the ice-skating fiasco.

Unwilling to just lie there and die, he'd yelled himself hoarse, but nobody had kum. He attempted to crawl to safety, but without the ability to use his legs, his upper-body strength quickly wore out.

As the sun rose a little higher in the sky, the fire burned closer and closer. Maybe fifty feet away from him now. Gabe was unable to peel his gaze from the flickering flames. If only he had one of those fire covers used by smokejumpers who parachuted from planes into the thick of wildfires. But that sort of protective gear wasn't issued to volunteers.

Gabe struggled to breathe in the oppressive heat. The fire was maybe forty feet away. *Gott, comfort my family and Bridget. I'm sorry I didn't listen to Daed, but that radio call made the fire sound so insignificant.*

Could he have done anything to prevent the fire from starting in the first place?

Entertaining such things was a waste of time and effort. He couldn't rewind the reel of life and redo any of his actions, never mind the actions of the Englisch teens he hadn't known anything about.

He eyed the fire as it crept closer and closer. Sweat beaded on his forehead and dripped into his eyes. He wanted to close them, but he decided to face the fire head-on, like a man. Like the early church martyrs. Maybe confessing his sins at this point would be wise. He'd done so on previous occasions, but not for his most recent sins, such as his irritation at Agnes.

Gott, please forgive me for my sins…even the ones I don't remember.

"Ye have not, because ye ask not."

Gabe blinked. *What?*

"Ye have not, because ye ask not."

It seemed Gott shared the bishop's habit of talking in riddles. Assuming what Gabe heard, or thought he heard, was the voice of der Herr.

Gabe bowed his head again after taking another glance at the flames flaring ever closer. Thirty feet now. "Lord, save me, or I'll die."

Did he really want to be saved? Even if he suffered third-degree burns? What kind of a life would that be? He cringed. *Living without any long-term injuries would be nice.*

Was his prayer as disrespectful as it seemed to him? Probably so.

He'd rather be escorted into the presence of the Almighty with praise on his lips than with disrespect and ingratitude for all the mercies Gott had granted him.

He tried to find the words he wanted to use. A verse from Revelation came to mind: "*Holy, holy, holy, Lord God Almighty, which was, and is, and is to come.*"

That seemed like a gut start. But he had a limited number of verses committed to memory. If he survived this, that fact would change.

Except…what about the words he'd spoken? *Lord, save me, or I'll die.* They reminded him of something read by one of the preachers last church Sunday. *Help me remember.*

It took a minute or two. The wind swirled in the opposite direction, halting the fire momentarily. Giving him time to think.

Yes, now he remembered. It was from the gospel of Matthew, the account of Jesus's calming the stormy sea when His disciples were with Him in a boat and feared for their lives. They said to Him, "Save us, for we die!" Jesus rebuked the wind and the waves, but not before rebuking the disciples for their lack of faith. "O ye of little faith," He called them. "Why do you fear?" And the disciples marveled at Jesus's power to command the wind and the waves.

The wind switched direction again, and the flames ignited some of the trees overhead. Sparks landed on the ground around Gabe. His shirt was probably soaked with sweat. He tried to recall the frigid feel of the water from the polar bear plunge in an effort to cool himself.

"What manner of man is this, that even the winds and the sea obey Him?" He spoke the words out loud, in spite of the difficulty of drawing a clear breath. "Gott, we have the winds, and three of the Great Lakes are nearby. Help me to have the faith to believe that You have all those elements in Your control, that You can change our weather. That You can calm the wind and send rain from the heavens. You said that I have not because I ask not. Well, I'm asking now. Help my unbelief. Help me to have faith in Your abilities. Not just faith, but a strong faith. Help me to…."

The wind changed direction, lifting the hairs on his head as it picked up speed. Shifting. Lowering the temperature from that of a fiery inferno to something like an arctic blast. Icy drops of water pelted his face. He held out his hands toward the sky to make sure he hadn't imagined them.

Harder and faster, Gott's answer showered down on his head. The fire hissed. Spit, then stalled, smoking.

Gabe lifted his arms higher. "Holy, holy, holy is the Lord Gott Almighty, who was, and is, and is to kum." Tears mixed with the freezing rain and rolled down his cheeks. "Help me never to doubt again."

A short time later, Gabe heard men shouting in the distance. He tried to call out but couldn't attain the necessary volume due to his coughing.

"Gabe!" The voices became louder as the men got closer.

Gabe coughed. "Here!" His own shout was raspy, but it would suffice. They would find him. After all, Gott answered prayer.

"Gabe!"

Noah and Patrick burst through the trees.

⁓

Bridget finished her lunch—an odd sort of soup made with root vegetables—and carried her dishes to the sink. She glanced out the window at the heavy gray smoke. Was that rain? It wasn't falling heavily, but it had to help, ain't so? The winds had calmed, too.

A pickup truck pulled in and parked. An Englisch man got out and went into the barn, where the bishop and Gabe's daed were working. Or praying. They'd said they intended to fast and pray.

Bridget wanted to go find out what was happening, but she couldn't kum up with a gut reason for being in the barn. If they were fasting, it wouldn't be appropriate to offer to bring koffee and cookies.

She turned away from the window, determined to stay busy, at least until the man left. She squirted a little soap into the dishpan and then ran the hot water while she went to collect the rest of the dishes.

Agnes stumbled into the room, her eyes bloodshot, her nose running, her lips quivering.

"I saved some lunch for you." Bridget went to retrieve the bowl of vegetable soup she'd set on the back of the woodstove.

"Is it lunchtime?" Agnes looked at the clock. "I'm not hungry, but danki."

The bishop's frau bustled back into the room. "You need to eat, dear, to keep up your strength. I started some water running in the basement tubs, and hooked up the wringer washer. Since we don't yet know when you'll be going home, I figured we'd get some laundry done today so you girls will have clean clothes. Won't that be fun?"

Fun? Bridget blinked and looked at Agnes.

"Danki, Katherine, but we don't have anything else to change into." Agnes's voice sounded hoarse. "And…and we'll be going home this evening, I imagine." She sank into a kitchen chair. "Any news?"

She didn't specify from whom. Gabe? Her family?

"Bridget's parents and younger siblings have evacuated due to her mamm's asthma. Maybe your folks did, too." The bishop's frau poured some hot water into a mug, added a tea bag, and then sat down across from Agnes. She pursed her lips as she ran her fingertip around the edge of the mug.

Bridget glanced away, thinking of going into the other room. If Katherine Brunstetter decided to follow the bishop's suggestion by telling Agnes about the destruction of her family's haus, Bridget didn't need to be present.

Just then the door opened, and three men came inside: Bishop Brunstetter, Gabe's daed, and the Englisch stranger.

"Bridget." Gabe's daed cleared his throat. "You might want to have a seat."

Bridget quivered. The grim expression on his face, the presence of the stranger, the heaviness of the atmosphere…. Her stomach knotted. She searched for the quiet peace she'd felt earlier. Grasped it and clung tightly. *Gott, let them both be okay.*

She sank into a chair. "Is it Gabe? Or Noah?"

27

The EMTs loaded Gabe into the back of the ambulance as some of the other volunteer firefighters looked on.

"I'm no doctor, but I'm guessing you'll need surgery on that ankle." One of the EMTs shook his head and muttered something else Gabe didn't catch due to another coughing fit.

"You inhaled a lot of smoke," another paramedic told him, his expression grim. "We'll get you started on oxygen."

Patrick reached out, folded one of his hands over Gabe's, and bowed his head. "Lord God, please bless Gabe with a speedy recovery and complete healing." He glanced up and met Gabe's eyes. "I'll follow you to the hospital and wait for you there."

That, coming from a man battling cancer, really touched Gabe. Tears burned his eyes. If Gott could turn the direction of a forest fire, He could heal people with grim diagnoses. *Gott, please heal Patrick.*

"I'll go with him," Noah said.

Friends such as Noah and Patrick were something to be thankful for. So was his daed. Gabe wanted to tell him about the miracle in the woods. Bridget needed to hear about it, too.

Gabe coughed. "Stop by the Brunstetters.' My daed's there. He needs to know. Tell him I'm alright."

Patrick nodded. "I already sent someone to notify your dad and your girl."

Gabe grimaced. Bridget was the last person he wanted seeing him like this. He wanted her to see him as strong. Invincible. Heroic. Not a man succumbing to weakness of the flesh. He exhaled as heavy a sigh as he could manage with his limited air supply. Except, even at his weakest, Gott had answered his prayers and sent rain.

"Of course, she probably evacuated with her family," Patrick said as he looked away. "The fire did destroy some property."

How far had the fire spread? *Gott, let the Behr family be okay. Even Hosea.*

They would've evacuated, ain't so?

And wouldn't he know, deep inside, if something had happened to Bridget?

An EMT fitted an oxygen mask over Gabe's face, making sure it securely covered his mouth and nose, then did something to turn on the portable oxygen tank. The ambulance doors slammed shut, and the vehicle took off. Nein siren blared, but they bounced over the ruts in the old dirt logging road with urgency, swerving sharply when they hit the main road. The lurching caused excruciating pain to Gabe's torn ligaments, which reminded him at every bump and turn that they hadn't had a chance to fully heal.

But at least he was alive. He should focus on the grace of der Herr, and count his blessings.

A roof over his head and a comfortable place to sleep. Food on his table and shoes on his feet. And now, new since Thanksgiving, loving family and friends. Hope of a future with Bridget. Answered prayers. And a relationship with Gott.

He was so blessed.

⁓

Bridget's hands shook. She glanced at the faces of the three men seated across the table from her, not knowing which one would deliver the bad news about Gabe or Noah, or both: the bishop, the visiting preacher, or the stern-looking Englischer.

Gott, help.... She cleared her throat. "Just tell me." She didn't dare glance at Agnes. If only she could ask her to leave the room. It was uncomfortable having her there to witness Bridget's private pain. "Is he...? Are they...?"

Gabe's daed reached out and rested his hand on one of hers, just long enough for her to register the warmth of his touch. "Gabe will be fine. They're taking him to the hospital for treatment for smoke inhalation. We'll go to the hospital later to see him. Noah is okay."

The knot in her chest loosened. Gabe and her brother were okay. The rest of her family had evacuated. Everything would be fine.

Gabe's daed nodded at the Englischer beside him. "This is Walter Carmen, one of the firefighters. He has something to tell you."

So, there was some other bad news. Unease skittered up her spine.

Walter Carmen bowed his graying head, then cleared his throat and looked up, a sheen of moisture in his brown eyes. "There's no easy way of saying this. Patrick asked me to stop by your home to tell you about Gabe. Some of the other firefighters were still there, and one of them told me he thought your family had evacuated to the Lower Peninsula. Do you know where they would've gone, specifically?"

Bridget swallowed a lump in her throat. "I don't think they know anyone there." She glanced at Frau Brunstetter.

"The Amish community is very close and will take care of their own," the bishop's frau assured her. "Someone would have taken them in."

"Do you have any way of getting in contact with them? I'm afraid I have bad news." Walter Carmen kept his gaze on Bridget.

"I have Daed's business cell phone number." Bridget squirmed. The news had to do with their home. Had to.

The man frowned. "We tried his phone. Left a voice mail."

Bridget braced herself. "Just tell me. I'll let Daed know when he returns."

Mr. Carmen hesitated. "I don't like this. Bad news shouldn't be delivered to a mere girl."

Bridget firmed her shoulders and straightened her posture. "I'm twenty-one. Hardly a girl."

Mr. Carmen raised an eyebrow. "To a man my age, you're a child. But…." He drew in a shaky breath. "The fact is, your place—the haus and barn—burned down. A total loss."

Their new haus, gone? The animals, gone? Her new, tidily arranged bedroom—gone? Her clothes…her Bible…all her important keepsakes. Gone. The pain of loss wrapped icy fingers around her heart and squeezed.

She mentally shook herself. None of that really mattered, since Daed and Mamm and her siblings were safe. Noah and Gabe were safe. Everything important had been left intact.

Daed would say it was the will of der Herr.

But what would they do now? Daed didn't have enough money saved to start over again. This meant they'd lost everything.

Everything.

She bowed her head and stared through a blur of tears at her gut hand, clenched tightly in a fist in her lap.

Agnes gently grasped the fingers of Bridget's broken hand. "It'll be okay," she said softly. "The community will help. My daed is the preacher in charge of—"

"Not now, Agnes." The bishop shook his head.

Mr. Carmen looked at Agnes and cleared his throat. "And you are Agnes Zook?"

Agnes's hand tightened painfully around Bridget's. Her eyes widened. Her mouth worked for a moment, two. Then she rose. "They died, didn't they? Gott took my home and my whole family. I knew it. I *knew* it. All nacht, I could sense them coming to say their gut-byes to me. That's why I cried. I couldn't help it. I'll never see my family again."

Bridget stared at nothing in particular, at a loss for what to say, or even think. But if what Agnes had said was true, then her "excessive" mourning could be understood and excused.

Agnes turned to Bridget, her eyes illumined by a strange light. Or maybe by fear. "We'll be sisters. We'll take care of each other."

Then Agnes collapsed in a heap on the floor.

⁓

After an eternity of waiting in the emergency room, Gabe was admitted to the hospital. The doctor wanted his oxygen levels monitored and mumbled something to his nurse about setting up a consult with a surgeon. Gabe didn't know whether the surgeon would visit him in the hospital or whether he would need to set up another appointment. It didn't matter. The IV pain medicine had relaxed him, making him extremely sleepy. And not at all in pain unless he moved. Something that was hard to avoid when the lingering smoke he'd inhaled caused him to cough.

At some point, he became aware of Patrick and Noah talking quietly nearby. Then of Daed, leaning over him with his hand on Gabe's shoulder, murmuring prayers Gabe couldn't comprehend.

Then Bridget sat beside him and held his hand as she whispered something. He didn't try to decipher her words, but the sound of her voice calmed him, and reminded him of Gott's powerful presence in the woods. He had something important to ask her, if he could sort out his thoughts enough to remember.

A short time later, a strangely quiet Agnes rubbed some smelly stuff on his feet and ankles. Hopefully, it wouldn't poison him. He tried to pray for her—and Bridget, too—but wasn't sure his prayers made any sense.

And then he heard Bishop Miah talking with whoever else was there at the time. He probably had many crises to deal with. Gabe had nein idea of the extent of the damage the fire had caused, only that acreage had burned, homes had been destroyed, and people had died.

All these details were like a confusing, messed-up puzzle, similar to the Rubik's cube popular when Daed was a teenager. Gabe had tried to solve the puzzle a time or two. He'd never succeeded. And the people who were there one minute and gone the next were more confusing pieces of the puzzle. Gabe wasn't sure what was real and what was part of a dream.

He tried to tell one of the nurses that his pain-medicine dosage might be off, because nothing should be this baffling. The nurse only smiled, patted his hand, gave him a sip of water, and left.

Hosea appeared in the midst of the madness, gesturing and speaking loudly, but even his statements faded in and out, and didn't make any sense. Hosea was shooed away by a man dressed in hospital scrubs the same color of the algae growing in the swamps near Gabe's home in Florida. The unidentified man adjusted Gabe's IV before two nurses wheeled Gabe down a maze of identical-looking hallways, then into a room.

The next time Gabe woke up, his entire lower body—from the hips down—ached, even without his moving. If they'd adjusted his pain medicine, they'd gone too far in the other direction. His throat was raw.

Daed sat at his bedside in a chair, his body leaning forward, his arms folded and resting on the mattress, his head bowed. Asleep? At least someone was. Maybe sleep would help with the pain.

Daed raised his head and looked at Gabe. "How are you feeling?"

"Not gut. My legs are sore. So's my throat."

"One of the nurses will be in soon with some more pain medicine. They've been checking on you routinely."

Gabe nodded. A myriad of questions came to mind, but it hurt too much to talk.

"Do you need ice for your throat? They had you hooked up to a breathing machine for the surgery," Daed told him.

That explained the sore throat, but it raised more questions. "Jah, ice. Danki."

Daed nodded and got up. "I'll be right back." A few minutes later, he reappeared. "Someone will be in shortly with ice."

"Danki." He glanced at the chair on the other side of the bed, empty now. "Bridget—"

"She's staying at the bishop's haus. He felt led of Gott not to take either Bridget or Agnes home that nacht. Gut thing, too. Both lost their homes." Daed grimaced, as if there were more to tell but he wanted to spare Gabe the details. Then he shook his head.

Gabe struggled to sit up as a nurse bustled in with a plastic container full of ice. He quickly quit trying to move because it was too painful.

The nurse adjusted the bed so he was sitting up a little.

Gabe thanked her, then looked at his daed. "What else?"

"The Behrs evacuated to the Lower Peninsula. Hosea has kum back. Nobody is certain if the Zooks evacuated."

Gabe frowned. The Zooks wouldn't have left without Agnes—or without telling her, at the very least. That didn't sound gut.

Daed looked away. "They likely died in the fire."

Gabe shook his head and said a silent prayer for Agnes before reaching for the dish of ice on the tray. He stuck an ice cube in his mouth. His throat needed moisture. Badly.

"Hosea is selling his business and moving back to Ohio," Daed said quietly. "His frau didn't handle the move here well. She misses her sisters and her parents. And she's expecting a life-changing addition to the family."

Gabe looked at him. The ice seemed to lodge in his throat. He coughed to free up his airways again.

"Noah wants to stay here because of Arie, though her family evacuated. He owns half the construction business, so he'll need a new business partner." A small smile slid across Daed's face. "Seems to me I know of a young man who might be interested."

If only Gabe could afford it. He shook his head. "Nein money."

"Ye have not, because ye ask not."

Did that statement pertain to other parts of his life, beyond the request to be saved from a fire?

Gott, if You could find a way to make it happen, I'd love to buy Hosea's half of the business.

"I might be willing to put up the money if you want to stay here," Daed said. "And since Preacher Zook and most of his family...well, there's an opening for a preacher here. Might even be willing to move the family north."

Gabe frowned at the reminder of the probable death of Preacher Zook. But then a slow smile started. That was a quick answer to prayer. "You'd do that?" It'd be great to be reunited with his family.

Daed nodded. "I have a solid construction crew in Florida, so I could manage business affairs long distance. And if there's some reason why that wouldn't be possible, then it would be a gut excuse for a vacation for your mother."

Gabe nodded. "I still need to talk to Bridget. She might want to go back to Ohio with her family." But Gabe hoped not. "And I need to pray." To discern the will of der Herr. To thank Him for His mercy. And to present his requests: a home, a business, and a frau, with his family nearby.

"Wise ideas. Hosea will bring Bridget by later to-nacht. He wants to talk to you about the business."

A nurse scooted into the room carrying a fresh IV bag. "Hi, there, Mr. Lapp. I'm Melanie, your nurse for the evening. How are you feeling?" She didn't wait for an answer but hooked the bag to the IV pole, then wrapped a blood pressure cuff around Gabe's arm.

Daed stood. "You pray. I'll see you later. Love you, Sohn."

EPILOGUE

Bridget filled the teapot with water and set it on the stove, then checked the fire. It needed wood, so she stepped outside onto the Brunstetters' back porch and grabbed a log. The odor of smoke still filled the air. Out of habit, she looked to the heavens. The skies remained gray and ashy, with a faint orange glow to the west. Despite the rain that had fallen the other day, the fires still burned. The wind had shifted again, compelling more local families to evacuate.

She was thankful her family had left, but she was saddened to realize she would never get to know the little brother or sister who would be joining the family. And she would miss Jonah, Shiloh, Roseanna, and her parents.

She whispered another prayer for Noah as she shoved the log into the woodstove. He refused to stop chasing fires. When she'd seen him briefly at the hospital while visiting Gabe, he'd talked about becoming a smokejumper. A necessary job, but dangerous, and her worrying over him nearly tore her up.

And Gabe...would he join Noah after he healed?

He'd managed to injure his groin muscles again, requiring surgery there as well as on his ankle. The surgeon had inserted a pin into his ankle and told Gabe he was not to bear weight on it for six weeks.

Six weeks!

How could Gabe be kept off his feet that long?

Right now, it was the hospital's problem, since Gabe would remain there for another day or two. Every time Bridget went to visit him, he was medicated and either asleep or so drowsy that he drifted in and out of consciousness without fully waking. Bridget wasn't sure if he ever knew she was there.

With Daed's having announced his plans to sell his business and return to Ohio, everything had changed. Bridget nein longer wanted to return to her former community, even though Daed had finally decided to adopt a dog to protect the family from nacht-time prowlers. She wanted to stay where Gabe was. If Noah stayed here, she'd be taken care of; and with Agnes's family missing and presumed dead, it seemed only right to take Agnes at her word and live as if they were sisters. Especially since they were still sharing a room at the Brunstetters'.

Except that she hadn't told Noah they had a new sister.

Or that she intended to stay.

They would have that conversation before Noah marched off to fight another wildfire somewhere else. Assuming Gott kept him safe as he battled this current fire.

And with Arie and her family having evacuated, Noah seemed to be taking more risks than usual.

A pickup truck rumbled into the driveway and stopped in front of the haus.

Bridget peered out the window. The driver was Gabe's friend and former boss, Patrick.

Bishop Brunstetter came out of the barn, tugging the curls out of his long, gray beard. He glanced toward the heavens as if in prayer.

Patrick said something, and Bishop Brunstetter frowned.

What crisis were they facing now?

Lord, help us through this. Provide for our needs.

Both men walked to the back of the pickup and peered at something. Then Patrick lifted a dead buck out of the back and carried it to the barn.

Meat.

Gott truly was providing, because the cupboards were bare, and nobody had taken the time to go grocery shopping. The local supermarket had closed due to the fire, and all able-bodied men were either fighting the fire or had evacuated, so there were nein drivers available to take the women to a larger town to shop.

Daed came into the kitchen as a van pulled into the drive. Gabe's daed climbed out, paid the driver, and hefted a big box out of the back. He carried the box to the haus, and handed it to Bridget. "Bananas. The store was selling the overripe ones real cheap. I took them all. We have other groceries in the back."

Bridget smiled. "Banana bread." *Wunderbaar.* Maybe Gott would provide chocolate chips and walnuts, too.

"You shopped?" Daed reached for his boots and tugged them on over his stockinged feet.

Gabe's daed shrugged. "I was the logical choice. I have some money and have been making daily trips to the hospital, anyway."

"I'll help carry in the groceries." Daed headed for the door, then paused. "When do you think your bu will be in any condition to make a business decision?"

"I mentioned it to him," said Gabe's daed. "He wants to pray about it. And talk to Bridget." He smiled at Bridget, and she grinned back. "I told him you'd be by later this evening."

She wished she could spend all day with Gabe, but such "idleness" would be frowned upon. She needed to help Frau Brunstetter with the all-encompassing job of haus-keeping: cooking, cleaning, doing laundry, and sewing dresses for those whose families had lost everything.

Agnes worked, too, though an aura of melancholy had settled over her. She'd tirelessly produced dress after dress using donated fabric, and once she and Bridget had enough clean clothes to wear, the bishop and his frau had started delivering the excess garments to others who'd lost their homes. The Red Cross had set up a shelter at a local school.

The remains of both the Behrs' and the Zooks' homes still smoldered, so nobody had been able to get in and search for anything that might've survived the fire. Or, in the case of the Zook family, their bodies. But that sounded rather morbid.

Daed returned with about five plastic grocery bags hanging from each arm. He set the stash on the table with a thump.

Food. Bridget reached into the first bag and pulled out a bag of milk chocolate chips. Gott had provided not only her needs but also her wants.

Danki, Lord Gott. Danki.

Maybe, if he thought hard enough, he would figure out a way to say it.

Gabe guzzled the glass of ice water a nurse had just delivered, plunked the cup down on the tray, and stared out the window.

I can't stop thinking about you.

True, but that didn't convey the emotion he wanted.

You're the only girl for me. Also true, but it seemed so blah compared to her comment about wanting him to feel "head over heels, can't-wait-to-kiss-her-again, please-Gott-let-her-feel-the-same in love with me." He didn't have that kind of imagination.

Jah, those words were seared into his mind. And his heart.

"Bridget, ich liebe dich," he tried aloud.

That might be a gut start.

A sound at the door caught his attention, and he glanced in that direction, hoping it wasn't Agnes who would appear from behind the curtain separating him and his roommate, an Amish man with severe burns. He had been taken elsewhere for some tests.

Gabe caught a glimpse of a pine-green sleeve, and then Bridget's face appeared. Bridget smiled brightly as she removed her black bonnet. "You're awake."

Had she overheard him practicing? Might as well assume so. "It's true," he blurted out.

She frowned as she dropped her bonnet on the bedside table. "It's true that you're awake?"

"Well, jah, but it's true that ich liebe dich. I am totally and completely head-over-heels, can't-wait-to-kiss-you-again, please-Gott-let-her-feel-the-same in love with you."

Her smile widened.

"Where's your daed?" He twisted as if to glance at the door, not that he could see it around the curtain.

"He went with the driver so he'd know where the van was parked."

Gut. So they'd have a few minutes alone. "Kum here."

She wheeled the bedside tray out of her way, reached for his hand, and started to sit in the nearby chair.

He shook his head. "I need to hold you. Lower the rails. I feel like a boppli in a crib with those up."

She raised her eyebrows. "I'll lower one side, but you need to stay in this bed. Your daed told me what the doctor said. Nein putting weight on your ankle for six weeks." The rail slid out of sight, then clicked into place.

Gabe reached for Bridget and tugged her down into his arms. Kissed her mouth. Her lips softened against his, granting him access.

In a moment, he pulled back. "Jah, but when those six weeks are over, we're getting married." Then he kissed her again. Longer. The need burned deep inside him, almost consuming him.

When he released her, she draped an arm across his chest and snuggled against him. A soft smile curled her lips. "Is that so?"

He shook his head. "Nein. I can't wait six weeks. How about as soon as I can balance on crutches? Unless you don't want to marry a wounded wannabe hero."

"You'll wait six weeks and marry her proper." Hosea came around the curtain.

Bridget stiffened and pushed to get out of the bed. Her face flamed red.

"That'll give both families time enough to make arrangements, and time for those who need to travel up to Michigan for your wedding." Hosea speared Gabe with a look. "Does that mean you'll buy my business?"

Gabe let Bridget go but grabbed her hand and held on tight. "That depends on Bridget. We still need to talk about it."

Hosea nodded. "I'm going to get some koffee. The bishop's frau, as hospitable as she is, cannot make a decent cup. Anyone else want one?"

Gabe frowned. He wasn't sure if he was allowed koffee yet. They were keeping him pretty much on a liquid diet until his throat healed.

Well, koffee was liquid, ain't so?

"Jah, get me one, please. Iced, if possible, with a shot of French vanilla syrup. The ice will be gut for my sore throat."

Hosea shook his head. "French vanilla iced koffee. Didn't know they made such a thing, but I'll see if they have it. In the meantime, you two talk about buying my business. I'll get your decision when I return."

"Impatient much?" Gabe muttered.

But then, who was he to talk?

There was nothing to talk about, really. Bridget just wanted to crawl back into the bed with Gabe, snuggle close, and kiss some more.

Though maybe she should give the conversation a try, if only because it would keep her from accidentally bumping into Gabe's newly surgically repaired parts and hurting him.

"Do you want to buy Daed's business and stay here? Or would you rather go back to Florida?"

Gabe shifted. Winced. "I like fish. I'm not so fond of deer."

Bridget blinked. "They have fish here. Everywhere, actually. And venison isn't bad if you know how to fix it."

"Michigan gets awful cold…when it's not on fire." Gabe chuckled. "Seriously, I thought I'd freeze to death. But then, I guess you could warm me up." He gave her a rakish grin.

Bridget's face heated. Her lips tingled. She peeked around the curtain at the door. Did they have time to kiss again before Daed returned?

"But Florida gets awful hot in the summer," Gabe went on. "You feel like you're melting."

"I notice Ohio isn't factoring in, here," she pointed out. Even though Michigan felt more like home to her, now.

He shrugged. Grinned. "I'm not willing to move in with Hosea."

"I've talked to Noah only once since Daed decided to move back to Ohio, but Noah didn't indicate he wanted to sell his half of the business. He also talked about how much he loves fighting fires, and that he's considering becoming a smokejumper." She rolled her eyes. "Truthfully, he knows very little about construction. If you bought the business, you'd be running it."

Gabe smiled. "I'd like to stay. Start our life here, if that's okay with you. We met here. I fell in love with you here. It just seems appropriate." He squeezed her hand. "Daed mentioned he might move the family up here, too. We'd just have to find someplace to live. Six weeks isn't enough time to get a haus built with me off my feet."

Bridget could hardly contain her excitement. "Bishop Brunstetter said the community might help with rebuilding, since so many people lost so much."

"He spoke to you about it?"

Bridget looked away, not wanting to admit she'd been eavesdropping. Again. "Nein. He was talking to your daed and mine. And he talked in general about rebuilding."

Gabe nodded. "You really okay with staying here?" His gaze searched hers for the truth, but the heat in his eyes stirred a storm of emotions within her.

"As long as I'm with you." Her face heated. "And I don't want to wait six weeks, either," she whispered.

Gabe smiled. "Gott used the fire to bring me back to a solid faith and to newfound maturity. And a beautiful frau, a new business, and a new home are rising out of the ashes."

Bridget nodded. The fire had burned away her own doubts and insecurities, leaving her with a stronger faith and a new resolve to trust God while taking a risk with her heart.

She marveled at how the fire had revealed what mattered most to both of them.

Gabe rubbed his thumb over the back of her hand. "So then, Bridget Behr…will you marry me? As soon as possible?" He winked as he added, "Kum on, Green Eyes. It'll be fun."

She laughed and snuggled next to him. "I can't wait."

"Neither can I." He tugged her closer. "Ich liebe dich."

She wrapped her arms around his shoulders, and they kissed again. This time, the kiss was everything she knew Gabe to be.

Wild. Dangerous. Passionate.

Fun.

And she wanted to live the adventure with him.

ABOUT THE AUTHOR

A member of the American Christian Fiction Writers, Laura V. Hilton is a professional book reviewer for the Christian market, with more than a thousand reviews published on the Web.

Laura's first series with Whitaker House, The Amish of Seymour, comprises *Patchwork Dreams*, *A Harvest of Hearts*, and *Promised to Another*. In 2012, *A Harvest of Hearts* received a Laurel Award, placing first in the Amish Genre Clash. Her second series, The Amish of Webster County, comprises *Healing Love*, *Surrendered Love*, and *Awakened Love*, followed by a stand-alone title, *A White Christmas in Webster County*. Laura's last series, The Amish of Jamesport, included *The Snow Globe*, *The Postcard*, and *The Birdhouse*. Prior to *Firestorm*, Laura also published *Love by the Numbers*, *The Amish Firefighter*, and *The Amish Wanderer*.

Previously, Laura published two novels with Treble Heart Books, *Hot Chocolate* and *Shadows of the Past*, as well as several devotionals.

Laura and her husband, Steve, have five children and make their home in Arkansas. To learn more about Laura, read her reviews, and find out about her upcoming releases, readers may visit her blog at http://lighthouse-academy.blogspot.com/.

RECIPE FOR MICHIGAN PASTIES

4½ cups all-purpose flour
1 cup shortening
1¼ cups ice water
1 teaspoon salt
5½ cups sliced potatoes
2 carrots, sliced
1 onion, diced
½ cup diced rutabaga
2 pounds venison (or stew meat or ground meat, either beef or pork)
1 tablespoon salt, divided
1 teaspoon black pepper
1 beef bouillon cube
½ cup hot water

In a large bowl, whisk together flour and 1 teaspoon salt. Cut in shortening. Make a well in the center of the mixture, and quickly stir in ice water. Form dough into a ball. Set aside.

In a liquid measuring cup, dissolve the beef bouillon cube in ½ cup hot water.

In a second large bowl, combine uncooked vegetables, uncooked meat, 2 teaspoons salt, and pepper with the bouillon.

Roll out pasty dough into rectangles measuring 6 by 8 inches. Place about 1½ cups of filling in the center of each rectangle. Bring the 6-inch sides together, and seal. Cut a slit in the top of each pasty. Place on dull, not black, baking pans and bake at 425 degrees F for 45 minutes.

Welcome to Our House!

We Have a Special Gift for You ...

It is our privilege and pleasure to share in your love of Christian fiction by publishing books that enrich your life and encourage your faith.

To show our appreciation, we invite you to sign up to receive a specially selected **Reader Appreciation Gift**, with our compliments. Just go to the Web address at the bottom of this page.

God bless you as you seek a deeper walk with Him!

WE HAVE A GIFT FOR YOU. VISIT:

whpub.me/fictionthx

WHITAKER
HOUSE